Anthony Gilbert and The Murder Room

››› This title is part of The Murder Room, our series dedicated to making available out-of-print or hard-to-find titles by classic crime writers.

Crime fiction has always held up a mirror to society. The Victorians were fascinated by sensational murder and the emerging science of detection; now we are obsessed with the forensic detail of violent death. And no other genre has so captivated and enthralled readers.

Vast troves of classic crime writing have for a long time been unavailable to all but the most dedicated frequenters of second-hand bookshops. The advent of digital publishing means that we are now able to bring you the backlists of a huge range of titles by classic and contemporary crime writers, some of which have been out of print for decades.

From the genteel amateur private eyes of the Golden Age and the femmes fatales of pulp fiction, to the morally ambiguous hard-boiled detectives of mid twentieth-century America and their descendants who walk our twenty-first century streets, The Murder Room has it all. ›››

The Murder Room

Where Criminal Minds Meet

themurderroom.com

Anthony Gilbert (1899–1973)

Anthony Gilbert was the pen name of Lucy Beatrice Malleson. Born in London, she spent all her life there, and her affection for the city is clear from the strong sense of character and place in evidence in her work. She published 69 crime novels, 51 of which featured her best known character, Arthur Crook, a vulgar London lawyer totally (and deliberately) unlike the aristocratic detectives, such as Lord Peter Wimsey, who dominated the mystery field at the time. She also wrote more than 25 radio plays, which were broadcast in Great Britain and overseas. Her thriller *The Woman in Red* (1941) was broadcast in the United States by CBS and made into a film in 1945 under the title *My Name is Julia Ross*. She was an early member of the British Detection Club, which, along with Dorothy L. Sayers, she prevented from disintegrating during World War II. Malleson published her autobiography, *Three-a-Penny*, in 1940, and wrote numerous short stories, which were published in several anthologies and in such periodicals as *Ellery Queen's Mystery Magazine* and *The Saint*. The short story 'You Can't Hang Twice' received a Queens award in 1946. She never married, and evidence of her feminism is elegantly expressed in much of her work.

By Anthony Gilbert

Scott Egerton series

Tragedy at Freyne (1927)
The Murder of Mrs Davenport (1928)
Death at Four Corners (1929)
The Mystery of the Open Window (1929)
The Night of the Fog (1930)
The Body on the Beam (1932)
The Long Shadow (1932)
The Musical Comedy Crime (1933)
An Old Lady Dies (1934)
The Man Who Was Too Clever (1935)

Mr Crook Murder Mystery series

Murder by Experts (1936)
The Man Who Wasn't There (1937)
Murder Has No Tongue (1937)
Treason in My Breast (1938)
The Bell of Death (1939)
Dear Dead Woman (1940)
aka *Death Takes a Redhead*
The Vanishing Corpse (1941)
aka *She Vanished in the Dawn*
The Woman in Red (1941)
aka *The Mystery of the Woman in Red*
Death in the Blackout (1942)
aka *The Case of the Tea-Cosy's Aunt*
Something Nasty in the Woodshed (1942)
aka *Mystery in the Woodshed*
The Mouse Who Wouldn't Play Ball (1943)
aka *30 Days to Live*
He Came by Night (1944)
aka *Death at the Door*
The Scarlet Button (1944)
aka *Murder Is Cheap*
A Spy for Mr Crook (1944)
The Black Stage (1945)
aka *Murder Cheats the Bride*
Don't Open the Door (1945)
aka *Death Lifts the Latch*
Lift Up the Lid (1945)
aka *The Innocent Bottle*
The Spinster's Secret (1946)
aka *By Hook or by Crook*
Death in the Wrong Room (1947)
Die in the Dark (1947)
aka *The Missing Widow*
Death Knocks Three Times (1949)
Murder Comes Home (1950)
A Nice Cup of Tea (1950)
aka *The Wrong Body*

Lady-Killer (1951)
Miss Pinnegar Disappears (1952)
aka *A Case for Mr Crook*
Footsteps Behind Me (1953)
aka *Black Death*
Snake in the Grass (1954)
aka *Death Won't Wait*
Is She Dead Too? (1955)
aka *A Question of Murder*
And Death Came Too (1956)
Riddle of a Lady (1956)
Give Death a Name (1957)
Death Against the Clock (1958)
Death Takes a Wife (1959)
aka *Death Casts a Long Shadow*
Third Crime Lucky (1959)
aka *Prelude to Murder*
Out for the Kill (1960)
She Shall Die (1961)
aka *After the Verdict*
Uncertain Death (1961)
No Dust in the Attic (1962)
Ring for a Noose (1963)
The Fingerprint (1964)
The Voice (1964)
aka *Knock, Knock! Who's There?*
Passenger to Nowhere (1965)
The Looking Glass Murder (1966)
The Visitor (1967)
Night Encounter (1968)
aka *Murder Anonymous*
Missing from Her Home (1969)
Death Wears a Mask (1970)
aka *Mr Crook Lifts the Mask*
Murder is a Waiting Game (1972)
Tenant for the Tomb (1971)
A Nice Little Killing (1974)

Standalone Novels

The Case Against Andrew Fane (1931)
Death in Fancy Dress (1933)
The Man in Button Boots (1934)
Courtier to Death (1936)
aka *The Dover Train Mystery*
The Clock in the Hatbox (1939)

The Looking Glass Murder

Anthony Gilbert

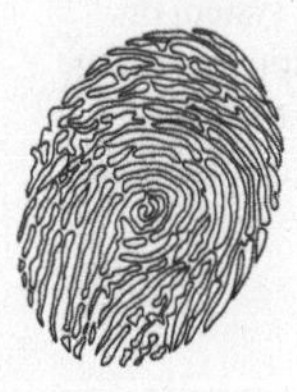

An Orion book

This edition published by
The Orion Publishing Group Ltd
Orion House
5 Upper St Martin's Lane
London WC2H 9EA

An Hachette UK company
A CIP catalogue record for this book is available from the British Library

ISBN 978 1 4719 1028 9

www.orionbooks.co.uk

1

IT WAS A GRAY DAY when I left Rome for the last time. Sitting in the air terminal, waiting for my coach to be called, I remembered a scandal that had taken place here a year before. A girl had been poisoned with coffee ordered and poured out by her lover. Few people had any doubt of his guilt; she had been pestering him to marry her, and the arrangement being clearly unsuitable, he had taken what to many had seemed the only possible way out. His defense was that she had taken the drug herself, intending him to be blamed. I don't know how the case would have gone in England but he won it here in Rome. Like a lot of other people, I had been convinced of his guilt. One of the lucky ones who got away, we told each other, nodding wisely. Now that I stood in his shoes I was less sure.

I found an empty table and sat down. When I had ordered coffee I opened my paper; my own name sprang into view:

SOLANGE PETERS FLIES OUT

and a double-spread picture. They weren't publishing pictures of Florian or the Marchesa any more; after today they wouldn't remember me either. Hurriedly I dropped the paper on the ground and looked about me. At the next table two Italian women, looking like exquisitely turned-out macaws, were chattering in the high rapid tones Romans can employ for hours on end, and it seemed to me they were staring directly at me. I moved at once. I knew that probably they weren't even thinking about me, but I was hypersensitive. After the Marchesa's sudden death, for which I knew they all held me responsible, I felt I had only to stand at a window of the palazzo and a crowd would instantly collect outside. They wouldn't throw stones or break glass, because it was Florian's property, but I could feel their hate and contempt pouring up at me like fog. It wasn't a palace in the English sense of the word, of course, just a big majestic house, rich in gloom, overlooking the olive-green waters of the Tiber. During the year and a half I had been acting as the Marchesa's nurse I had often stood at those windows watching the world go by. Life in Rome never stops, it's like being on a wheel. Even at night there is movement, whispers, a sense of excitement, a perpetual kaleidoscope.

When the waiter brought my coffee he told me that my coach departure was delayed. Thanks to freak storms in Europe, various flights were being held up, and some were being rerouted, but he promised to let me know when the time came for us to depart. I sat sipping the hot black coffee, wishing I'd ordered a cognac, even this early in the day. I couldn't contemplate the future, I felt like someone in a cul-de-sac, slap up against a blank wall, so inevitably I brooded on the past.

"You have been very fortunate," my Italian lawyer had told me, the lawyer Florian had engaged to defend me in case I found myself facing a murder charge. This was after the inquiry, when it had been decided there wasn't sufficient evidence to bring me to book. "If there had been a prosecution, then"—he shrugged—"even though you had not been found guilty, there would have been nowhere for you to hide. As it is . . ." He shrugged again, the elaborate gesture of his race. "Your other piece of good fortune," he continued, "is that you hold a British passport."

I had my mother to thank for that. It's what your father would have wished, she told me. It was almost the only time I ever heard her mention him. He had been killed on D-Day, when I was two years old, and immediately after the war she had met and married her adored second husband, Victor Manuelli. The two were completely wrapped up in each other. I had what might be considered a luxurious childhood, but it was a desperately lonely one. Even on holidays I was always farmed out to some family with children of my own age. My mother never wanted anyone but Victor. They were killed instantaneously in a car crash when I was sixteen, and the lawyer told me, long-faced, that though we had appeared to be rich people, it would now be incumbent on me to earn my own bread. The Manuellis accepted no responsibility for me, and Victor had made no provision. Of course, he hadn't expected to die at forty-eight.

I wasn't at all disconcerted. From childhood I had

wanted to nurse. My mother had been appalled when I told her.

"I suppose you are attracted by the uniform," she said. "There is nothing romantic about sickness, nothing heroic either. Sick people are deformed people." She and Victor enjoyed the most radiant health.

I started working at a children's hospice until I was old enough to be accepted at a training hospital. The three years I spent there were the happiest I had ever known. I made friends, I loved the work, I skated over the disagreeable sections of it without disgust, I passed my examinations without difficulty. I was twenty-three when I came to the Palazzo Polli as resident nurse to the widowed Marchesa.

At that time she was a vigorous woman of fifty-two, crippled by poliomyelitis. The attack had taken place four years earlier, and after a brief period of recovery, deterioration set in and she lived the rest of her life between her bed and her wheelchair. She was the busiest and most competent of women. The Polli fortunes would have been at a very low ebb but for a thriving business in the export of local marbles. This business had been inherited by her husband through his mother. No patrician herself, she had had no difficulty in marrying into the Italian nobility, and she handled her fortune with the skill of a man. Her husband, the late Marchese, had taken little interest in this commercial undertaking, confining his energies to the family properties that her energies supported, and his dogs. He had had three magnificent Saluki hounds who accompanied him everywhere. When they died they were buried in the grounds of the palazzo, beyond the orchard, each with a tombstone as big as a Christian's. The heir was a cousin of the second generation, Florian. The Marchesa had only two daughters, one well married and established in Milan, and a much younger girl, Perdita, who lived at home and spent most of her time playing stormy music in the enormous, shadowy music room of the palazzo. I don't know when I realized that it was her mother's ambition to marry this sallow, secretive little creature to her beloved Florian. She made no secret of the fact that she cared more for him than the rest of the world put together, and he had inherited her business proclivities. The palazzo was nominally his, but no one would have dreamed of asking her to change her address; she was its chatelaine, and in any case Florian was away a great deal, sometimes on business, sometimes, presumably, on pleasure. He had an ardent and almost notorious personal life. It was said he couldn't walk from the Ponte Victor Emmanuel to the Ponte Garibaldi without treading on half a dozen hearts flung passionately in his road. He was dark, handsome and had a charm that could wheedle a bird from its nest. When he came for one of his lightning visits the whole house seemed to kindle into warmth. I suppose it was inevitable that I should fall in love with him and equally inevitable that the notion he would take me seriously would never occur to the Marchesa. When he was gone again I would wait in a sort of golden haze of impatience for his return. The first time he took me in his arms and told me that he, too, loved, I could scarcely accept it. I would have told the world, I had a vision of myself standing on the terrace of St. Peter's making the announcement.

"I love Florian." Here there would be a roll of trumpets. "Florian loves me." And here the fireworks would begin to fall, a rain, a hail, a cataclysm of color and light.

"And we shall be married soon?" I would urge.

And Florian laughed. "Well, not tomorrow."

"But perhaps the day after tomorrow." Meaning the autumn—I'd always loved autumn better than spring.

"Perhaps."

He explained that he was negotiating a very important contract, if he could pull this off he would be able to impose his own terms, would conciliate the Marchesa.

"Why should she not welcome me as your wife?" I asked jealously. I knew, of course, that the Pollis were Catholics and I was a Protestant, but they sat very lightly to their religious duties. When he was in Rome, Florian didn't even attend Mass.

"Oh come, carissima, you know better than that," Florian teased me.

"You would never give me up, would you?" I pleaded. "We shall be married?"

"Well, not tomorrow," Florian said. "How British you are!"

He had been in England, found them an incalculable race, dead to passion, so self-contained as to be scarcely human.

"They have abandoned their belief in God, yet think of themselves as gods," he told me. I supposed he meant they didn't believe they could ever be defeated. If that were so, I thought, then I was British to the backbone.

The Marchesa found out about our "affair," as she called

it, in the most unfortunate way. A letter from Florian, intended for me, found its way into the wrong envelope. Soon after I had taken in her mail that day, her bell rang imperiously, and I hastened to answer it. My heart was like a soap bubble in those days, as radiant, as light. That was the last instant of happiness I ever had in that house.

She showed me the letter—it had the slightly guarded tone of all Florian's letters to me. I wondered later if he was afraid they might be intercepted, he always got someone else to address the envelopes, but the Marchesa was quite sharp enough to see through that trick. This morning she showed no mercy, put me through an examination as grilling as the one I was later to face in regard to her own death.

Did I, she demanded, really expect Florian to marry me?

Yes, I did. We were in love . . .

She disregarded that. How long, she said, has this intrigue been in force?

There was no intrigue, I said.

If that was true, why had she been left to discover the position in this underhand way?

Because Florian wanted to see the results of his latest enterprise, it would mean he had more to offer me.

She laughed then. "The Marchese has nothing to offer you but what I choose to give him. Deprived of my business interests, my directorships, he will be as poor as a clerk."

"It won't matter," I told her obstinately. "We can both work."

"Pah!" she cried. "You talk like a peasant. Men like the Marchese recognize their obligations. In England, perhaps, a people of mongrel blood . . ."

"I've never been in England," I told her. I felt my head and heart beating like drums, as though tides of blood inflamed them; if the whole atmosphere had exploded at that moment it would hardly have surprised me.

I expected her to tell me to pack my cases and get out the same day, but she always took the long view, it was the secret of her great success. "I shall write to my lawyers," she said. "I shall show the letter to Florian when he comes. He is a free agent, he is of age; if this marriage is what he desires no one can thwart him."

"You may be surprised," I told her.

"We shall see."

But we didn't, because before Florian arrived three days later, the Marchesa was dead.

I was away from the palazzo at the time of the tragedy, having gone on an errand to the Corso to match up some silk. It would have been more normal to send Perdita, but I knew she would take the first thing that was offered, and I should be saddled with the duty of returning the unsuitable material and trying to persuade the shopkeeper to accept the length and find me something more in accord with what was required. She was in the music room as usual when I left the house, and long gloomy chords came pealing down the stairs.

Like a Requiem, I thought, not guessing how close to the truth that would be.

It was a glorious afternoon. For some days previously the weather had been overcast. When it rains in Rome it can be like the Flood. I had settled the Marchesa in her chair in the garden, close to the house. I knew I had plenty of time, since shops in Rome close at noon and don't open again until three o'clock. The Castel St. Angelo, that grim prison, glittered in the sun. I went by the Borghese Gardens and down past the sugar-icing statue of Victor Emmanuel and so into the Corso. It took me some time to find the right color, and I came back also on foot. Already the crowds were cramming the Roman buses. It must have been almost five o'clock when I returned. Florian was due the next day, and when he came all my troubles would dissolve like the snow.

As I approached the palazzo I was startled by the buzz of voices and the noise of feet. I wondered if Florian could have returned early, and I almost ran through the gate. A man in uniform stopped me.

"Who are you? No one is allowed in."

"I'm the nurse," I said. "What's happened? The Marchesa . . ."

The Marchesa cannot see you, I was told. I was led into a room that seemed remarkably full of people and asked a fusillade of questions. They passed over my head like a flight of birds.

"What has happened?" I insisted. "You must tell me."

What had happened was that the Marchesa had met with a remarkable accident that might well prove fatal. As I said, I had left her in her wheelchair in the gardens of the palazzo. She was a very energetic woman, despite her disability, and she liked to keep everything under her eyes. At any time she could probably have told you how many pairs of sheets there should be in the linen cupboard, it was even whispered she knew how many sprigs of thyme there should be in the herb garden. In this chair she was quite mobile; she could take it along the path, by the flower beds and through the entrance to the kitchen garden. Lower than this she never went. The grounds sloped steeply to the orchard, and beyond the orchard were the famous dog tombstones and the enclosing wall. What appeared to have happened was that she had gone on one of her normal tours of inspection, but when she applied the brake, as she must do, at the head of the gentle slope leading to the vegetable garden, the brake didn't work. Although the incline was not steep, the Marchesa herself was a very heavy woman who had put on considerable weight since the onset of her disease, while the chair itself was not light. Once it started on its descent, there would be no stopping it. By the time she realized there was something wrong it would be too late to do anything about it. I shivered to think of the chair and its helpless occupant whirling down the path; no matter what skills she employed, she couldn't avoid the ultimate collision. She had crashed into one of the tombstones, the shock had jerked her forward, she had struck her head with some violence on the stone itself.

A gardener had found her; there was no knowing precisely how long she had been there. Gardeners, like everyone else in Rome, sleep during the siesta; it was regarded as a little strange that the Marchesa should prefer a routine presumed exclusively British and sit in the hot afternoon sun. Perdita later declared she heard nothing, she had been busy at her practicing, and indeed no scream could have penetrated that hideous cacophony. The gardener had summoned help—no one person could have pushed the chair back up the steep lower slopes—a doctor had been sent for—the police came later. It was the gardener who discovered the faulty brake. I said it had been in good order the last time I saw the chair. I had established her in her usual place. Yes, I agreed, it was no surprise to me that she should have moved, she was accustomed to propelling herself in the grounds when she was alone. I added that I should like to see my patient, I had the right . . .

The look in the eyes of my interrogator gave me my first hint of the way the wind might blow. No one could see the Marchesa, he said, she was unconscious, and the medical opinion was that this condition might obtain for some days. Perhaps, he added, she will never regain it. "How would that suit you, signorina?"

"What a question!" I cried. "It couldn't conceivably suit me. She is the only one who can tell us what happened."

"We know what happened; what we have to learn is how it happened."

The chair had been handed over to experts for thorough examination. It must have been that night, I think, that I realized they were going to suggest the damage to the brake was deliberate.

Police swarmed in the hall when I came out and went up to my room. There was another officer on the landing. He intimated I had better stay where I was, unless and until I was sent for again by the authorities.

"What is happening to the Marchesa?" I demanded. "Has she been removed to a hospital?"

"Unfortunately, that is not thought wise." Special nurses had been summoned, my services would not be required.

Perdita came out of a room onto the staircase and saw me standing there. "Don't let her loose," she said to the policeman as she went by.

So I realized I was being kept a prisoner in my own room. Later a tray of food was brought me, handed to the officer and passed through my door. I had my own suite here, so I had no excuse even for venturing onto the landing. When later I asked if there was any change in the Marchesa's condition, my only answer was a shrug. No one, it appeared, would speak to me. The next morning I asked whether Florian had arrived. I was told that if my presence was required I would be summoned. Later I received such a summons, from the man I had seen before. Another rain of questions fell upon me. It had been discovered that the chair had been willfully damaged. It was absurd, I said, no one could do such a thing without my realizing it. I asserted it had been in good order when I left the palazzo. Did I then suggest that some member of the household was responsible? It was quite as probable as that I had had anything to do with it, I retorted hotly. I refused to accept the theory that the damage was deliberate. By some unforeseeable accident the chair had got out of control. The Marchesa herself might have exerted too violent a pressure—she had great muscular strength in her arms—but I didn't believe that, either, I simply couldn't find any explanation. Why had I deserted my post for so long? I had the right to a certain amount of time off; in any case, I used a good part of it in the Marchesa's service. Who had suggested my going to the Corso that afternoon? I couldn't be sure, it might have been myself. Was it true that I was under notice to leave her service? No. Nothing of the kind had been said. They showed me a letter in the Marchesa's handwriting, addressed to her lawyer. In it she said that owing to unexpected developments, she would be making new arrangements in the household, she would send him the details in a day or two, it seemed probable that Signorina Peters would be replaced. This put me in a dilemma; I didn't wish to be the first to mention Florian's name. I realized he was expected that afternoon. I said it was true that I might be resigning from my position, I had spoken to the Marchesa about marriage, but nothing definite in the way of dates had been mentioned. Presumably I sounded halting and looked guilty, for my interrogator gave me a very searching look. I asked for news of the Marchesa and he said briefly that there was no change.

"If she could recover consciousness," I said, "she might be able to solve the mystery."

I was allowed back to my room. Reporters still clamored at the entrance of the palazzo. When they saw me the clamor rose, but I was not allowed a word with them. I saw the flash of a bulb as some enterprising fellow brought his camera into play. I threw my arm over my eyes and ran up the stairs.

Florian came back that night. I heard his voice in the hall, sprang to my feet and went to the door. The inevitable policeman was on guard, though this man was a stranger to me. He said if my presence was required I would be informed. I went back impatiently to wait. I supposed Florian would have to cut a lot of red tape, be subjected to the usual hail of questions, before he would be free to come to me. It was more than an hour before I heard his foot on the stairs. Once more I sprang from my chair, stood beside the door.

The feet went past, down the steps.

They can't have told him I am here, I thought, and wrenched the door open. My love was disappearing down the fine marble staircase. I called to him.

"Florian! Florian, I am here."

He didn't turn; he made no sign that he heard me. Perhaps, I thought, I've lost the power of speech, I only think I cried out. I ran past my guard to the head of the staircase. The guard tried to impede me.

"It's the Marchese," I panted.

Below me a door closed.

The next morning I insisted that I should suffocate unless I were allowed to leave my room and get a little fresh air. To my surprise, no objection was made. The house seemed wrapped in silence, not a voice, not a footstep. My apartments had never been as close to the Marchesa's as (I discovered) is usual; she had a bell beside the bed that rang in my ear if I were wanted in the night. I supposed the strange nurses were still with her; if so, none of them appeared. The doors were closed as inexorably as the doors of family tombs. I went out into the grounds; the sun was peeling the morning shadows from the lawn. I thought, I will go a little further, soon Florian will come and join me. He will know we're not under surveillance here—by which I meant even the police couldn't eavesdrop. I waited, but he didn't come. The silence was enormous. Suddenly I switched around to face the house and was aware of a number of faces melting from windows. I knew how freaks must feel in exhibitions, peered at remorselessly by strangers who can't be repelled because they've paid for the privilege. When I reached the herb garden a police officer sprang up to bar my way.

"No further than this," he said.

"I'm trying to find some reason for the defective brake," I insisted. But he wouldn't let me proceed.

When I got back the man who'd interrogated me on two occasions said that I had a right to send for a lawyer in my own interest. I said I knew no lawyer. He said a name would be supplied. I said I should prefer to get one from a less-prejudiced source. Back in my room I rang furiously. After a very long time a servant answered my bell. I said I wished to see the Marchese.

The Marchese was not available. Oh yes, he knew I was still on the premises. The speaker was acting under his orders.

In that case, I said, I should like the use of a telephone. There wasn't one in my apartments. I had, or supposed I had, friends in Rome who would support me, but I was told no telephone was available, either. Later perhaps—the Marchese was extremely busy, no message could be delivered. In desperation, later that day, I wrote him a letter and gave it to my jailer to be delivered. Some time later it was returned to me, unopened. I think that was the hour when hope died.

I was told once that there is an instant in every nightmare when the dreamer can free himself from the veils of horror enclosing him and break back to the normal world, but let that instant pass unperceived and he has to pursue the road to the end. There must, I supposed, have been a moment when I could have escaped from this maze of horror, and I had let it go. At all events, the nightmare went on and on.

The next day I had an unexpected visitor, a lawyer sent by Florian to protect my interests. He took me through my story once again, and seemed as dissatisfied as the police had been at my answers. He probed more deeply, though, into the situation between me and the Marchesa. I said he had better address himself to Florian, and I asked once more why I hadn't been allowed to see him. He said it was in my own interest, that it would be fatal if a rumor got about that we had been accessories . . . "Accessories in what?" I demanded. "Oh, this is ridiculous. The Marchesa may have resented the idea of a marriage between me and her cousin, but she would be the first to assure you . . ." He gave me such an odd look then that I paused.

"The Marchesa can't help you," he said. "She died this morning without recovering consciousness."

Florian had sufficient influence, I suppose, to have the funeral before the public inquiry. I heard the noise of arrivals, footsteps, voices, but no one came near me; no one, of course, suggested I should attend. When all was quiet again I was allowed out of my room. It was like entering a crape-hung world to walk down the staircase and through the hall. The Italians are sometimes accused of taking nothing seriously, but this isn't true so far as death, at least, is concerned. Even the marble birds on the staircase newel posts were draped in black. I walked around the grounds, avoiding the herb garden. Today no one watched at the windows. I might have walked in an empty world. Already my existence seemed to have been blotted out.

I heard sounds later in the day, the high Italian voices bouncing off the marble walls.

"Still here?"

"Does she think Florian . . . ?"

"Of English parentage—it is well known they are barbarians."

"The inquiry—at the inquiry—" That word was repeated over and over. I had opened my door an inch or two just to establish my connection with a living world, but I soon closed it again. I preferred the stifling atmosphere of my room to those cruel voices.

And after the funeral the public inquiry. I was allowed

out for that all right, was compelled to attend. In a way I was glad, for surely Florian must be there, I should see him at least, somehow he would give me reassurance, explain his strange silence of the past days.

He was there all right, I suppose you could say it was he who saved me.

My appearance was the signal for a rain of hisses; if it hadn't been for the police who clustered around me, it might have been a more spectacular rain. Once more I told my story, was grilled and tricked till I scarcely knew what I said. When at length they let me go it was Florian's turn. All this time he hadn't attempted to catch my eye or send me a message. Looking back, I can see he was as much on tenterhooks as I. He told the court it was absurd to suppose I had any hand in the Marchesa's unfortunate death, since I had no motive. The result to me would be the loss of a position I had occupied for eighteen months and in which he believed I had been happy and secure. He laughed at the idea of any marriage contract between us, had never spoken of it to the Marchesa because he had never entertained any such notion. Letters he had written to me, that had been taken from me by force, were produced in court. They contained affectionate, even passionate, phrases, but nowhere, he insisted, had marriage been suggested. He couldn't say whether the Marchesa had been aware of his relationship until, unfortunately, a letter of his had gone astray, but she would not have been surprised or distressed. There was a sort of chuckle at that. Everyone present knew of Florian's colorful private life; it might have been indiscreet to include one of the Marchesa's servants, but—the incident could be shrugged off. As for the letter to the lawyer, he could explain that. He had his cousin's permission to announce an engagement between them, it had been the Marchesa's wish and generally accepted. He and Perdita—the names revolved like blinding suns—he and Perdita.

I didn't for an instant believe the story he was telling the court; he'd never looked at her, no, he was making this sacrifice for me, and I didn't want it, I didn't want it. I thought triumphantly, When they come to read my letters to him they'll know it's a lie. But those letters were not produced. Florian told the court he never kept letters from ladies—there was another snigger there. The letter to the lawyer referred to the new conditions that would obtain after the wedding. Changes would be made in the household, the Marchesa wished the lawyer to arrange for a small present to me as a return for my devoted service. I had spoken to him more than once of wishing to return to my native country. And it was true, it was true. You will take me to England after we're married, I'd pleaded. I would like to see my father's country. I never thought of it as mine. Finally he made the point that no nurse will risk injuring her patient, she holds the honor of the profession, as well as her private honor, in her hands. He was very eloquent; I could understand how he was so successful in his business dealings, you could feel the atmosphere of the court lightening. Florian went on to say that he'd had no communication with me since his return, and there was plenty of evidence to support that. He even persuaded Perdita to go into the witness box and say that she had never heard any suggestion of an alliance between us; she had realized there was an amorous situation, perhaps, but once the engagement was announced I should be leaving the household.

My lawyer produced some witnesses to speak of my attentive care for the dead woman. The doctor said he had always had implicit faith, the Marchesa herself had always spoken well of me . . . and I suppose it occurred to a number of people that if I'd wanted to murder my tyrant there were safer, more certain ways. She might have been injured but not killed; she might have recovered sufficiently to bring a charge herself—the general view was that the case against me was Not Proven. I wouldn't care to put it much higher than that.

"You have been very fortunate," my lawyer said to me.

"A matter of opinion," I told him. "Where do I go from here?"

He told me that the Marchese, in consultation with his lawyers, had made a certain provision for my future. Clearly I could not hope again to find work in Rome, equally clearly my presence there would be an embarrassment to Florian and also to Perdita. A single ticket to London would be supplied to me, together with enough British and foreign currency to cover my journey. In London a sum of money would be lodged at a London bank and could be claimed by me on receipt of a letter the lawyer would have signed. In England I could make a fresh start. A very generous offer, my lawyer said.

"And now," I suggested, "how about my side of it? What am I to give in return?"

He told me—all Florian's letters, any gifts he had made

me and an assurance that I would leave Rome immediately and not return for at least ten years.

"Am I not to see Florian again?" I inquired.

He widened his eyes in astonishment. "To what end, signorina?"

"I should like to thank him myself for the sacrifice he has made on my behalf," I said steadily.

The lawyer looked as if he couldn't believe his ears. "Sacrifice, signorina? The Marchese has behaved as any man of honor would do."

But I thought, No, only what a man in love would do. There could be no going back from his declaration of a betrothal between himself and Perdita, and never, never would I believe that this is what he had wished.

"All the same," I said, "I should like a final word. Remember, I shall not be crossing the frontier even for ten years."

I don't think he approved, but he made the arrangement. Florian looked unbelievably pale and remote; his lawyer was with him.

"The Marchese has to leave in a few minutes," said this man.

"I shan't keep him more than a few minutes," I told him. "Florian, I wanted to thank you and to say how grieved I am to have—have involved you . . ."

He shook his head. All the fires were damped today. "Not you, Solange."

I thought that was his way of telling me he knew I had had no hand in his cousin's death.

"And one other thing," I continued. "There has been a lot of gossip, but I wish to say in the presence of witnesses," for my lawyer was there also, "that I know there was never any thought in your mind of marriage between us."

It was an effort to say the words, but for his sake they must be said. And I had no sooner spoken them than I realized that they were true. Probably I was the only person in Rome who had ever supposed the notion had crossed his mind. He had loved me, I knew that, but he was a man to whom love came easily. He had warmth and charm and he expected love as poor men look for daily bread. When he saw that my mind was set on marriage, how disturbed he must have been, and by then I was so deeply involved it was difficult for him to extricate himself. In a way, I thought, his cousin's death had cut a knot for him, since any thought of marriage now must be out of the question.

He said, "Naturally, I never believed ill of you, Solange. I hope in your own country happiness awaits you."

It was like putting a coin into a machine and getting a printed card in return. I put out my hand and he held it for a moment, but the electric current that used to run between us had been switched off. I thought I was crazy to have imagined I could ever be his wife, the mother of the future Marchese. He had been bred to a certain manner of living, he could no more escape it than he could leave his skin. I tried to see him going to some office each day, returning to the equivalent of a suburban home. It was fantastic. Now I felt all the blame should lie on my shoulders. I even began to believe that he had always meant to marry his cousin.

There was nothing more to say. I returned to my room. Florian left the palazzo that night. It was his wish that I should stay at the palazzo until my departure, that is, two days hence. I should keep a guard, I should in no circumstances allow myself to be interviewed by the press. Next day I called a cab and was driven to a hairdresser near the Colonna, where I had never visited. I had my hair restyled and darkened. It had been the thing about me Florian had sometimes seemed to love best. The Italians are a dark people; all the Pollis were as black as night. Florian used to take my hair in his hands. It's like living gold, he would say. When I returned, the lawyer, who was to remain on the premises until my departure, congratulated me on my good sense. I packed my clothes and had the box forwarded by train to a London station. Take care of your receipt, the lawyer said. It is your passport to your new life. That last day seemed to go on forever. Most of the servants had been put on half wages, Perdita had gone to her sister in Milan. I had my single air ticket, the travel agency had booked a room for me in a hotel in the Cromwell Road near the West London Air Terminal. I was to remain here for a week, after which my connection with the Pollis would be as though it had never existed. I would be on my own. The money in the London bank would tide me over until I found employment.

Indeed, between them Florian and the lawyer had covered every contingency except the one they could not possibly have foreseen.

2

SOMEONE SPOKE URGENTLY in my ear, a hand touched my elbow. It was my waiter telling me that my coach was about to depart for the airport. I snatched up my small case and pouch bag and hurried between the tables. The two Italian macaws had vanished; they were already on board. When we reached the airport we learned that owing to the vagaries of the weather, our through flight to London had been canceled, we would touch down at Bordeaux, where we would take up a number of passengers. Others had been transferred from another flight to this plane; they were those who wished to alight at Bordeaux. There was a lot of loud chatter and complaint, to which no one paid any heed. It made no difference to me. I still felt like someone existing in a void.

I took a seat near the front, feeling that this way fewer people would have to pass me, which would reduce the likelihood of my being recognized. The airplane was about two thirds full—some superstitious passengers had canceled their journey, preferring to wait for better weather. I had a seat beside a window, but overlooking a wing. By straining I could catch an occasional glimpse of the world, a long way below, looking like a sheet of postage stamps in greens and browns, with black lines that were walls or hedges and white streaks that were water. My Italian pair were sitting just behind me. They were still talking nineteen to the dozen and after a little I heard the name of Polli.

"It was the daughter, I daresay," said one. "It is known she intended to catch her cousin, and this was her opportunity. Once the nurse was out of the way—she was in the house, yes? There were no witnesses."

"It is no wonder they did not wish to press the prosecution," said the other. "But—what a Borgia—her own mother."

I was sure that if there had been a little more evidence they would have spoken quite as confidently of my guilt, nevertheless it was a solution I could not ignore. It was some time before it occurred to me it mattered very little to me what had happened. Perdita had always made me think of Hermia in *A Midsummer Night's Dream. I may be little but I can scratch.* There would be no servants about at that time of day. She had only to offer to wheel her mother into the herb garden, let go of the handles of the chair, and quite a small push would send her flying . . .

"No," I said aloud, but I knew I would never be able wholly to obliterate that vision from my mind. I remembered what she had once done to a dog who had displeased her.

I turned to the window again, but now we seemed to be flying through murky cotton wool, a condition which endured until we touched down at Bordeaux. Nearly all the passengers left the plane. I decided to buy some custom-free brandy and have some more coffee. The other passengers drifted past; I didn't pay any attention to them. Mostly they were businessmen, with a few married couples, one or two commercial representatives. I was the only woman traveling alone. I couldn't guess that this change of direction by the airplane company was going to alter my whole life.

I found I couldn't face the possibility of being recognized in the café, so when I had bought my brandy I went out and found a row of chairs facing onto the airstrip, and here I sat down to wait. The plane looked like a great silver bird stretching its wings in the sun which had suddenly rolled away the clouds.

"Could you be British?" said a voice in my ear in an accent I didn't recognize.

I looked up in instant suspicion to find a girl of my own age taking the chair beside me. She was dark and gay and full of a kind of serene joy.

"I heard you ask for brandy," the girl explained. As I was traveling on a British passport and wanted to air my English, which, I suspected, might have got a bit rusty, I had asked for the bottle in what was, I suppose, my native tongue. "No sense being solitary unless you have to," the girl went on.

It occurred to me she might be from some newspaper.

"This is my first time out," she told me. "I'm from Australia, but I reckon you guessed that, they say we give ourselves away every time we open our mouths. You going to London?"

I said yes.

"They say it's a great city. You got folk there?"

I said I'd been working abroad for some years, my folk—instinctively I used her word—were all dead.

Her hand, warm, confiding, touched mine. "I know, bvoney. Gives you a funny feeling, doesn't it? Even if they were old and you knew they couldn't last, it doesn't seem to make all that difference. Like finding yourself alone in the nest, when there's always been someone up till now to lift a wing between you and the storm."

I thought it an unusual simile, but apt. Except that Florian had been my wing.

"They tell me I'll feel as if I'd got into a dolls' house after our wide-open spaces," the girl went on. "But I reckon living in a dolls' house could be as much a part of a person's experience as anything else."

Over the microphone passengers were asked to take their seats for the flight to London. We walked together to the plane. The girl, who said her name was Julie Taylor, stayed at my side. I saw with relief that the two macaws had remained behind at Bordeaux.

She had been a schoolteacher back home, Julie confided, living with Aunt Marty, just the two of them. Like me, she had been an orphan for some years, only unlike me, she'd never felt the iciness of that estate. Aunt Marty had died a few months before, leaving her a little legacy. "See the world while you can, she always advised me, it doesn't pay to put things off. She'd always meant to travel herself, but she kept putting it off. You'll think as I did you've all the time in the world, she told me, then something happens, you fall in love with a local boy, you marry, you have a family, and one day you find yourself dying in the hick town where you've spent your whole life. And it's not," Julie wound up, "as if I had anyone but myself to consider now."

I told her my name; I said I'd been working in Rome. It didn't mean a thing to her. I knew I could have said the Marchesa Polli and she wouldn't have blinked an eyelid. That was the moment I began to realize Rome wasn't the whole world.

"I mean to see Rome on my way back," Julie said, "but I reckoned I'd start with England. Our plane sprang a leak or something, anyway, we had to come down at Bordeaux.

There's always a meaning in everything, Aunt Marty says. Maybe it was meant for you and me to meet."

While we were talking the plane had carried us away from the sun and we were once more back in a world of cloud. What could be seen beyond the window, which wasn't much, was dark and menacing. A woman a few seats away was starting to panic.

"I can't see a thing, Arthur," she declared. "How can the pilot . . . ?"

"They have radar, dear," Arthur said.

"I don't see how it can change so suddenly," she wailed. "In Bordeaux . . ."

"Not long now, dear," said Arthur. I heard a newspaper crackle.

"I guess they're British, too," Julie confided. "They were in the bar. There was another Britisher there, on his own. I talked to him for a bit; to hear the way he went on you'd think London was the gate of heaven."

"It's natural to think that about your own city," I suggested, remembering my love for Rome and the conditions of my exile. It sounds melodramatic but at that instant I thought my heart would break. Up till now events had moved so fast and so catastrophically I hadn't had the time to evaluate my own sense of banishment.

I drew a long sighing breath. "Nervous?" asked Julie in gentle tones. "I guess the pilot knows his job."

I stared helplessly out of the porthole. Now the cirrus cloud was all around us, I knew we must be flying utterly blind.

"I'm cold," I conceded.

"Maybe we could get you some coffee."

I saw her look around, then she lifted her hand and waved in an indescribably gay little gesture. "My Briton of the bar," she explained.

"Don't worry about the coffee," I told her. "The stewardess will have her hands full."

The nervous woman behind me called out, "I'm going to be sick, I know I'm going to be sick. Arthur, I want to get down."

Two or three people laughed heartlessly, others were impatient. "I told you it was dangerous in this weather," the brittle voice whined on. "The forecast . . ."

The air hostess appeared, looking as cool as a painting. "Drink this," I heard her say, though I couldn't see what was being offered. "We're in an air pocket, it makes the plane a little unsteady, but there's nothing to worry about."

She was a good linguist, that girl. When she had to make an announcement, as she did not long after, she made it first in Italian, then in French, then in English.

Another voice, this time as English as roast beef, observed heartily, "It's what I've always said, if we were meant to fly we'd be given wings, just like if were meant to walk we'd have four legs."

A few people laughed, but the woman at the back was beyond relief. She began to scream, you could feel panic spreading like water stealing over a flat surface. Julie Taylor put out her hand and touched my arm.

"It's going to be all right," she said. "I'm wearing my mascot—look!"

She pushed up the sleeve of her coat and showed it to me. It was a bracelet made of copper, shaped like a snake, with small turquoise eyes. "It belonged to Aunt Marty," she said, "she wouldn't walk the length of the garden without it. Wear that and you'll never come to harm, she told me. I wanted her to have it buried with her, but she said no, she was through with luck and all such, now it was my turn. She was wearing it when she died," she added softly.

"How did she square that with never coming to harm?" I asked.

Julie gave me a strange look. "She wouldn't call that coming to harm, she was an old woman, my uncle had died years before, she lost her only son, but she never felt —bereaved."

"She had you," I said, and Julie gave me her lovely smile.

"I guess that worked both ways. I don't know how I'd have gotten on without her."

There was a sudden terrific lurch and then a crash, as though a trayful of china had fallen over. It was no longer possible to pretend everything was going smoothly. I heard a quick crackle as one or two paper bags were opened. The stewardess went to a man sitting nearby and asked him if he'd mind putting out his pipe, the fumes were upsetting one of the lady passengers. He made rather a fuss about it; people who became airsick shouldn't travel by air, he said. Why do they do it?

The loud accented voice of the man who'd talked about having wings boomed out again. "People who haven't any consideration shouldn't go on breathing," he remarked, "but they do."

Julie laughed, and the man put his pipe out. "He's just an

old sweetie," Julie told me. "We got talking while we waited. I'd give you one of my cards, he told me, only they're a bit in short supply just now, and I can see you're one of the ones that'll never need it." She smiled. "I told him about my bracelet, and he said I suppose that's what they call a symbol, not that I go for this hightoned talk myself."

I thought I knew what he meant. All I knew of Julie was what I'd been able to gather during our short conversation, but she gave out the most extraordinary sense of security, as though whatever happened she could never be mortally wounded in herself, as most people are, a sort of armor . . . Impulsively I put my hand over hers. It was the first human contact I'd felt for ages. You couldn't count Florian, it was like touching a stone, and even the lawyer who'd represented me hadn't offered his hand when he said goodbye.

"You're my mascot," I told her.

In a flash she had removed the snake from her wrist, and before I realized what she was going to do she had slipped it onto mine.

"Now you'll be safe," she said.

"But you—I can't take your luck," I protested.

"I reckon you could do with a bit," she said. "You've had trouble—bad—haven't you?"

I muttered something.

"Maybe one of these days you'll feel you can talk about it," she said. "It's a help sometimes. Up to you, of course. You got a place to stay in London?"

I told her about the hotel room that had been booked for me.

"You reckon they could find a corner for me, under the bath or somewhere?"

It seemed to me characteristic she hadn't even bothered to that extent.

Then the lights in front of us flashed on. While we'd been talking I hadn't noticed we were plunging more wildly than ever. Pieces of hand luggage started to fall all around us; the woman at the back set up a steady scream.

"We're going to be killed, all of us," she declared.

"Please fasten your safety belts," said the hostess, walking down the aisle as prim and unruffled as if she'd just stepped out of a bandbox. "I'm going to have a word with the pilot. In the meantime, please don't panic, it only makes things more difficult for everyone."

That calmed most people but not the woman in back. "How can he tell where to land in weather like this?" she cried in her high piercing voice. "He could drop us all into the sea."

"By guess and by God," said the imperturbable cockney voice behind me. "He carries a lot of responsibility, don't he?" It was difficult to tell whether he meant God or the pilot.

The hostess came back with the second pilot, who proceeded to address us, also in three languages. This time he spoke in English first.

"Ladies and Gentlemen," he said, "I'm sorry about this delay, but it's due to weather conditions over which we've no control. We've struck a spot of bother and it appears it's not possible to land at the London Airport, so the pilot is trying to locate another airstrip where we can get the word to come down. I'm afraid this is making us a bit late, and I'm very sorry. It's rather murky outside, so if there's anyone who hasn't fastened a safety belt I suggest this is the time to repair the omission."

"Where are we?" someone shouted.

"It's difficult to say with any certainty, because we're cloud-bound. If we could descend a bit we might be able to get our bearings, but believe me there's nothing to worry about. The pilot's a very experienced man, and he doesn't want to break his leg or anything any more than anyone else. At the moment he's playing safe, which may hold us up a little, but I'm sure you'll agree it's best for everyone."

He repeated this in Italian and in French. Like the air hostess, you'd think he was just telling us the bus was being delayed a few minutes because the conductor hadn't turned up, something a little tiresome but nothing, as he said, to worry about.

"Poor man!" said Julie's voice in my ear. "I reckon God's not the only one with responsibility."

Arthur's wife was belying all I had ever heard about British phlegm by dissolving into a fit of hysterics. The air hostess asked coolly if there happened to be a doctor on board. Miraculously there was.

"You don't want me to knock you out, I suppose?" he said brutally. But she was past caring: "I told my husband—I don't want to fly, I said—this absurd meeting of yours—if you're so important they can hold it up, can't they?"

"Who'd be a married man?" inquired the indomitable cockney voice. "A life sentence, that's what it is."

Someone laughed.

"Straight up," said the Englishman seriously.

For a moment the tension lifted. Then a French voice said something angrily about the British—like children—and that started Arthur's wife off again.

"Put her out, for God's sake," urged the second pilot. "Toni's got enough on his plate as it is."

I suppose the doctor gave her an injection, because she quieted suddenly, stopped in mid-scream as it were. Julie's hand was still on mine, warm yet cool. The great healers must have had hands like that, I thought, and what a nurse she'd have made and lucky children who had her for a teacher.

Now the only noise we could hear was the grinding of the engines; outside, the wind seemed to be rushing past like a horizontal torrent, darkness had come down and smothered the world. Then the noise altered, quieting, and the plane dropped a little. A fresh voice behind me said, "That's nice. One of the engines cut out. Still, he'll probably manage all right. I've come in more than once in the old days on a single engine. What they want at the controls these days isn't a pilot, it's a bloody magician."

The machine was limping now, like a wounded animal under pursuit. For the first time it occurred to me we might all be doomed. Perhaps I shivered at the thought, because Julie's voice in my ear said, "You're bound to be all right, you have your mascot." Those were the last words I heard before we crashed—all the lights went out, for an instant we seemed to have the noise of a collapsing world in our ears, the drums seemed as if they must break under the pressure. Then the noise died and the hand that had been holding mine went away, but it didn't matter, because this was the end of the world.

I opened my eyes to find myself in a narrow bed with what looked like thin sheets of metal all around me. I wondered if it was some sort of coffin and I must have spoken or cried out, because one of the walls was pulled back and a woman in a white uniform and cap came and stood beside me.

"Come round at last, have you?" she said coolly. "Well, you've taken your time, and with beds at the premium they are . . ."

I didn't think she was heartless or cynical, I knew that was the way nurses often rallied their patients. "I'll get Sister," she said and disappeared.

Sister came and took the place beside the bed. "We've been waiting two weeks for this day," she said. It didn't make sense. It was only a short time since I'd been in a plane with Julie beside me. "When you feel up to it we'd like to ask you some questions," she went on, "but no one's going to hustle you. Only if there's anyone you'd like sent for . . ."

"There isn't anyone," I said. I hadn't got the situation fully in focus yet; it was like a television screen with the picture gradually taking shape. "This is a hospital, isn't it?" I said. "What happened to the plane?"

"It came down," said Sister briefly. "You were hurt, but you're doing nicely now."

"My head," I told her. "It feels very strange."

"That was one of the things that got injured in the crash," she told me. "Don't try and force yourself, it'll come back in due course. Nature's never in a hurry."

I remembered a nurse at my training hospital saying just the same thing. "Nature's never in a hurry, just you be thankful you're not an elephant," she told an expectant mother. "They take two years."

I giggled at the recollection. "I'm glad I'm not an elephant," I said.

Someone else, a man, came around the side of the screen. "So you've decided to come back to us, Julie," he remarked. "That's good. Up to now we've been doing all the work, now you'll be able to lend us a hand."

I was feeling rather fogged, but something he'd said jarred. I couldn't place it. I looked down at my bare wrist, and I held it with the fingers of the other hand. There should have been something . . .

"You're thinking of your bracelet," said Sister at once. "It's all right, it's quite safe. We had to take it off, of course, but you shall have it back later. It was lucky really that you were wearing it, it helped us to identify you. It was about the only clue we had."

I realized what had been wrong with the doctor's speech. "No," I said painfully. "Julie Taylor . . ."

"That's right. Luckily there was someone on board who remembered your wearing it."

I was fighting some mysterious obstruction in my throat. Sister's words seemed to come across in slow motion, and my reactions followed suit. And yet I was sure conversation shouldn't be like this. It should sparkle like a river and flow like light.

"The girl sitting next to me," I enunciated with extreme care. "She's the one."

Doctor and Sister exchanged glances. Then the doctor said, "Listen, Julie, whenever you hear this it's bound to be a shock, you may as well take it first as last. I'm afraid your friend was killed when the plane crashed, together with a number of others. It was a miracle, really, you got out alive."

"Not a miracle," I insisted. "The mascot."

"Mascot? Oh, you mean the bracelet. Well, perhaps." I could see they were going to humor me. "She can't have known a thing about it."

Someone giggled again. It had to be me. I couldn't help it, it didn't make any sense. I was the lucky one who had got away to a future that held little hope; Julie had been blotted out at the beginning of a new phase of existence. I'd only been with her a little over an hour, but I realized she was one of those who light lamps wherever they go. Being a nurse makes you a shade more sensitive than other people, perhaps; you can nearly always tell which patients are going to live in spite of everything, and which will die simply because they haven't got the will to overcome. Julie had been made for life, and she was dead. It was absurd and wrong.

"You don't understand." I knew this was my final effort, for the moment at least. The picture was beginning to clot again. I hung on to the side of the bed, I was afraid I might be going to fall or float away.

"You can explain better when you've had a bit of a sleep," Sister promised.

"No sense fooling yourself," said the doctor robustly. "It was a frightful thing, but this is a world in which frightful things happen. There were only three survivors . . ."

"The two old women," I began, before I remembered they'd stayed at Bordeaux.

"Both the others were men. That's enough for today. You've been a very sick girl, but just remember you've started to get better. Hang on to that. I'll be seeing you."

And he was gone. A nurse brought me something to drink. I didn't know if it was a sleeping draught, but soon afterward the clouds came down again. I thought, I can't argue any more now, and anyway the doctor's gone. There's plenty of time. If Julie's dead I can't do her any harm just using her name for a few days. She had no people, she'd told me that. I had the doctor's word that I wasn't really fit for argument, and then I remembered those faces in Rome, I didn't want to see the faces around the bed change from human to vulpine. The doctor was right, I'd be able to straighten out the situation when I was a bit stronger.

I don't know if it was the next day or the day after that they took the screens away and I saw I was in a ward full of people. "You've had a world to yourself long enough," Sister said. "You're our star patient, Julie, everyone's interested in you."

I must have flinched at that, because she said reassuringly, "It's all right, no one's going to eat you. We're very proud of you."

Later one of the walking patients came and sat on the bed. "You gave us ever such a nasty feeling, dear," she said, "expecting you to peg out. How are you feeling now? No visitors yet, I suppose. But people have been calling to ask after you ever since they brought you in."

"I don't know anyone," I said.

She gave me an enormous wink. "More people know Tom Fool than Tom Fool knows. There was a piece in the paper about you. I'll show you." She pattered off to her locker and came back with a newspaper cutting. "I'll read it, shall I? 'Julie Taylor, one of the three survivors of the Phoenix plane that crashed in thick fog on Wednesday night, is still lying unconscious in Kingswell General Hospital with severe head and other injuries. Miss Taylor was making her first journey from Australia to England. She was one of three passengers thrown clear of the burning wreckage . . .' "

"I don't want to hear any more," I said. I couldn't endure the thought of that bright spirit consumed in the flames.

"Well, I was only telling you." The voice sounded offended.

Here was my chance to say, It's all a mistake, I'm not Julie Taylor, but at that instant a nurse came bustling up.

"What's going on here?" she demanded. "Mrs. Blount, what's the paper?" She snatched it out of the woman's hand.

"I thought she'd want to know," explained Mrs. Blount in an ingratiating whine. "It's not every day you get your picture in the papers."

"There's no picture," said the nurse firmly. She drove the woman away. "Everyone on that plane must have been killed outright. It's a miracle you're alive. And I don't mind telling you we didn't expect to save you. You put up a great fight and we're very proud of you."

I couldn't believe that. I'd been lying there like a log, with about the same amount of sense. Nevertheless I smiled and said, "It doesn't seem fair, though."

"Why not?" demanded the nurse. "Why shouldn't Julie Taylor be saved as much as anyone else?"

I suppose that was my first real chance to put matters straight, but I told myself she was a stranger to me, I wanted to explain to Sister or possibly the doctor, and there'd be plenty of time. I see now that at the back of my mind was the thought that perhaps I could skip the explanations altogether, though I'd have been shocked to know it at the time. If I'd really been Julie I'd have told the truth then, whatever the consequences, but I'd realized from our brief meeting that Julie was worth ten of me. She'd never have taken the coward's way. I'm not really up to all that argument, I told myself weakly, I shall only make a mess of it, and probably she won't believe me. When I'm a bit stronger I'll clear up everything. I supposed it might mean having recourse to Rome to prove my identity. I'd realized that Solange Peters was officially dead and buried in a mass funeral. It was even possible that news of the crash had been received in Rome, doubtless with relief—another proof that God was on the side of the big battalions. Coming into the open now would mean more trouble for Florian—and all the confusion about the money in the bank and the box of clothes at the railway station. I mulled the situation over this way and that until, when Sister appeared carrying the snake bracelet, I was in a positive fever.

"What's all this?" demanded Sister, gimlet-eyed. "What's upset you, Julie? Look, I've brought you your mascot. You must have had it a long time."

"I've been thinking," I said, making a final effort. "That other girl—Solange Peters—"

"She told you her name, did she? H'm. I wonder if she told you her history. I hadn't meant to discuss this with you, Julie, but I can see you're getting all worked up. Now we know her story. She was coming to a country where she had no friends, coming under a cloud, she'd have faced a very hard future—I don't mean that reconciles one to what happened, of course, but . . ." "She didn't do it," I said. "Kill the Marchesa, I mean."

"She seems to have been very confiding. Well, perhaps

she didn't, and in any case it's not for us to judge. But that sort of accusation is very hard to live down. You go on thinking she was innocent—poor girl, she needed some friends."

"She wouldn't have done it," I urged. "She was a nurse."

"Some people don't have much luck, do they?" agreed Sister briskly. "Here's Doctor."

"How are you this morning?" the doctor said.

Sister answered, "She's worried about that girl who shared her seat on the plane."

"She didn't do it," I repeated.

"Perhaps not," the doctor agreed. "She was never officially charged, was she? Still, whichever way it was, it's not important any more, not to you, anyhow. Her life's over, poor thing, yours lies ahead. You owe it to yourself as well as to the rest of us to make the most of it."

I reminded myself that I was probably going to be questioned later by the police or whoever was conducting the inquiry into the crash. I could tell them. The hospital wouldn't want reporters and photographers all around the place, which was bound to happen when the news broke. My lawyer had been wrong, I saw, in telling me that the British would know nothing about the Marchesa's death. I was deceiving myself, of course, but at that stage I still believed (half-heartedly) that I was going to try to establish the facts.

(Actually, I was hardly questioned at all. Of the three survivors, I had sustained the worst injuries, and one of the other two had given a clear account, so far as anything could be clear, of what happened. The disaster hadn't been due to the failure of one of the engines; the machine had hit a tree while the pilot was trying to come down, and had broken apart. There was no one to blame, just sympathy for the bereaved; the matter was closed. Another aircraft disaster to be classed with cars that had collided in that night's fog, pedestrians run down with fatal results, no need to badger a girl who clearly wouldn't be able to add anything.)

It was crazy, of course. I couldn't really have imagined I could keep up the deception forever and ever, and every day that passed made the truth seem more remote, more difficult to expose. Nevertheless, the sense of respite remained. Sister had brought me the dead girl's bag, a big olive-green affair that I had last seen on Julie's lap. I took out the Australian passport, inspected the photograph. I saw a girl not unlike me, though seeing us together no one could have doubted whose this was. For the first time I wondered how far my injuries might have changed my appearance. I hunted through the bag for a compact, but there was none. The Sister would have removed that, of course, and there was only one reason. I knew they'd cut my hair, though I didn't think it could have grown enough for the dye to be obvious. Anyway, lots of girls dyed their hair, that wouldn't mean a thing.

"I had a compact," I told the nurse when she came around. "It seems to have vanished."

"I'll speak to Sister," the nurse said.

"Could I have a mirror?" I asked.

"All in good time," said Nurse. She moved on. "Now, Miss Ayscroft, we can't have you playing us up. You can't expect to have an operation without feeling a little discomfort later. You lie there and reflect how fine you're going to feel when we do let you out."

Later the woman Sister had snubbed, Mrs. Blount, came stealing down the ward and sat on my bed.

"Feeling better, dear? Coo, your poor face."

"How bad is it?" I asked.

By the swiftness of her reply I realized how bad it might be. "You don't want to worry, dear, they do wonders with plastic surgery these days. A cousin of mine had her face practically reconstituted, and the advantage to her you'd never believe."

"Get me a glass," I whispered.

"I daren't," she told me. "Sister'd murder me."

"It's my face," I pointed out, and she gave a sort of horrified giggle. I had a ghastly feeling that perhaps I hadn't got a nose or something.

"Get me a glass," I snapped, and she went away and came back with a hand mirror. I stared at myself. There wasn't as much to see as I expected, there were so many bandages, but I saw I needn't have worried about being recognized. I hadn't known till now—at least I hadn't thought—that I'd suffered from burns. I didn't feel anything much after that first glance, but this was a stranger, someone I'd never seen before; and whether I thought about it or not, I knew what plastic surgery can do, I'd seen it in Rome.

Mrs. Blount was looking nervous. "It'll be all right, dear," she insisted. "It's not as though you were blind or anything." She took the glass back.

"Mrs. Blount!" said an awful voice, and Sister appeared on her morning rounds, like a spirit of vengeance.

Mrs. Blount was a big woman but she jumped where she sat. The glass fell out of her hand and cracked across.

"Seven years bad luck!" she whispered, appalled.

"You deserve it, every minute of it," Sister told her. "Pick that up and—*go away*. If you know how to turn yourself into a mouse, hide in the wainscot."

I never saw anyone so deflated. The awful thing was I wanted to giggle.

"You're much too sensible to let that upset you," Sister assured me in her cool voice.

"I asked for it," I said with belated justice.

"She should have had more sense. This is a halfway house."

I nodded. "It's all right, Sister." I could see she thought how well I was taking it; she couldn't guess that in my (temporary) disfigurement might lie my salvation.

After she'd gone I examined the handbag. I thought it might contain some clues to Julie Taylor's past. Of course, if there were letters there, then my deception couldn't hope to succeed, because letters have to be answered, also they're written by living people who may suddenly turn up and blow the gaff. But there were none. Only a few snapshots in an envelope—some of an elderly woman with the words Aunt Marty on the back, one of a cat labeled Sam, two or three of a house, the house where Julie had lived, I suppose. No pictures of relatives, no pictures of friends. There was a wallet containing a wad of Australian pounds which could be cashed in England and a book of letters of credit. I didn't bother to count them, I knew I could never cash them. The Australian pounds I'd use, I had to have some currency and I couldn't touch the allowance made to me by Florian, any more than I could collect my clothes. As soon as I was well enough I must look for a job—not nursing, because I'd be asked about training and diplomas, and those belonged to Solange Peters. Julie had been a schoolteacher, but I hadn't any references there either. There must be something I could do. I could find that out when I was able to leave the hospital.

Mrs. Blount, who had the epidermis of an elephant, came stealing back. "I wanted to ask you, dear," she said, "what does it feel like to sit next to a murderer?"

"I never did," I told her.

Her huge face was transformed with pleasure; the red color suffused it. Here was a bonus indeed. "You mean, no one told you? My dear, she was a nurse, she killed her patient, in Italy this was, poison or something—" she hadn't even bothered to get her facts right—"lucky not to stand trial, but it was an influential family and they say they were afraid of what might come out. So they packed her off —and see what happened. It's what I always say, you can't escape the justice of God."

"You really think a planeful of people had to die in a horrible way because of one girl who may have been innocent?"

"It's like the war," said Mrs. Blount vaguely. "Lots of innocent people are killed in that. There was a bomb in my sister's street that didn't miss her, and she never killed anyone in her life."

"I can only assure you," I said, and by the way my voice trembled with rage I knew I must be getting better, "if she was a murderer she looks exactly like everyone else. You or Nurse or . . ."

In her indignation Mrs. Blount missed my change of tense. "Well, really!" she said. I had offended her past forgiveness now. She stopped at half a dozen beds on her way back to tell them I took murder in my stride. I daresay by the time she reached her own place she had cooked up a separate murder for me.

Soon after that I left the hospital for the Godsmere Clinic to have my face patched up. Here there were cases so much worse than mine, I felt ashamed of even a grain of self-pity. Though the treatment was painful and sometimes frightening, in a sense I was glad, because it gave me a breathing space, a chance to grow into Julie Taylor. The fact that everyone here took my identity for granted was a help, of course, and by the time I left—I was there a little more than two months—I really did feel I was Julie. Solange, poor girl, had died and was best forgotten, and with her went all the tragedy and heartbreak of Rome. There was a good library at the clinic and I spent a lot of time reading up about Australia, particularly the district where Julie had come from. I used to practice her signature, too, though I didn't intend to use her letters of credit. It didn't seem to me particularly wrong to take her name, it was no use to her any more, and you only had to meet her once to realize she'd give you anything she had, even her life if it came to that, but taking her money by forgery, somehow that stuck in my craw. I had one piece of unexpected good fortune. It appeared that Julie had taken out an accident insurance policy and the company honored this once they'd satisfied themselves I was the true beneficiary. It's odd how the mind works, I didn't feel dishonest taking that. But it did give me a jar, because it seemed as if she would have named a beneficiary of her own. However, I found out that she was only insured against accident; I supposed she thought there was no one to benefit by her death. The money was very welcome. I knew it would tide me over while I looked for a job. I still wasn't sure what residue of scar tissue there would be when all the bandages and dressings were removed, but I proved to be one of the fortunate ones. I didn't look like the twin sister of the girl who had left Rome, but there was a considerable likeness and such marks as there were were almost invisible.

"An exhibition job," Matron told me. "You won't have to worry about being looked at, except for the nicest possible reason."

That matron was kindness itself. She asked if I had a place to go when I left the clinic; she knew I couldn't have any plans. When I said no she rang up a friend of hers, a Mrs. Stafford, who kept a boarding house, mainly for young people, near Streatham Common. "Better for you than right inside London," Matron explained, "till you've found your feet, anyway. The air's fresh, too, not just Diesel fumes, which is all you can look for in a city these days, and you can easily reach town by underground or bus." She added that it would be cheaper than staying in London, and that was an important consideration.

When I asked about payment at the clinic she said there was nothing to pay, it was all covered by the National Health. She told me about getting insurance cards and said as soon as I had a job—she seemed to think I'd get one immediately—I should go to the Ministry of Labour and ask for a card. I could explain about the clinic, and if there was any trouble she would write herself. I went out for a bit before leaving Godsmere, bought myself a suit and some cashmere jumpers and the sort of shoes other girls were wearing. I also bought a suitcase, since no landlady would take me in without one, and Matron herself saw me off on the London train.

She said a car would meet me at the station and take me to Streatham, since I didn't know my way round and Mrs. Stafford was expecting me. She didn't ask me to keep in touch, I could see she wanted me to put this part of my experience behind me with all the rest.

I can't explain the confidence I felt as the train drew out. Dick Whittington setting forth to conquer London might have understood.

3

PRIDE GOES BEFORE A FALL. My confidence was to be gravely shaken before I reached London. At first all seemed well. I had a carriage to myself, the weather was good, if I got bored I could walk along to the buffet car and get myself a cup of tea. I traveled on a second-class ticket. Begin as you mean to go on, Matron said. At first I amused myself looking out of the window, seeing the English landscape for the first time. It was a bright day. I liked seeing the fields and trees and cottages, the squat Saxon churches, and the little cars running about the roads like colored beetles. Presently we drew up at a terminus and people started climbing in. The door of my carriage bounced open and a big rubber ball of a man fell into a corner seat. He was wearing very bright brown clothes and a brown checked cap. I thought he might be a farmer—when I knew England better I realized he looked more like a bookmaker, but I hadn't met any then. He had a pile of papers in his hands and a shabby little bag that he dumped on the seat. For some time he seemed obsessed with his documents. I had a book and pretended to read it, flicking over a page every few minutes but not taking in a word. I hadn't expected to feel nervous with strangers, and certainly no thought of assault of any kind came into my head, but I felt nervous, for all that. Perhaps it was because from now on I'd be standing on my own and I wasn't certain of my capacity.

After a while I saw that my companion had put his papers on one side; he seemed to be watching me with unusual interest. I thought fiercely, I'll outstare him, and lifted my eyes. The next second he was leaning forward, a huge smile wreathing his big red face.

"Remember me?" he said.

I shrank away. "I think you're making a mistake," I told him, but I felt disturbed. Though so far as I knew I'd never set eyes on him before, the voice seemed familiar.

"I don't make that sort of mistake, sugar. The Phoenix flight from Bordeaux . . ."

I remembered at once, the man with the resonant voice, Julie Taylor's "old sweetie." I thought I'd heard few less apposite descriptions.

"You said if we'd been meant to fly we'd have wings."

"Did I, sugar? Well, it's true, ain't it?" I thought, and was horrified at myself, that it was just my luck he should be one of three survivors. "I was sorry about your girl friend," he went on. "It was too bad."

"It was too bad for everyone," I told him jerkily. "I don't know how you recognized me. I've been in the clinic at Godsmere, I've only just been released."

"They made a very nice job, sugar," he assured me gravely. "And I knew you all right—it's like Cleopatra and her asp." He nodded toward my wrist and I realized I was still wearing Julie's bracelet. "Your mascot carried you through all right that time."

"It's changed my appearance," I said breathlessly, "but some people think that's for the better."

"The world's full of dames who think they can improve on nature's handiwork, and being dames, they're sometimes right. Not that you had much to worry about."

"I keep thinking about that other girl," I told him. "Her name was Solange Peters, she'd flown from Rome . . ."

"I read about her in the paper," the man told me.

I thought, If he knows who I really am, let him come out with it now. I can't stand any more suspense. I wondered if he might try blackmail. I couldn't see what good it would do him to denounce me as an impostor, he didn't look the heroic type that's governed by a social conscience. If I'd shrunk from appearing in my true colors at the hospital, now the thought was intolerable. I'd thought myself into Julie Taylor's skin, it was Solange Peters who seemed the stranger.

"It's rum how things work out," the man was saying. "Maybe it's better this way."

"That's what Sister at the hospital said."

"Who am I to contradict a sister? They give me cold shivers down my spine. Where are you bound for now?"

"I shall be looking for a job, of course."

"Let's see—schoolteacher, wasn't it?"

My relief was so great I didn't know how to control it. "That's right. Of course, I haven't got any papers or anything, they were all lost, but I shall find something temporary until I can get established."

"People live who mean to live," he said to me, "and chaps work who won't take no for an answer. Got any chums?"

"I've been in hospital ever since I arrived. And Australia's a long way off. They were very kind to me, especially at the clinic," I added breathlessly. "Matron taught me as much as she could."

"Taught you how to speak like a limey," said my companion. "Pity, really. That Aussie accent made a nice change." He hauled a big silver watch out of his pocket.

"Talking's thirsty work, ain't it," he said. "Think I'll see if the bar's open." He pulled back the door. "Send anything up for you?" he inquired.

"I'll get a cup of tea later," I told him.

"Your bar's the other end," he said.

I gave him a minute after the door had closed before I jumped up and dragged my small case from the rack. That and the big olive-green bag was all the luggage I'd brought with me. There was more than an hour before we reached London, but I'd no intention of returning to the carriage. That he meant to do so was obvious, since he'd left his papers higgledy-piggledy on the seat. It seemed rather careless, but I suppose he thought no one would be interested. I knocked against them trying to open the door, and a card fell down. I stooped. It was like an outsize visiting card, I supposed he was some sort of a commercial. The card was peculiar enough to hold my attention. It said Arthur G. Crook and gave two addresses and two telephone numbers. And underneath: "Your trouble our business. And we never close."

I wondered if I was wrong, he was on the music halls, I'd seen that sort of turn on the television screen at the clinic. I peered up and down the corridor; no one was moving. We were hurrying through a semi-industrial area, there was nothing much to be seen from the windows.

"What a funny place to leave a card," I reflected aloud, and as clearly as though she stood beside me I heard Julie's voice.

"He said he'd give me one of his cards, only they were in rather short supply, and anyway he could see I'd never need one."

I began to shiver. Second sight? I didn't think so. This Mr. Crook wasn't the sort you associate with mysticism. Of course it wasn't that. He hadn't had a notion she was going to die, he'd simply known she'd never need his services. She was armored already.

> Joy and woe are woven fine,
> A Clothing for the soul divine.
> And when this we rightly know
> Safely through the world we go.

I had had the same conviction. If she had lived to be eighty and been faced with every conceivable vicissitude, she would always have been safe. It was the first time I had realized that perhaps even death cannot ultimately destroy.

All the same, Crook had left one of his rare cards just where it was bound to attract my attention if I went near the door. And—I now understood—he had known I'd make for the door the instant he disappeared. But why? There was only one answer to that. He knew I wasn't Julie Taylor and he wasn't saying a word. I could fool myself as much as I liked that the skin grafting had changed my appearance, and that was true, but it wasn't the answer. He must have noticed me on the plane, probably because of Julie, or perhaps because he always noticed everyone. I pushed the card into my purse. It was always useful to know the whereabouts of your enemies, I thought. I'd been careful not to tell him my destination. I charged down the corridor, banging against closed doors with my suitcase, inviting exasperated glances from travelers in other compartments. As I reached the end of the corridor I threw a rapid glance over my shoulder. Mr. Crook must have drunk his pint or whatever in double-quick time, or perhaps the bar wasn't open, I hadn't got the hang of British drinking hours yet; anyway, there he was leaning against one of the windows, staring at the uninspiring landscape, a great humpy ginger-colored British lion. I found myself giggling quietly, a habit I'd acquired since the plane crash. They should put him on the engines instead of that yellow horror, I thought; that might speed up the trains.

In the tea compartment I made myself unpopular by joining a party of three who'd only just sat down. There were various tables with only one occupant or two women together, but they were all getting near the end of their meal, whereas this trio was only just beginning. I wasn't going to give Mr. Crook an opportunity to come prowling in and join me at an otherwise empty table. When at last I had to move I thrust my way into a compartment already containing several other people. There was no sign of Mr. Crook when the train drew in. I let everyone leave the carriage first, and so I saw him getting out further down and marching over to the taxi rank. I was so dilatory I didn't get a porter and almost missed my car. I was told the driver would be carrying a board marked *Carbright.* When I identified him and he saw I had so little luggage, he said disapprovingly, "You could have taken this on the tube."

I explained I'd been ill, I wasn't allowed to carry things. He said his wife had just had her appendix out, thrown out of the hospital within ten days and expected to be back on the job. I had expected to sit next to him on the journey, but he threw open the back of the car and made it clear he expected his privacy. I suppose it was stupid of me not to realize I had to pay for the car; somehow I'd thought that was arranged for. When I said falteringly I was only just over from the Continent, he said, "That's right, all the foreigners are the same, come over here to get our National Health and not so much as a stamp."

He dumped my luggage on the pavement, didn't say thank you for my tip and huffed away.

Mrs. Stafford came hurrying out to meet me. "I suppose the train was late," she said. She insisted on carrying my bag. "You'll be able to meet some of the boarders this evening, and you don't have to be sensitive about your appearance, they all know you've been in an accident, they won't stare."

Actually, I don't think they'd have noticed if I hadn't had a head at all. They were all engaged in their own concerns, never spent any time in the house, dashing off to work or rehearsals and spending the evening in coffee bars or cellar dance halls or night classes. There was one middle-aged woman who came over to sit beside me and say, "Well, you could have fooled me, I'd never have guessed. And they say every new experience is a milestone." Then she sighed and said, "It must be nice to see a different face in the glass in the morning."

She herself looked rather like a horse, her name was Ada Holloway and she was a buyer for a big multiple drapers.

"Back to the treadmill?" she suggested, and I said I supposed so, and she said what's your line? and I said I had to wait for copies of my diplomas to come over from Australia and in the meantime I'd take whatever offered.

"You'll be all right," Ada said. "The difficulty nowadays is to stay unemployed." She gave me the names of two or three employment agencies where I might apply and went off to listen to a program of classical music on television.

I didn't have any luck with the agencies. Right off I was presented with an immense questionnaire asking for all manner of information that couldn't conceivably be relevant to the job in hand. My replies seemed to be a procession of "No's" running all down the page. The young woman who interviewed me said impatiently, "This is absurd, there must be something you can do, you're not a moron, are you?"

I snapped back that I could speak a number of languages, drive a car . . .

She won that round by saying I couldn't do that till I'd passed my English driving test, and it would be weeks before I'd get my name on a list. She asked what I'd done in Australia, and when I murmured something about teaching she slapped her appointments book shut and said, "This isn't the right place for you," and started to question me about A and O levels. When I said things weren't the same in Australia she said I was wasting her time (not my time, she made it clear that was of no importance), and before the door had closed behind me she had torn up my application form and put it in the wastepaper basket.

I didn't have any more luck at the second agency and I hadn't the courage to brave the third. There must, I decided, be other ways of getting work. I'd noticed advertisements outside stationer's shops asking for domestic help or babysitting.

"Don't touch 'em with a barge pole," said Ada Holloway. "They ask you for references, but what about their own? Never know what you may be getting mixed up in, and there's a lot of truth in the saying that you can't touch pitch without being defiled. No, read the ads in the evening papers or the *Record*, they give box numbers, that gives you a chance to make inquiries, too."

I answered one or two advertisements—most of them were beyond my capacity—comptometer clerks, computer clerks, receptionist (shorthand essential), lady's maid (references essential), assistant in infant school (copies of two testimonials to be enclosed with application)—I got sick of that word Refs. In the meantime I had bought a map and started finding my way about London. I came to a motor-driving school and went in to inquire about my test. I was told I should have a few refresher lessons first, particularly if I'd never driven in England before; they couldn't, they explained, apply for a test for me till they had some idea what I could do. I'd had two lessons and was becoming used to the right-hand drive—"we'll put you down for a test as soon as poss., might be a time lag of six weeks, though"—when I saw Oliver Duncan's advertisement in the Personal column of the *Times*. At last it seemed to me there might here be something I could do. A companion, not over thirty, wanted for an invalid lady recuperating from an illness. No nursing experience necessary, but someone willing and cheerful. No housework but an ability to do a little cooking three evenings a week appreciated. Car driver essential. No children or animals to be cared for. Regular domestic help. Nothing, surprisingly, about references.

I answered it at once, explaining about my motor lessons. (Julie presumably hadn't driven, there was no license in her purse.) If my patient, as already I thought of her, was herself a licensed driver, it wouldn't matter, because even a learner-driver can go out with an expert. Anyway . . .

Ada Holloway came in while I was penning my application. "You're never going to answer that," she said in shocked tones, putting down the *Times*. I'd bought a copy after reading the advertisement in the public library.

"Why not?" I asked. "It sounds the sort of thing I could do."

Ada said in her flat kind voice, "You must have lived a very sheltered life in Australia. Anyone with half an eye can see what this chap's after. Cook, nurse, gardener, chauffeur, bottle-washer, for a tweeny's wages. Nothing said about those, I note, and no indication where this mansion of bliss may be."

"If it's someone convalescing," I pointed out, "they wouldn't want unsuitable applicants ringing the bell all day."

"I don't think they're likely to be bothered," Ada said. "They're just waiting for a mug like you." She made a sound like the honk of a goose. "The only people who're going to answer that are going to be women born the same year that I was, with daughters of your age, who go round telling everyone that the world always takes them for sisters.

Sometimes I wonder there aren't more domestic murders than there are."

There it was again, the word that seemed to crop up everywhere. You can get away with murder, people said. My dear, it was murder. If that woman at the greengrocer sauces me again, I'll murder her. No one else seemed to notice. Perhaps when you've been involved in a murder case yourself you become a bit sensitive.

"This must be his first effort," Ada Holloway went on, "or he'd have dressed it up a bit. I mean, there it is all laid out, as plain as a pound of sausages. All those chores and not even a dog for company. I daresay in your spare time you're expected to sweeten the situation for the master of the house. Still," she allowed generously, "there's one thing, he doesn't say send a photo. Never trust them when they say that."

In spite of her warnings I posted my application. Although I believed I had buried Solange Peters, the mere mention of nursing brought all my professional feelings into play. If I did get the job I must be careful not to be too professional. I decided to say I knew nothing of gardening, though I supposed I could turn up a few weeds, assuming I could distinguish between weeds and newly sown plants. The Marchesa's gardener would have chopped off the head of anyone (barring his underlings, of course) who tried to interfere in his province. There I went again, I noted, chopping off someone's head; the violent phrases seemed to pop up like rabbits out of burrows.

Ada was probably right about there not being many applications, because Oliver Duncan rang me up as soon as he'd read mine and asked me to meet him at the big station hotel at Paddington at twelve-thirty next day. Nothing was said about lunch.

"He'll buy you a drink," said the knowledgeable Ada, "then if he thinks you're napoo he'll give you your fare home, possibly enough to buy a bun and a cup of coffee at a Lyons, and no hard feelings on either side. If he offers you lunch it means you're in the running for the job, and before you accept it make sure it's what you want."

Oliver Duncan was a man in the late thirties, pleasant-spoken, good-looking in a rather conventional way, who seemed relieved at the sight of me. One thing was obvious, he was distracted to get somebody to fill the vacancy. It was for his wife, who had been ill for almost a year.

"What's wrong?" I asked. "And shouldn't she have a nurse?"

Mr. Duncan shook his head. "We've tried that, it didn't work. You see, there's nothing organically wrong—I've had her examined by specialists, it's a kind of nervous reaction and no medicine's any use for that. The specialist's term to me was 'mental conflict.' " He suggested I should finish my drink and we'd go in to lunch. So far, so good. During lunch he told me the rest of the story. It was rather strange. It seemed that Bianca Duncan had what he called a guilt fixation. She had been a nurse before her marriage—I didn't like that much, it was coming uncomfortably near home—and she had lost a patient.

"She wasn't in any way responsible," Oliver Duncan insisted. "She wasn't even on the premises at the time of the accident, and at first she seemed to accept that. Then I suppose she started brooding. I can only surmise from what she's told me since. A nurse's life can be a very solitary one, particularly if she's doing private work, not on a big staff. Anyhow, she began to think she might in some way have prevented what happened."

"But nurses can't be on duty twenty-four hours a day," I said. "They need time off like anyone else."

"You said that with real conviction. That's precisely the line to adopt. Mind you, you'll need to be careful, I don't want her to get the idea I've been prompting you. But if she could accept the fact that no situation is absolutely foolproof and we all have to take our chances, she might get back to a normal life. She's thirty-six and in perfectly good health otherwise."

"And how long . . . ?"

"Almost a year. Unfortunately, she saw some report in a newspaper that bore the very slightest resemblance to her own case, and that seemed to start the trouble up again. It's all so futile. Nothing anyone does can restore Evelyn to life, and she knows, and so do I, that it was only a matter of months at any time. But she got this idea that new patients regarded her rather oddly, didn't altogether trust her. I don't know whether anything was ever said, she hasn't told me. I hadn't seen her for about a year until we had this chance meeting in Salisbury. I recognized her at once, of course. I thought she looked tired, as if she'd been working too hard. She'd had a bit of a holiday after Evelyn's death—well, it hadn't been a sinecure, she needed a change—"

I interrupted. "Mr. Duncan, may I ask you? Was Evelyn your first wife?"

He looked surprised at the question. "Didn't I say? Oh, that's how Bianca and I met. Evelyn thought the world of her, nothing I could do would repay Bianca for the care and the affection she gave my wife during those last months. It must be an exhausting life, a nurse's, going from one sickroom to another, the demands made on her—not that there would be anything of the kind here," he added quickly. "It's her suggestion that she should have a companion, not a nurse. She doesn't need professional attention, she just wants someone to—to haul her up out of her slough of despond. That's why I asked for someone young. You'd be surprised how lively and enterprising she used to be. The change had started by the time we met in Salisbury, a purely fortuitous meeting. I asked her how she was doing, could I give her lunch, and suddenly it all came out, how she'd assumed responsibility for what had clearly been an accident, and couldn't shake off the feeling. She said it wasn't only patients, no one would trust her, she wouldn't dare marry or have children, not unless the man knew, and she'd never dare tell him."

I didn't like to ask for more details, but I couldn't help wondering if there was something Mr. Duncan didn't know. I didn't doubt that Bianca was a sick woman, but that didn't have to be due to disease. A lot of illness, I knew, is due to a defense mechanism. People want to retreat from a fact or a situation, and they can actually induce a form of invalidism which absolves them from further responsibility, the responsibility of taking decisions. I'd opened my mouth to explain this to Mr. Duncan when I remembered just in time I wasn't a nurse. Anyway, he was plowing on with his story.

"I told her that was nonsense, and she said well, put yourself in his place. Would you marry me? And I said of course I would. A man would be very lucky . . ." He fell silent. So that's how it was, I thought. I was definitely curious about Bianca by now. Had she set him a trap and he'd walked in, only, if so, what had gone wrong? Why was she a neurotic invalid within two years? Or perhaps it hadn't happened quite the way he told it.

I noticed he'd refilled my wineglass. It was the best meal I'd had since I left Rome.

"How do you feel about it?" he said. "The job, I mean? I felt I had to tell you so much, though I hope I've not given you the wrong impression. I'm afraid having Nurse Adams was a mistake. She talked in words of five syllables and she rustled and crackled till it sounded as though the house was on fire. And she was full of stories about her other patients. Very few of them seem to have recovered," he added.

"At least I shan't be able to do that, shall I?" I said.

He looked at me eagerly. "That sounds as though you were really considering it."

"I need a job," I told him. "I'd like to be out of the city—anyway, for a time." To me a city implied Rome; I didn't want to think too much about Rome, not just yet. "I'm used to looking after people . . ."

I wondered how he'd square that with my story of being a schoolteacher, but he took it all in his stride.

"Your aunt? She was an invalid?"

From what I had gathered from the real Julie, Aunt Marty had been as strong as the proverbial horse, it seemed a shame to sacrifice her now, but it couldn't hurt her.

"Only toward the end," I stammered. "Anyway, it would only be a stopgap wouldn't it? I mean, she's going to get well."

"Yes," said Mr. Duncan in heartfelt tones, "she's going to get well—if you'll lend a hand, that is. It was the doctor's partner who suggested we might try for someone young this time," he continued. "Let her see how much life has to offer to a healthy woman in her mid-thirties. Not that I mean you, of course . . ." He lost track of that sentence and sensibly abandoned it. "What I'm trying to say is—who'd make the effort to recover her health in order to be like Nurse Adams? She really was—voracious. What's the name of that flower that opens its heart to suck in all the insect life around it—the sundew? Yes. Well, she was like that."

I thought if Ada had been present at this meeting she'd have caught me by the hair and torn me into Praed Street, but I told myself it was a beginning. I had to have references, a background, and though I didn't particularly cotton to the job, I had to begin somewhere. Besides—and here with a shock I discovered a bond between myself and the absent Bianca—I also had a feeling of indebtedness. I knew it wasn't my fault that the Marchesa had died—I wouldn't let myself think about Perdita in this connection. I didn't believe that providence could crash an entire airship because a suspected criminal was on board. I didn't really feel guilty about using Julie's name, because I knew she would have given it to me without reservation. Nevertheless, I felt I owed someone something, perhaps because in spite of all my mishaps I was still alive. And pulling Bianca out of her slough, as her husband had said, might be the way for me to pay my bill.

Mr. Duncan gave me details about pay and conditions. It wasn't exactly handsome, but it wasn't niggardly. I longed to ask how much Nurse Adams had had, but of course Bianca, having been a nurse herself, wouldn't expect to pay an amateur at a professional's rate.

"I suppose it all depends on her now," I said. "It wouldn't be any good my coming if she didn't take to me."

"Well!" He sounded a bit dubious. "You do appreciate she isn't the taking kind. I mean, she's like those fellows in the hymn who always had their armor on. Your job will be to help her to disarm, and I have the feeling you may be the person who can do it."

"Parsley round the dish," Crook was to say later, when I told him that. "Well, he could hardly tell you she was an impregnable fortress. Even you, who don't seem to have all your marbles, would hardly have jumped into the pit then."

After lunch he drove me down to his house at Hotham St. Mary. He had a very handsome car and he drove it as easily as most people breathe. He said there was another car that Bianca used to drive, but since her illness she'd refused to take the wheel or even to go out. He told me not to worry about the driving test, as he had a friend at court who could probably shove me in a bit early.

Bianca Duncan was up and dressed when we arrived. A tall gray woman met us at the door to say she (Bianca) was in the drawing room. A languid voice called, "Is that you, Oliver? Any luck?"

She was a tall, very dark-haired woman, and if her voice was casual almost to the point of boredom her eye was like the eye of the prophet that misses nothing. I felt after a first glance she could have told you every stitch I was wearing, the color of my eyes, the way my hair was done. It was a raking glance and for some reason I felt excitement ripple through me. I had always enjoyed a challenge, more perhaps than I knew. Being nurse to the Marchesa had been challenging—I must have known the chance I took daring to fall in love with Florian; already I could see I'd overreached myself expecting to marry him—and now this woman, who would always keep one on one's toes. I could feel that this woman would fight every inch of the way, which made it all the stranger that she should have succumbed, as, clearly, she had done, to a private dread. Of course, I reflected, she might secretly have cherished the death-wish, have been in love with Oliver Duncan. I wondered if she would bring herself to confide in me, assuming, that is, that she approved of me sufficiently to agree to my being her companion. And in due course so she did, but what she had to tell me wasn't in the least what I'd anticipated.

Her first question, and it took me by surprise, was "Why do you want the job? It's very monotonous and we live a very quiet life."

I said I wanted to be in the country, and Mr. Duncan intervened with an eager reminder of the plane crash. I had told him about that, to explain why this was my first job since my arrival.

Mrs. Duncan waved her hand impatiently. She wore beautiful rings, and she had the long clever fingers of an artist.

"If we do come to an arrangement it must be understood that I am the patient. And that doesn't imply you can try and rule me with a rod of iron, as Adams did." Then she told her husband she'd like some tea. "Tell Mrs. Dotrice, will you?" Mrs. Dotrice was the gray woman who had met us in the hall.

There was a bell at hand and she could perfectly well have pressed it, but she wanted to get her husband out of the way. It was the most transparent excuse imaginable, and I suppose he saw through it, because he didn't come back immediately but left us to ourselves.

"How much did he tell you?" she demanded, and when I'd answered that, she said, "I can see you view yourself as St. Christopher or someone, lifting me out of the morass."

"That's what I'm here for, isn't it?" I said with more spirit than I'd realized I possessed. "There's not much sense my coming otherwise."

Her big, rather thin-lipped mouth parted in a smile. "What a self-opinionated girl! You're sure you'll succeed, aren't you?"

"No," I told her, "but I can try, and if I'm no use I'll move on somewhere else. But I don't see why it shouldn't work out." I could hear my own voice throbbing with energy.

She lay back, nodding. Mrs. Dotrice must have had the

kettle on the boil, because she brought in the tray almost at once. She put it at Bianca's elbow.

"Why did you really leave Australia?" she asked, handing me my cup.

"I had this little legacy, I thought I'd like to see something of the world."

"Do you mean to go back?"

"I hadn't thought," I said.

She smiled again. "I suppose it was a man. Oh come, a girl with your looks doesn't go out as companion to an invalid without some good reason. Did you work there?"

"I was a teacher, but I thought I'd like a change," I said lamely.

"And you think this might be an easier way of earning your living? If you're coming to me we may as well start straight. What happened? Was he married?"

"No," I said, "but it turned out he didn't want to marry me."

"Then you're well out of it, aren't you? These fortune-hunters . . ."

"I didn't say he was a fortune-hunter."

Her finely plucked dark brows rose. "What other reason could he have for shirking the issue? I suppose you weren't in the family way?"

"Certainly not," I cried.

"I suppose he's not likely to come after you? I don't want any melodrama here. We can supply all that ourselves."

Ever since I set eyes on her my interest had been engaged; her last words simply whetted it. Not that I wanted any melodrama either, I assured her. And . . . the man wouldn't be following me.

"If you've been dealing with children you must have acquired patience," Bianca went on. I noticed she didn't eat anything; she lighted a cigarette, which she smoked in a long holder. "That was what Adams lacked. What she knew she knew, and what she knew was right. I'm not a clinical case, you know."

"Your husband told me. I suppose you could say I should be here to help you to cure yourself."

"So that your job would really be a sinecure. You're very outspoken. I suppose you don't really care whether you get this job or not. There are plenty of others."

"It doesn't matter how many there are if they're not the ones you want."

"Adams wanted this one," she said. "She was a real man-hunter. Oh, I don't mean she made passes at Oliver, but she liked being in authority. That woman doesn't want me to get well, I told the doctor. Send her away." She blew a long cloud of smoke. "Of course, it was an easy job for her."

I opened my mouth to say no nursing job is easy, then remembered just in time and shut it again.

"Have you a family over there?" Bianca went on.

"Not now." I took a picture of Aunt Marty out of my bag and offered it to her. "I lived with my aunt."

She glanced at the photograph and handed it back. "She looks a regular old battle-ax. Looking after me should be child's play. Did you arrange all the details with my husband? You realize it's not a permanency, of course."

"I'm not looking for permanency."

"On the other hand, I don't want you to get yourself established here and then discover something more amusing."

The door opened and Mr. Duncan came in. "All set?" he asked.

"What doctors call the climax has just come. There's one more point, Julie. I shall call you Julie, the other would remind me too much of Nurse Adams. If you're looking for a place where you can lie up and nurse a broken heart, this isn't the place for you. I have to be the center round which your interests revolve. There's no need to look at me like that, Oliver. I don't want anyone here under false pretenses." She sent him a long dark look. I didn't know what that meant. Not then.

"What price your feminine intuition?" Arthur Crook was to ask me later. "Gone to sleep for the winter, like a dormouse?"

Certainly on that afternoon when I said I could start work as soon as I was wanted, I had no notion what I was letting myself in for. And I still don't think I was entirely to blame.

4

NOT THAT I WASN'T WARNED.

"You're joking, of course," said Ada Holloway that evening, when I told her the result of my interview. She threw up her thin horsy head. You could almost say she neighed her disapproval.

"No, why?" I asked. "I have to get my foot in somewhere."

She said, as Bianca Duncan had done, "What a self-opinionated girl you are! Just make sure you don't get your foot into a coffin, that's all. I daresay you do need a job, but you don't have to take the first that offers, like some terrified mousey, jumping out of a wainscot to find itself between the cat's paws."

"I hoped you were going to congratulate me," I said lightly. "This is the first job I've applied for in person." Because of course there'd been the others I'd written for, without getting any reply.

"And you're surprised they jumped at you? Well, I'm not. You're God's answer to the hypochondriac—young, good-looking, inspired by the martyr spirit . . . what's really wrong with the woman?"

"I told you, she has this fixation. She thinks she was responsible for her patient's death. Nurses don't like losing patients," I added.

"Then they shouldn't be so careless. Any proof that she wasn't, by the way? responsible, I mean?"

"She wasn't even in the house at the time."

"That's what she told you—huh?"

"It's what her husband told me."

"Not that that's anything to go by. You don't read enough detective stories, my girl. Death by remote control gets more popular every day."

"By computer, I suppose?" I suggested.

"Why not? They're the ultimate power that's going to run

the world. One of these days they'll take over completely, even wars won't be between individuals. Press a switch and a million men on the moon will drop dead."

"You'll still need the human finger to press the switch," I pointed out.

"I can see I'm wasting my breath," remarked Ada shortly. "Leave an address and telephone number, won't you, then I'll be able to stand in as your next-of-kin. Good heavens, Julie, this is your first job in a new country—do you have to go and work for a suspected murderess?"

I felt myself go white, with anger as much as fear. "You've no right—there's never been any suggestion of murder."

"How can you be so sure of that?" She was quite unmoved.

"Would Oliver Duncan have married a woman who might have murdered his own wife?"

"I don't know. It might have been part of the bargain. Oh, go if you must, but it all sounds as fishy as Billingsgate to me. Not that I think there'll be any attempt to murder you," she added. "Only—take my tip. Leave your brains at home. Don't go round trying to be a clever dick and sort things out. The dead should be allowed to lie in peace, and that goes for facts as well as people."

"You're in the wrong job," I said. "You should be writing thrillers."

"Or perhaps she's blackmailed him into marriage," Ada continued in absorbed tones. "Wouldn't care to be in his shoes. Is he a rich man?"

"It looks a rich sort of house."

"Who poured out the tea?"

"She did, of course."

"I wonder he dared take a cup."

"He didn't come in to tea."

"You see?"

"Have you any reason," I inquired with elaborate patience, "to suppose she wants to be a widow?"

"You'd be surprised at the people who do. Why do you have to be so original? Why can't you marry a nice young man and settle down?"

I stood up. "Perhaps," I said, "because the nice young man doesn't want to marry me."

Even that didn't cause her to come unstuck. "Should have his head examined," she said.

I grinned suddenly, I couldn't help it. If anyone was

being led up the garden path it was the Duncans. One whisper about the Marchesa Polli and I'd find the chain up when I arrived. It was up to me to see that that whisper never circulated.

In effect, the job was easier than I had anticipated. One of the trials of the nursing profession is the patient who runs a mental temperature one day and is down below par the next, dropping plumb from the seventh heaven to the seventh hell. I didn't know whether Bianca Duncan had assumed she was entering the seventh heaven when she married Oliver; if so, she was certainly disillusioned by now. Not that I ever heard them quarrel, they didn't even argue, he was out a good deal—I suppose there isn't much encouragement to come home in the evening when your wife's always in bed, and if he wanted to entertain, it was easier at the country club. No, what was inclined to get me down was what she'd warned me about that first day—the monotony of the job. It was like living in a house where everything is the same tone of gray—gray walls, gray carpets, gray curtains, even a gray porcelain bath. I used to think if there were such things as gray flowers, she'd have had those, too. And somehow it didn't seem in character. She'd shown such flashes of spirit that first day, there was obviously turmoil under the surface calm.

It seemed to me my first job was to persuade her to get up and go about like an ordinary person.

"What a bully you are, it's Nurse Adams all over again," she said pettishly one morning. "I should have thought I was much less trouble to you under the bedclothes. If I have to get up and dress I shall expect to be entertained."

"Bed's for invalids," I told her, "and only the helpless ones at that."

She flashed me a glance of pure malice from her long dark eyes. "Did Oliver tell you to say that?"

"I don't discuss you with your husband."

"What do you talk about when I'm not there?"

"I hardly ever see him alone."

"Anyway," she went on, "who are you to expect miracles? You've only been here a couple of weeks."

"According to some people—my Aunt Marty was one—the world was made in less time than that."

"Your Aunt Marty sounds like the mother of Rip Van Winkle. Tell me this, Julie. Why are you so keen to see me on my feet? It would simply mean you were out of a job."

"It's such a waste of energy," I objected. "Not just yours, mine."

"I thought your energy was what I was paying for."

"If I baked you a cake," I said, "and you just threw it on the fire, wouldn't I have a right to feel cheated?"

"Not if I'd paid for the ingredients and I didn't complain of your cooking. No, no pep talk please about the starving millions. Tell me, how do you get on with Mrs. Dotrice?"

"She hardly speaks to me," I acknowledged.

"I don't trust her. Oliver engaged her, you know."

"Your husband engaged me," I pointed out.

She stared at me in amazement, then broke into laughter. "If you believe that, you'll believe anything. One word from me and you'd have had your return ticket home. Now, Julie, don't try and rush me, and don't make the mistake of thinking you have God's private ear. I like you and I want you to stay. I don't stop in bed because I enjoy stopping in bed, but because so long as I'm here, Oliver will agree to your remaining."

"You can't mean you're putting on an act just to keep me here?" I exclaimed incredulously.

"Not putting on an act. But if you ask would I sooner live this invalidish existence, with someone I trust on the premises, or bounce about alone in this big house just with Oliver—after Mrs. Dotrice has gone home in the evening, that is—the answer is yes."

I was so flummoxed that I forgot a nurse's first duty, which is never to show personal feeling.

"But you married him," I exploded at last. "And he doesn't hold you responsible for the death of his first wife."

"No," said Bianca in an odd voice, "I don't suppose he does. He's probably the only person living who could testify on oath that I was not involved."

Here the telephone rang and she answered it, while I went down to get her some beef-tea which her pussycat old doctor, Dr. Mitchison, had ordered for her.

When I came back she started talking about something else. She didn't revert to the subject of Evelyn Duncan's death until more than a fortnight later. By then I had been in the house just over a month; it seemed like a year. I can't remember precisely what started her off again; I think perhaps I had spoken of going to London one evening, I was feeling suffocated by this narrow regime. I had taken my driving test by now and passed, but so far I hadn't persuaded Bianca to let me take her out in the car. I wondered secretly if that was how Evelyn had come by her death.

I couldn't have been more wrong.

It seemed that she had known hers was an incurable case, but she didn't want to die in a hospital if she could help it, and Oliver said he could manage with the aid of a nurse, which was how Bianca was introduced into the household.

"It was quite a heavy job," she told me. "I was the only nurse, so of course I couldn't stick to the letter of the law where hours were concerned. But I didn't really mind, she was the nearest thing to a saint I've ever met. Not in any tiresome dogmatic way, it was some quality I can't explain. She said if it got too hard for me I must tell her, but I promised to stay as long as I was needed. Then one day I got this letter from a friend in London asking me to come up for the evening." Bianca moved restlessly in the bed. "I mulled it over and over but I still don't see how I could have guessed what would happen. She'd been deteriorating, we all knew, she was writing to her lawyer about some codicil to her will—and it was she who insisted I should go. I said I wouldn't stay late, but it would be nice to have a gossip. I meant to be back about eight. The housekeeper would be there to get the dinner in any case, and Oliver was spending the evening at home. I put her hot milk in the Thermos and left the biscuits she liked, and her last words to me were, 'If you want to stop on, don't bother.' She was like that, the most considerate patient I ever had.

"When I got to London—perhaps it was the change of air that intoxicated me; anyway, my friend had managed to get two tickets for a play everyone was dying to see, and I might never get another chance—the long and the short of it is I rang up and Oliver said of course, stay, he'd be home all the evening and he'd sit with her for a bit, so that seemed all right. I enjoyed the dinner, I enjoyed the play, I enjoyed the contrast, only toward the end did I feel a sense of unease. I told myself it was absurd, but as soon as the last curtain came I refused a final drink and got a taxi to Paddington. Oliver came into the hall when he heard my key in the door. Had a good time? he said. It was all right, no alarms. She'd had her milk and the omelet Mrs.—what was her name? the housekeeper of the day?—anyway, she'd eaten those and he'd read to her for a while—he's got a beautiful reading voice, you must have noticed it, I used to tell him he should have been a clergyman." She laughed *abruptly*. "Oliver a clergyman! Well, I went up and Evelyn was awake but rather drowsy. She said Oliver had almost read her to sleep, but she wanted to know about the play, so we talked for a little, and then I gave her two sleeping tablets, and I came down and had a nightcap with Oliver—I never did as a rule, but this was to make up for the drink I'd missed in London. Everything seemed perfectly normal and I went to bed. There was a bell in Evelyn's room that rang in mine. She didn't use it often but I'd made her promise that if she couldn't sleep or if the pain got too intense, she'd call me. I don't know whether she rang that night, that's one of the things that worries me. I slept like a log . . ."

"Then she didn't ring," I assured her firmly. "A nurse would wake at the first sound, it would be instinct."

She looked at me oddly, and I realized I'd spoken more trenchantly than I'd intended.

"I had a friend in Australia," I went on, not blinking an eyelid. "She was a nurse and she told me it's like a sixth sense, and over the years it becomes automatic. She said," I elaborated, "that sometimes she'd wake and go into a sickroom and find her patient longing to ring but not wanting to disturb her."

"I hope that's right," Bianca said. "I shall never know for certain, because when I went in next morning she was dead."

I ought to have anticipated that, but I hadn't. I gave a start. Then I suggested, "Wasn't that a blessing, really? I mean, if she couldn't get well and the pain was cumulative?"

"Yes, if it had been a natural death," Bianca told me. "But it wasn't. When the doctor came he told us she'd died, in his opinion, of an overdose of sleeping pills, and he wouldn't give a death certificate."

A lot of things that had puzzled me hitherto became clear in that moment. "You think she took them—could she reach them?"

"They were in a bottle, a phial, by the bed. They made a lot of that at the inquest. The coroner was a new man, who hadn't known her, and was out to impress. He agreed that she might have taken them, when she knew I would be back late, and then forgotten—it has happened. But, of course, no one let it rest there."

"You mean they thought she might have taken them deliberately?"

"She'd never have done that; she was a religious woman. And even if she'd have overcome her scruples or been desperate, she'd have left a note. She'd never have left that mess for other people to clear up."

"Then what other explanation . . . ?" My voice faltered away at the scorn in Bianca's face.

"Don't play the innocent, Julie. You know better than that. Of course they considered the possibility—of murder."

The word was out. It made me shiver.

"But who did they think . . . ?"

"There were only two people who could have given them to her. Oliver or I. And I knew it wasn't I."

"But why should he? It was taking such a risk."

"He's an ambitious man, Julie. He wants to be regarded as a tycoon. And Evelyn had most of the money. He needed money at the time to increase his interests. Evelyn had given it to him before; she used to say my money's all I can give him now. Only when he made this last proposal, she refused. It was all right, she told me—we'd become very intimate, I was her one real confidante by that time, she couldn't bear other people to see her, so deteriorated and in obvious pain—so long as it meant the business would belong to Oliver, but if he took this further step he'd belong to the business, just a part of the machine."

I said, "But you married him, you said you felt responsible."

"Because at that time I no more suspected Oliver than I would have suspected myself. What I thought had happened was that she had put out her hand to take a pill of another kind, a perfectly harmless mixture that she could have at any time—which sometimes did help with her sleeplessness, the other was more of a pain-killer—and she'd picked up the wrong bottle. I couldn't find any other explanation, and I felt myself responsible because I'd left the two bottles within reach. If I'd put the sleeping tablets on the shelf, this couldn't have happened. It was only later I began to realize there could be another explanation. And there, again, if I'd come back earlier, it couldn't have happened."

I took my courage in both hands and asked her what she supposed had happened.

She said simply, "It was in the milk, of course, it had to be. She liked her milk sugared." She made a little grimace. "It sounds horrible, I know, but she was a great sweet-tooth. It would have been so easy for him, while she dozed off perhaps, or he could accidentally have knocked the bottle off the table and abstracted the necessary tablets."

"But this is all supposition," I urged. "You don't know he did anything of the kind."

"I know she had the additional tablets," said Bianca steadfastly. "I know she would never have taken them herself, certainly not without leaving a note, and I know I didn't give them to her."

I was silent for a minute; I thought this was a kind of obsession. I had to admit the explanation wasn't an impossible one, but so far as I could tell, she had nothing positive to back it up. That's what I thought then, but she speedily disillusioned me.

"If he's so mercenary," I hesitated, "why did he marry you? Why not another rich wife? Isn't that the usual pattern?"

"He married me for something all the money in the world couldn't get for him, an alibi. Wives can't give evidence against husbands, at least they can't be forced to, and if they do it's usually looked on rather poorly by a jury—the revenge motive, you see. I suppose he thought at the end of a year he was safe."

"Were people talking then?"

"My dear, he didn't give them a chance," said Bianca bitterly. "Almost immediately after the funeral he put two counties between himself and the district. He'd practically insisted on my taking a holiday abroad, where I wouldn't be available; and in this part of the country he was simply known as a recently bereaved widower, and, as such, ultimately available. A widower's the next best thing to a bachelor. Then I suddenly turn up and start resurrecting the past. I was in rather a state about it, I admit that. He knew I might be talking to get some reassurance and sooner or later the whole thing might flare up again. Oh yes, I think marriage was his only choice. I never fooled myself that he was in love with me," she added in quieter tones.

I felt appalled. Here was a situation that found me right out of my depths. It seemed highly improbable that this quiet-spoken, pleasant man should be a murderer, but I knew how deceitful appearances can be. And my problem was less what Oliver had or hadn't done than how to calm his wife. No wonder she was in a state of perpetual nervous tension if she really believed what she said.

And that she did believe it was made abundantly clear in the course of the next few minutes.

"They say it's always easier the second time," she said quite calmly. "I watched Oliver waiting for Evelyn to die, but she was so slow, she lingered and lingered, and he had to have that money. And now," she wound up, "he's waiting again, and this time it's me."

"He's got a long wait," I said with brutal candor. "You've got nothing wrong with you; you could easily outlive him, in the course of nature."

"Ah, but is nature going to be allowed to take her course? I think not. I told him I didn't want a nurse this time, I wanted a companion. What I really meant, as you'll have realized by now, is a police guard—to make sure I don't die suddenly through some mysterious accident as Evelyn did."

I'd heard sick women say this before. They want sympathy, attention, to be the center of your universe, to insure that you don't forget them night or day. But this, I decided, wasn't that type of case. She spoke with such matter-of-factness, such an absence of hope. And whether she was right or wrong in her suspicions, the fact remained that she'd been living with them for months. She'd had no one in whom to confide—naturally not Oliver, nor Nurse Adams. I knew her type of nurse, clap someone on a psychiatrist's couch within the hour and, worse still, repeat everything word for word to the husband. Dr. Mitchison wouldn't be any good either. He was one of those rosy-faced Santa Claus-looking people, sixty-plus, probably pushing seventy, with a theatrical bedside manner which presumably patients liked. I'd heard he took over the private patients, leaving the National Health roster mainly to his partner, a much younger man called Gregg. Bianca had met this young doctor and taken an instant dislike to him. Pushing, she said, obviously with no time for sick people who hadn't a definite disease to be labeled like a butterfly in its case. Since she had no disease, it didn't matter so much (from her point of view) that Dr. Mitchison was probably behind the times, if not actually incompetent, but I could see he'd be no good to her in a situation like this. I could visualize him patting her hand, talking about "We mustn't get fancies, must we?" and reassuring her attendant that it was all right, it often happened, nervy women frequently turned against those they loved most, but not to worry, wait for the nicer weather when she can get out more, and so pussyfooting his way down to the hall where Mrs. Dotrice always met him with a small silver coffee pot and some homemade biscuits.

And she—Bianca, I mean—didn't appear to have any relatives or intimate friends. During the time I'd been at the house she'd had practically no visitors. She refused to see the vicar, who, she said, came only once a year to collect a subscription. The neighbors around about thought what bad luck on that charming Mr. Duncan having a droopy-drawers for a wife. The fear had been boiling up inside her like pus in an abcess; it was a good thing it was being lanced now. And it occurred to me for the first time to wonder just how Oliver did spend his evenings. He was very seldom at home. Bianca never came down to dinner, and I usually ate with her. She might distrust Oliver, but it seemed to me she was still very jealous of him, always wanting to know what precisely he'd said if we only exchanged half a dozen sentences. I wondered why Dr. Mitchison had never suggested she should go away, get out of this festering atmosphere. I wondered if I dared drop him a hint.

"Julie," Bianca broke in, "open that drawer"—she indicated it—"and bring me my album."

The album was a big leather-bound book filled with newspaper cuttings. When I began to examine them I saw they all had one thing in common, though they had been clipped from a variety of sources. They all dealt with sudden death—through murder, accident or what was sometimes called an Act of God. And all the protagonists were husbands and wives. I shuddered. The poison was even blacker than I'd realized.

"One of these days," said Bianca, "if you're still here, you'll be able to add my record to the list. Oh, I'm quite serious." (I didn't doubt that.) "If I'm not included already it's not Oliver's fault. He's a great trier."

You couldn't mistake her meaning and she backed up her statement with what she considered unassailable evidence.

"The first time was the classic example of a husband and wife going for an affectionate stroll on a cliff top, and the husband coming back alone—distraught, naturally. Well, I suppose that's what you'd expect. There's always the one chance in five hundred that the victim will live long enough to make a statement. There's even a case where someone in a low-flying plane said he saw the fatal push, though I don't think the jury accepted that as evidence. We'd been married a few months and we were having a few days off in Cornwall. Cornwall is Oliver's favorite county. I don't care for heights myself, but he said, 'hang on to me and you'll be safe.' Presently he peeped over the edge and he exclaimed, 'Bianca, this you mustn't miss, you may never get such a chance again. The whole of the cliff face'—which was practically perpendicular—'is papered with sea birds.' I remember the description particularly. It seemed so expressive. I laughed and said, 'I'll take your word for it,' but he insisted on my coming to the edge. I peered over hurriedly and I said, 'It's a pretty sparsely patterned paper,' and he told me, 'You're not near enough,' and he gave me a little jerk. 'Now look down,' he said, and then I felt the cliff giving under my feet. I knew I was going to fall. I screamed—and he must have been right about those birds because they rose in a great white cloud, like some immense snowstorm between me and the sky, they seemed to blot out all the world's light.

"Somehow I managed to twist back—he had his hand under my armpit. I came down on my knees and fell face downward on the cliff. I was shaking and sobbing. It wasn't only the fall, it was the birds, the way they dived straight at me. I thought they were going to attack me, and I couldn't cover my face because I needed my hands for balance. Have you ever been very close to a pack of distracted sea birds? All you can see are piercing beaks and little round eyes full of malice. Oliver got down on the grass beside me, pulled me back onto my knees. I said to look, he told me; he sounded exasperated. I didn't say pitch yourself over. Afterwards he said I'd given him the shock of his life. 'What on earth happened?' he said. 'I slipped,' I told him. 'I thought I was going over.' He told me to stay where I was and went and tested the cliff edge. He said it seemed firm enough. 'Lucky for you I was there,' he told me. He walked me back to the village and in the pub he bought brandy for us both. He said to the barman, 'That cliff of yours is none too safe, my wife almost fell. Why don't they put up a railing?' The barman said, 'There's a warning board, isn't there?' You hear how friendly Cornish people are, but this one wasn't. Or perhaps he thought we were foreigners criticizing local efficiency. Oliver said, 'I didn't see any board,' and later he walked back to make certain. When he came in he said, 'There was a board all right, but it was lying on its face in some bushes. Someone's idea of a joke, I suppose. I've reported it to the local police. Of course, they blame the removal on the tourists, but it may make them a bit more careful from now on.' "

"But it could so easily have been an accident," I protested. "Why should you even think it might be anything else?"

"I didn't—at the time. We came back, got into our regular routine. I almost forgot about it. I mentioned it to one or two people; I couldn't understand why Oliver didn't like to hear me. 'It was a near-miss, perhaps,' he said, 'but you don't want to brood on it. That's how people develop obsessions. Before we know where we are we shall have people saying I tried to shove you down among the fishes.' He actually said that. Of course, it was the most disarming thing he could have said. You'd argue that only a husband at once innocent and relieved would make that sort of joke. And I really didn't give it much more thought until the incident at Auxerre some months later. Oliver's one of those men who don't settle comfortably to long holidays. After a few days he gets bored and then impatient. A week in Cornwall, a week in France, a week in Scotland perhaps, that's what he prefers. Well, we'd gone to Auxerre for the week. On about the fourth day we were crossing a cobbled street. It had been rather bad weather and the stones were inclined to be greasy. Just as I stepped off the pavement a motorcyclist came whirling up from nowhere, clearly not intending to stop, even for President de Gaulle. Oliver had me by the arm; he gave me a great shove. 'Get over quick,' he said. But I pulled back. I nearly knocked him off his feet. The cyclist described a sort of arc and went zooming away like a mammoth bee. 'That chap shouldn't be on the road,' Oliver cried. 'He might have killed you.' That was when the thought went through my mind for the first time: Not the cyclist. You. And I remembered the incident on the cliff top.

"You can say, if you like, I was simply being neurotic, it was coincidence, and in neither case had I come to harm, but my inner self told me I hadn't got Oliver to thank for my safety, only my own quick reactions. He made light of it, after a bit. 'All's well that ends well,' he said, and—you know what a charmer he can be, naturally I wanted to save my marriage—anyway, I persuaded myself it had been a lightning error of judgment on his part. But I don't think I really believed it then, and I certainly don't now. I'm certain he's only waiting for the opportunity to strike for the third time. Now you see why I want you to stay. You're the one person I can trust, though if Oliver had the least suspicion I'd confided in you, you wouldn't last long."

I decided to assume she meant Oliver would hand me my walking papers, but she wasn't sparing me anything.

"I'm telling you this as much for your own sake as mine, because from now on you must be on perpetual guard. Don't breathe a word to the doctor either, he'd simply go running to Oliver and suggest I was suffering from a complex."

"Does your husband realize what you suspect?" I asked. I had to know.

Bianca shrugged. "If he does he's covering up very well, but he's probably like most criminals. You know what brings them down in the end? Vanity! They're so clever they think no one can catch up with them. If he tries to be confidential about me, listen to what he says, but don't give anything away."

I hadn't been a nurse, even for a few years, without realizing what a large part delusion plays in the lives of patients. Sometimes they foster it deliberately, it gives them a sense of added importance, insures more notice. Sometimes they're convinced that what they tell you, no matter how horrific, is the truth. Now and again it is.

I wasn't sure from that first conversation into which category Bianca would fall. I reminded myself not to be hoodwinked by consideration and charm of manner, both of which Oliver had in plenty. I'd heard that Charles Peace, that arch-criminal, though slovenly in his person, was irresistible to women, a fact which had lured I didn't know how many to ruin. So I didn't propose to let Oliver's surface virtues cloud my mind. All the same, I couldn't lose sight of the fact that Bianca was an obvious neurotic, who could draw fantastic conclusions from the smallest event. I decided to bide my time. I didn't have to bide long.

It couldn't have been more than a week or ten days after this conversation that the weather, which had been cloudy and uncertain, suddenly cleared and enticed one into the open. I had been suffering my usual shock at the realization of how quickly the human mind can assimilate even aspects of horror, and this may have made me poorish company. Anyway, Bianca urged me to go out while I could, that is, while Mrs. Dotrice was in the house. Some afternoons she stayed till five, twice a week she stayed on and cooked the dinner. It was tacitly understood that if it could possibly be avoided, Bianca shouldn't be left alone in the house with her husband. I hadn't then achieved, as I did later, regular times off, so I jumped at the idea of getting away from the house.

It was on a Tuesday that I saw the mushrooms.

I was crossing a patch of open country and I saw them, beautiful, sturdy, a sort of leprous-white in the sunshine, springing up in great clumps behind wire fences. But I knew at once they were the wild variety. I thought I remembered hearing that in England wild mushrooms may be picked by anyone, though it's supposed to be courteous to ask the farmer's permission. But these, though wild, had been fenced in. I asked Oliver about them that night, and he said, "That would be Russell's Common. He won't mind our helping ourselves. I'll ring him up tonight, and we might go along tomorrow before the hordes appear. They come down like locusts and strip the field before half the world's awake. He's done what he can by putting up wire enclosures, but I doubt if those give him much legal protection. Of course, if they were cultivated, it would be different."

"So would the mushrooms," I insisted. "The wild ones have much more flavor. At home . . ."

"In Australia? Yes. Somehow I hadn't thought of them growing there. You need a damp climate . . ."

I knew a pang of dismay. I found it a strain to be perpetually on guard. When I spoke of home I meant Rome of course.

"I thought you never saw anything but sun in Australia," Oliver continued. "One of those enviable countries where they have to pray for rain."

"Drought's no joke," I assured him sharply. I was remembering a Roman summer when for three months we got no more than a teacupful of water, and prayers had been offered in all the churches then. The peasants had even brought proprietary gifts, as simple men have done long before the Christian era.

"I'll run you over tomorrow," Oliver went on. "It's a long time since we had mushrooms. I don't know why. They're on sale in the shops."

When I told Bianca she gave me a long, strange look. "Whose idea was it?"

"The mushrooms were my idea, driving me over to pick them was Oliver's."

"Don't say anything tonight," Bianca counseled me, "but if the weather holds up tomorrow I might come with you. It's Mrs. Dotrice's afternoon off, and in any case she's not the most cheerful company conceivable."

The next day was as good as you could look for. Mr. Russell had said yes, of course, help yourself. I found a nice square basket and off the three of us went. Oliver drove the car onto the grass verge and Bianca said she thought she'd sit there, we mustn't be too long, though. I reassured her:

"We haven't got far to go. Are you sure you won't come?" But she said no, she couldn't stoop and pick, and there would be nowhere to perch nearly so comfortable as in the car.

"I suppose you do know the difference between real mushrooms and the poisonous fungi," she added. "I don't want to die of agaric poisoning."

"Well, anyway, *I* know," Oliver said.

"You can check them over when we bring them back," I offered. Glancing over my shoulder as we moved away, I thought she looked rich, composed, but lonely, sitting there waiting. It seemed to me that for the past few years her life had been nothing but waiting, waiting for threats against it by Oliver or anyone who might be in his pay. I knew she sometimes suspected Mrs. Dotrice of knowing on which side her bread was buttered, had had an eye cocked even for clumsy, tactless Nurse Adams. Though even Bianca could hardly suspect that old dodderer Dr. Mitchison.

Oliver and I passed a small clump of mushrooms, and he stooped, picking one up and holding it out to me.

"I hope you wouldn't have been deceived by this," he said. "It's called deadly nightcap round here, and it's remarkably like a true mushroom. But there's a sort of fluting under the cup you have to look for . . ." He turned up the nightcap to show me what he meant. Then he threw it down and we moved on a little way and started to pick.

It gave me an odd feeling to be able to fill a basket without putting down a penny, but Oliver said lightly, "Oh, this isn't like the market place of some sordid city. How people live and breathe there I'll never know—the breath of corruption." His passion startled me, it seemed so genuine. "It's axiomatic for me to mistrust anyone who comes from a town," he explained a minute later. "I know some of them can't help it, poor beasts, and others who've never breathed anything but Diesel fumes don't know what they're missing, but my prejudice remains."

This was a new side to Oliver. It occured to me I really knew very little about him, and what I did know was mainly gleaned from what Bianca had told me, and she was hardly an unprejudiced observer. It was a queer thing, but this was practically the first time I started to think of him as a person, to wonder what made him tick. People are so contradictory, one shining virtue offset by a corrupting vice: they can be good but not sympathetic, generous but not kind.

"I really think I ought to be getting back to Bianca," I said after a while. I always had a secret fear that Oliver was less simple than he liked you to think, that he rather than Bianca might discover the truth about me, in which case he'd be perfectly in order in drumming me out of the house, and within his rights to hand me over to the police. False pretenses—entering the country on what was to all intents and purposes a forged passport. Set a thief to catch a thief. I would appear much blacker in the eyes of the law than he. And I felt that whatever happened I'd got to defeat him, keep him in the dark. I had that curious vanity, found in women so much more often than in men, that I had a destiny no one else could achieve. I was Bianca's shield between her and great danger; anything I did, any fraud I chose to perpetrate, was justified so long as I kept her safe. And so long as I was on the premises, safe she would be.

Oh well, you know what they say about pride going before a fall.

When I got back to the car I found Bianca walking up and down rather restlessly, swinging her big leather bag.

"I was just going on safari," she announced. "I decided you must have met Mr. Russell and he'd invited you in to tea."

"We'd never have left you on your own," I protested, half laughing. "Look!" And I showed her the basket.

"What happened to Oliver?"

"He stopped to get a few more. They're growing like—oh, like Wordsworth's daffodils—ten thousand saw I at a glance."

We got back into the car. Bianca began to examine the mushrooms. "They're certainly beauties," she allowed. "You have been careful?"

"Oliver showed me the poisonous ones I mustn't pick. I think all these are all right, but you can vet the lot before I cook them. Still, I think Oliver is very knowledgeable."

"Oh, I'm sure," she agreed in an odd bitter voice.

Oliver came hurrying up with some more mushrooms wrapped in a clean handkerchief, which he tilted into the basket. It was such a lovely afternoon we decided not to go straight back, but ride around for a bit. We stopped for tea at a place called The Peacock's Feather.

"I don't know how they dare," said Bianca. "Tempt providence, I mean. Everyone knows peacocks' feathers are unlucky."

"Except the peacock, I suppose," murmured Oliver. "Surely you don't subscribe to that superstition."

"You can laugh, but Mrs. Dotrice saw the new moon through glass, and her husband died within the week. She told me."

"Was that supposed to be good luck or bad?" asked Oliver flippantly.

Bianca's manner stiffened. "It wasn't a joke to her."

"Oh come," he protested, "you mustn't attach so much importance to my every word. I'm not on oath."

"Anyway," I put in, with that officiousness nurses so easily develop, "there's nothing unlucky about the tea."

It couldn't have been better—homemade scones, homemade jam, home-baked cakes. We all did it justice, then got back in the car and drove home. Mrs. Dotrice had been gone for some time, leaving cold stuff for the evening meal.

"Let's have high tea tonight," Bianca suggested. "Mushrooms, and there's the cold ham and Mrs. D. will have left a salad. Put the mushrooms there, Oliver, and I'll go through them."

"She doesn't trust me an inch," Oliver said, laughing, doing what she asked. "Sometimes I think she suspects I've got some fell plot against her."

He said it in a deep voice and rolled his eyes, but neither of us laughed.

"What can have put that notion into your head?" Bianca inquired composedly.

"I saw a film the other day, an old Hitchcock, I think it was, a wife going in fear of her life. A good film," he acknowledged, "but I could have shaken the woman. If she really believed she was in danger, why did she stay? She was quite young, she could have got a job, but there was something about her, something spineless . . ."

"Perhaps she was in love with her husband," Bianca offered. She had discarded two or three of the mushrooms, I couldn't see why, they looked just as good to me as the others.

"That's what I call being spineless, being in love with someone you know can't get rid of you fast enough. He made his situation perfectly clear."

"If he disliked her so much, why didn't *he* just walk out?" I asked.

"Oh, I don't think he could have," Oliver told us

seriously. "There was the question of the money. In this case it was mostly hers."

"Very complicated for him," Bianca agreed. She stood up. "I must wash my hands. These all pass the test, Julie. I must say I'm quite looking forward to them. It's a long time since I went mushrooming."

"Do we peel them?" Oliver asked, but I told him no, it wasn't necessary, not when they were so clean. I still couldn't get accustomed to the British passion for washing away all flavors, peeling vegetables whose goodness was only retained by the skins, or cooking them without flavoring.

I got out the big iron pan and melted butter in it. Bianca came back. "Is that butter you're using?" she asked in quite a sharp voice.

I looked surprised. "Of course."

"I don't know what Mrs. Dotrice will say."

"Mushrooms should be cooked in butter," I insisted. "What would she have used? Lard?"

"Have you never heard of margarine?"

In Rome, of course, everyone cooks with butter. "It 'ud be like dressing a beauty in rags," I protested. "It's worth the bit of butter it takes."

"I wouldn't have called that a bit." Bianca looked critically at the great chunk that was turning a pale golden brown in the pan.

"Yes, it does take rather a lot," I acknowledged, "but you really don't need to butter the bread, so you save there." It was another of those petty contradictions that used to puzzle me. She wasn't normally "near" with her money, she liked things to be good quality, would order fruit and vegetables even when they were out of season, but I could see she was genuinely shocked that I was using the best butter, though the difference in cost couldn't be more than a few pence.

"Why don't we eat in here?" suggested Oliver, looking around the kitchen. "I never understand our British way of life. Everything comes piping hot off the stove, and then for the sake of gentility or some such fiddle-faddle, it must be carried, often uncovered, through a draughty hall and into another room."

"It's not everyone who wants to eat with the smell of cooking round them," Bianca pointed out. "Julie, would you set the table, and, Oliver, how about some wine?"

"Watch the toast," I urged, cutting the slices and putting

them on the grill. I collected knives and forks and hurried through the hall. Bianca was turning the toast when I came back—there was an electric toaster but Mrs. Dotrice wouldn't use it, she said the only proper way to make toast was on the end of a fork in front of a coal fire. Oliver had opened a bottle of white wine and fetched in the ham, still on its bone, from the larder. I put the toast on hot plates; Bianca started ladling out the mushrooms. There had seemed so many when we picked them it was alarming how they'd shrunk. I thought of saying I was allergic to mushrooms, but I knew I'd never be able to keep that up. I put two plates on a tray and at that moment the telephone rang.

"I'll get it," I said. It wasn't anything important, a message from a man about some work that was being done in the garden. I went back to the kitchen, collecting the smallest plate of mushrooms.

"Here, I was going to have those," said Oliver. "After all your work you deserve the lion's share."

"That's the plate I fancy," observed Bianca coolly.

"But you know you adore mushrooms. I'd picked this one out for you."

"What lovely natures we all have," she said. "Each of us tyring to give the biggest plate to the others."

"My dear, they're all exactly alike," Oliver protested.

"Then it can't matter which one I have. Julie, you take those two plates on the tray, Oliver bring the wine, I'll carry my own."

What for a moment had threatened to be awkward drained away. We were three normal people who'd had an enjoyable afternoon luxuriating in what Oliver called the fruits of our labor, though, he added, I suppose some of the credit should go to Russell. After the mushrooms we had the ham, and we all agreed that Mrs. Dotrice had surpassed herself with her mayonnaise.

"It always seems so simple," Bianca said. "It should be delicious, but half the time it's like the stuff you use to polish the table. There's no doubt about it, that woman may look like Rachel mourning for her children, but she's a first-class cook."

After dinner we played pontoon for a little, then Bianca said she was tired and I took her up to bed. Oliver washed up—he was very good about the house. I went down to warm Bianca's milk and he gave me a cup of coffee. I carried it up with me. Bianca said she'd take a sleeping tablet.

She was looking a bit worried. "I hope those mushrooms weren't a mistake," she said. "All that butter. So rich."

I waited till she dropped off, then went back to my own room and started a letter to Ada. It was nearly twelve o'clock when I put out my light.

I couldn't have been asleep more than a couple of hours when the bell from Bianca's room began to ring with a sort of furious tremulousness. It was such a long time since she had disturbed me in the night that I let it ring for a moment before I realized it wasn't a part of my dream. Then I was up and flashing into her room. She had switched on the bed-side light, and a single glance warned me that this was no whimsical appeal for company, or the aftermath of a night-mare. Her face had a shining stretched look, the skin pol-ished; her eyes were wild with pain and she was retching and vomiting. "Don't try and talk," I said. She was quite limp and heavy in my arms, and the pain was so severe she could only gasp and moan. The only word that came through clearly was mushrooms.

"There was nothing wrong with them," I coaxed her. All the same, I didn't like her looks. With one arm still sup-porting her, I reached for the telephone. It wasn't easy to dial the doctor's number, but I managed. The voice that answered was as strange as a foreign tongue.

"Dr. Mitchison?" I said, and the voice replied, "He doesn't take night calls. This is his partner, Dr. Gregg, and I only take them in cases of emergency."

"This is an emergency," I said. "Food poisoning." I described the symptoms.

"Who are you?" asked Dr. Gregg. "Nurse?"

"Companion. But I have done a certain amount of nurs-ing."

"God preserve me from the amateur nurse," he said piously. "Now listen. I take it you can do what you're told?" He proceeded to give me some instructions. I let him run on, though some I'd already carried out before I rang him, and the rest I had been going to do as soon as I hung up. But I'd just told him I wasn't a nurse . . .

"How did he do it?" whispered Bianca in a drugged voice. "Don't go away, Julie."

"I wouldn't dare," I said.

The doctor must have traveled faster than light. In no time at all he was making a tremendous commotion with the front-door bell. Bianca hung on to me, but it was all right, because the noise awakened Oliver and he went staggering down to let the doctor in.

"You the husband?" said Dr. Gregg. You could hear him all over the house. "Stay down here and put some kettles on, will you? Fewer people in the sickroom the better. I'll call you if you're wanted." (He told me later he always put distracted husbands on to boiling kettles. Sometimes the hot water really came in useful, mostly the kettle boiled dry. He gave a heartless chuckle when he said that. "That'll teach 'em to be careless.")

A greater contrast to soft-voiced, soft-palmed Dr. Mitchison couldn't be imagined. For one thing, Dr. Gregg—I learned afterward his name was Lionel and it seemed ideal for him—was much younger. He was very dark, with a brisk manner and a keen thrusting face. But he knew his job. He got to work right away without asking a lot of questions; he said the time for that could come later. One way and another it was a messy affair; I couldn't help reflecting it was a good thing I was a nurse. You develop a kind of protective covering; it doesn't necessarily harden your heart, but it does harden your nerves. When he'd got Bianca as comfortable as possible—no question of removing her to a hospital, he said—he asked me what precisely had happened. I explained about the mushrooms.

"It's very mysterious," I said. "We all examined them. But I suppose somehow a fungus got in. I don't see how it could have been anything else."

"H'm." He stroked his long powerful chin. "Do you want me to try and send in a nurse for a few days to help you carry on? You said you're not a trained nurse?"

"That's right," I agreed. I had said so.

"Well, you could have fooled me. Any other women in the house?"

I told him about Mrs. Dotrice. "Make her lend a hand."

He had a reassuring word with Oliver, but you could see he wasn't really interested in him. If Mrs. Dotrice had to take turns in the sickroom she wouldn't be able to keep up with her normal job, but that didn't bother him. I should be preparing the pap that would be all Bianca would have for a day or two, and if Oliver wanted anything solid he could go to his club. As doctor and nurse, we were only concerned with the patient. I privately thought it was rather heartless of him to have consumed more mushrooms than any of us and be so aggressively well.

"I still don't understand why it had to be Mrs. Duncan," I

said, taking the doctor to the door. "Why not her husband? Or me?"

"Why did a buzz-bomb hit one house and leave the one next door unscathed?" Dr. Gregg demanded.

Oliver caught me in the hall as I turned to go back to Bianca. "I won't delay you, Julie," he said, "but there's one thing I must say. And you're to take this to heart. How this thing happened, I don't know, I thought we'd examined every mushroom, but something obviously went wrong. But don't start blaming yourself. Oh yes, that's what's in your mind. I saw your face when the doctor confirmed the cause of Bianca's collapse, and remember, I've seen that expression on a woman's face before. When Evelyn died and Bianca chose to believe—because at the beginning it is a choice, never lose sight of that fact—she chose to believe she was responsible, she brooded over it till at times she practically convinced herself she'd mixed an overdose for Evelyn. I saw what that did to her. You've never seen Bianca as I remember her. I don't understand the reason for it, though women do appear to have a kind of inbuilt capacity for martyrdom, which does neither them nor anyone else any good . . ."

"It's all right," I interrupted. "I don't blame myself. And I must get back to Bianca now. You're the one who shouldn't worry; Dr. Gregg says she's going to be all right."

The first thing Bianca asked me when she was able to talk at all was where Oliver was. "Keep him out of here," she mouthed at me. "Keep him out, I don't care what you tell him."

So I promised to do my best.

It must have been on the third or fourth day that Dr. Gregg—he was continuing the case, to Bianca's disgust; Dr. Mitchison had gone to bed with a heavy cold that might well turn to pleurisy—asked me, "What's she like, Mrs. Duncan, I mean, when she's not indulging in poisonous fungi?"

"All the details are on her card," I said before I could stop myself.

"Why should I wreck my eyesight trying to read my partner's hieroglyphics when you can tell me just as well?"

"She has a sort of persecution mania," I acknowledged. "She's afraid . . ." I stopped, I didn't know how far I should go.

"That's often a sign of the death-wish," said Dr. Gregg,

cheerfully. Bianca would have had a heart attack to hear him. "How long's she been married?"

"About five years, I think. She was the first Mrs. Duncan's nurse."

"What happened to the first Mrs. Duncan?"

"She died. Bianca holds herself responsible because she wasn't there at the time."

"Who's she to suppose she'll never make a mistake? Most of us would have to admit responsibility for a death that with more knowledge, more experience, sometimes even a greater degree of care, need never have happened. It's a mere morbid luxury brooding over it. And nurses are like doctors, they can't afford luxuries."

"I hope Dr. Mitchison is soon back on his feet," said Bianca icily. "This young man may be very intelligent, but that gallow's-foot manner won't get him far."

Dr. Mitchison, however, didn't come back. "Bronchitis," said Dr. Gregg. "That's what I call it, but it's non-U to have bronchitis these days, it's pneumonia now. Just the same way no one will confess to a common cold. Oh, Doctor, they say, crowding my surgery that's already bursting at the seams, I think I've got the flu. I tell 'em to go back and stick their feet in a bucket of hot water and take an aspirin and knock off the drink. I don't see many of 'em twice."

"That," Bianca remarked after he'd gone, "is scarcely surprising."

Dr. Gregg might have been an unconventional doctor but he certainly added some spice to the household's rather monotonous routine. "How much longer do you expect to be here?" he asked me.

"She needs me," I explained.

"Like I need a hole in the head. There's a poem by Rudyard Kipling, about the sons of Mary who cast their burden upon the Lord, and the Lord He casts it on Martha's sons. Your employer, Julie" (he called me by my first name always, "any young woman in a sickroom is Nurse to me, and if she can't claim that title I use her given name. I'll have no Miss this-and-that in my sickroom"), "is a son of Mary, and she's seeing to it that Martha's kith and kin are carrying the can night and day." He growled. "You're about the only person I meet these days who doesn't ask me for a prescription and the one person for whom I can recommend one."

"Oh yes," I said, "I meant to ask. Is there a prescription for Mrs. Duncan?"

"There is not. And the first chance you get you throw out that chemist's shop she's got in her room. I don't know what it is about women, they will hoard love letters, locks of hair, dance programs, photographs of a favorite kitty, half-bottles of medicine which probably aren't much more than colored water at best." He began to laugh. He had a good healthy bellowing laugh; Bianca said it made the flesh crawl on her bones. "Patient of mine complained of a bellyache the other day. Said she'd taken a dose of something, she wasn't explicit, something she'd had recommended the previous year, so she thought. Label had fallen off the bottle but that didn't bother her. Turned out it was the puppy's worm mixture." He roared heartlessly and off he went. I heard the echo of his laughter right down to the gate.

"Why were you so long?" Bianca demanded when I got back to the sickroom.

"I was asking if there was a prescription, and he said no."

"Not one I'm going to take," Bianca agreed. "His idea is that I shall go abroad for a while."

"But why not?" I cried. "You'd feel safe there, surely."

"I might get there all right, I'm much more doubtful as to whether I'd ever get back. Anyway, this is my home, why should I be driven out of it?"

The doctor's car suddenly sprang to life and went hooting down the road. "I know who he reminds me of," Bianca exclaimed. "That poem by John Betjeman.

The doctor jumps in his Morris car
The surgery door goes bang.
Clash and whirr down Colleton Crescent,
Other cars all go hang.
My little bus is enough for us
Till a tramcar bell went clang.
They brought his in by the big front door
And a smiling corpse was he . . .

Can't you imagine him, Julie, smiling in his coffin, still certain he was right?"

I sat down on a chair beside the bed. "Why don't you give his suggestion a bit more thought?" I urged. "You really should get out more. At least," I added desperately, "start going out in the car again. If you're worried about its condition I'll take it along to the garage and have it thoroughly overhauled. I've passed my test now . . ."

I had seen the little black Parker in the garage when

Oliver beached his nobler specimen. Bianca used to drive it a lot, she told me, but it hadn't been used for some time. Nurse Adams didn't drive, and Bianca had become nervous. Now, however, she seemed inclined to listen to me.

"It would be a start," she conceded. "I'd trust myself with you, Julie."

"Presently you'll be driving yourself around again, just as you used to," I prophesied. "Dr. Mitchison . . ."

"He's all set for the Riviera as soon as he's fit to travel. Dr. Gregg seems quite pleased about it. Perhaps he hopes he won't come back either. Not that that young man will ever be much of a success with private patients."

Before the doctor called again I'd taken the Parker down to the local garage for a thorough going-over. If the tires were the least bit worn, fit new ones, I said. I even wondered about having it resprayed. I was spending my spare time persuading Bianca that however much of a tycoon he was, Oliver couldn't buy up everyone—the doctor, the garage proprietor, Mrs. Dotrice. I had to humor her a lot. It was like teaching a child to walk after an accident; it's a slow process, you need a lot of patience and an inexhaustible store of encouragement, but unless you persist, the child may remain a cripple all its days.

It was after I'd left the car at the garage that I discovered the existence of The Motive.

It was Market Day when the buses were all crowded anyhow; you had to be at the bus station twenty minutes before they took off to hope to get a seat, especially on the 12:30. They only ran every two hours and on some days less often than that. The shops mostly closed for the lunch hour, too, and this annoyed some people, who complained of the inconvenience, but it didn't surprise me. In Rome shops all closed at noon till three o'clock and some later still. Of course, they stayed open later, too. I missed the 12:30 bus and I knew all the teashops where the shoppers congregated would be packed. Even the museum was closed, and there was nothing much to see there but a few arrowheads in any case. I decided to go into the bar of The Huntsman and buy myself a drink and see if I could get some sandwiches. The Huntsman was the most considerable of the local inns. In fact, it called itself an hotel. The bar wasn't very full and I ordered my drink and took it over to a table. Before I could order any sandwiches the door was pushed open and Oliver came in accompanied by a girl who almost took my breath away. She was one of those golden girls you find in

England, as pretty as a picture and as radiant as spring. She had so much vitality you'd have thought the sun was shining outside even on a wet day. She and Oliver went up to the bar, where they collected two stools and he gave an order. I was watching the girl, fascinated. It occurred to me she probably was only about ten years younger than Bianca, but it seemed as if a whole generation separated them. At least, I thought, she doesn't know about her, and I had a sudden vision of Dr. Gregg saying, "Let her come out and see the sort of competition she's up against. That might knock some sense into her," and I found myself agreeing with him.

The couple at the bar were so absorbed they had no eyes for anyone else. I changed my mind about ordering sandwiches. I didn't want Oliver to get the idea that Bianca had put me on to trail him, so I slipped out unobtrusively and had a very nasty meal at The Copper Castle, where all the waitresses were dressed as dwarfs and the quantities of food were obviously intended for dwarfs, too. I thought that if Bianca did know about this girl, she had good reason for fear. For if Oliver Duncan had married his first wife for money and his second for expediency, if he ever got as far as his third, this time it would be for love.

I chewed soggy macaroni and cheese and drank pale coffee and then went to the bus station. The 2:30 wouldn't be so crowded as the one before, but it would be full enough. Shoppers, many of them, enjoyed the change of a lunch they hadn't had to cook and wouldn't have to wash up, and they liked different company from that they usually had to put up with. I got a seat, still obsessed with my vision of Oliver and the lovely girl whose name I didn't yet know.

The bus was very late getting us to Hotham St. Mary, mainly due to a dog whose mistress always traveled by this bus, bringing him with her. He had gone out for a stroll on his own account—"He does enjoy a little private life," his owner confided to us. "I'm sure he won't be long." No one seemed to mind. It didn't occur to the driver to tell her to wait for the next bus. After about five minutes the dog appeared, not hurrying itself, walked up to the bus, lifted its leg against one of the wheels and entered the door before its owner. Everyone treated it as though it had done something miraculous. The conversation buzzed all around me: these excursions were like an additional woman's institute meeting, a sort of bonus to good housewives who took the trouble to go to market and look out for bargains. There was a lot of talk about trading stamps of various colors—thank goodness, Bianca never expected me to collect those. When I did get home Bianca said rather shrilly, "So you're back at last? I quite thought you must have eloped."

"Who with?" I asked. I showed her the silks I'd got for her petitpoint; it was her one relaxation and she did it rather well. I suppose she'd acquired the knack during those long nights all private nurses know, when you find yourself wondering if it will ever be day. It's easier in a hospital, of course, with people around you and something going on all the time.

"You've a very good eye for the color," Bianca congratulated me. "Adams never had the patience to match anything right. Good heavens, Julie, what's happened? You're not going to faint, surely? Didn't you have any lunch?"

"Yes," I told her, "and of course I'm not going to faint. It was rather stuffy in the bus, that's all."

Why at that instant did I have to remember the Marchesa and what happened when I went matching silks for her in the Corso? There was no similarity here, nothing had happened to Bianca, nothing was going to.

"You didn't happen to see my husband, I suppose?" The words were intended to be light, but they came out as heavy as a soggy cake.

"Not to speak to." If she hadn't bugged me, making me recall that afternoon in Rome, I'd have been watching my words more carefully. Of course, she was on to my half-admission like a knife.

"What does that mean?"

"I mean, I caught a glimpse of him in the distance."

"How far distant?"

"I was having a drink at The Huntsman . . ."

"By yourself?" She sounded incredulous.

"Of course. In . . ." I stopped dead. I was about to say that in Rome it's usual to have an apéritif.

"Well, go on."

"In the bar. I thought I'd see if I could get a sandwich. Every place was so crowded."

"And could you?"

"No. I went to The Copper Castle. They could do with a new cook there. This one . . ."

"I hope you made Oliver pay for your drink."

"He didn't even see me."

"You should have attracted his attention."

"I couldn't, he was busy. Some business connection . . ."

Bianca laughed; it was the jangling laugh that always sent shivers up my spine.

"I've heard it called a lot of things, but never that. Oh, stop trying to be diplomatic and loyal, Julie. Do you imagine I haven't known for ages about my husband and the entrancing Miss Fiona Lane? It's not Oliver's fault if the whole neighborhood doesn't know about it."

"I thought perhaps she was his secretary," I offered desperately.

"His secretary is a woman of forty with a face like a chopping-block. Very efficient, though, I understand. Oliver has the good sense to seek his entertainment outside the walls of his office. You're sure he didn't see you?"

"I'm sure he didn't."

"Too much engrossed, I suppose. Do they know you at The Huntsman?"

I stared. "How can they? I've never been inside the place before."

Abruptly she changed the subject. "I meant to tell you—you missed your friend."

"*My* friend?" I couldn't think who she was talking about.

"You say that as if you didn't know you had any."

"I didn't know I had any here." Oddly enough, the only person who came to my mind was the strangely named Mr. Crook, and it couldn't be him, because he wouldn't know where I was. "Who was it?"

"Very cagey," said Bianca. "Wouldn't leave a name. What a woman of mystery you are, Julie. Two months under this roof and not a single letter, not even a phone call until today. What happened to all your Australian buddies?"

"They'd hardly be ringing up from the other side of the world," I said.

"They might put a pen to paper occasionally."

"There really isn't anyone much, not now."

"Aunty gone to her rest and the young man . . ."

"That's all over," I said sharply. Something in my voice warned her.

"Anyway, whoever it is, is going to call again at six." She began to pull at the fringe of a rug she had on the bed. She hated eiderdowns, wouldn't have one.

"You're not in any sort of trouble, are you, Julie? I mean, it's so strange a girl with your looks being contented to bury herself in a hole like this. You're not wanted by the police or anything, I suppose?"

My laughter at that was so spontaneous she seemed to be reassured. "All right," she said, "I'll come clean. I thought that phone call might be from someone about a job."

"I've got a job," I pointed out.

"You could have a more exciting one."

"As long as you want me I'll stay," I said. There was nothing heroic about it; I was a nurse, it was as prosaic and obvious as being a sentry. I showed her a guidebook I'd bought at Levers, the big bookstore, that gave details of local drives up to a radius of a hundred miles. Of course, she wouldn't be up to doing such distances at present, but there were shorter spins, and some National Trust properties with gardens where she could have tea and just glance over the ancient walls. It was high time she put herself into circulation again. Mr. Leverson at the garage had promised to make the overhaul a top-priority job. I imagine he'd charge for special service, but that didn't matter. If Oliver had funds to take lovelies out in The Huntsman bar he could pay a sizable check for his wife's renewed mobility.

On the stroke of six my correspondent came through again. Why I hadn't thought of her before, I don't know. It was Ada Holloway, the only person who had my address, if I'd stopped to think, but somehow since coming to the Duncan household I'd felt like an embryo enclosed in an egg; the rest of the world went on as usual, but I didn't seem a part of it.

"What gives?" she demanded. "I've been quite worried about you, my girl. Eight weeks and not a word. They're not keeping you prisoner, I suppose?"

"In a job like this you don't have a lot of free time," I said evasively.

"You should join a union," Ada assured me. "I can see just how it is, that woman's fastened on to you like a land crab. She sees you're good-natured and she's cashing in. Does it never occur to you what an occasion for sin an unselfish person can be? It's a good thing there's one human creature who knows you're alive. I'd have called before but I had flu. Okay now, though. Which is your afternoon off?"

"I don't exactly have a special afternoon," I explained.

"Then assert your rights and demand one. Next Wednesday would suit me. We could meet in London, there's a good train service, I've looked it up."

"Wednesday wouldn't be any good," I blurted out. "It's not one of Mrs. Dotrice's late nights."

"You don't have to be all that late. We could meet after

lunch and have an early meal in town. What did your delicate Duncans do before your arrival?"

"There was a nurse . . ."

"Don't make me laugh," said Ada scornfully. "Nurses don't work all round the clock, not unless they're blacklegs. Wednesday then. You've got my telephone number?" She repeated it in case I'd forgotten it. "It'll be a good thing for Mrs. Whosit to realize you're not alone in the world."

I wasn't enthusiastic. I was rather nervous about this plain energetic woman with her gimlet glance and outspoken ways. I felt she'd get everything out of me before I even realized I had told her the facts, and I certainly didn't propose to share Bianca's secret with her. Besides, I still assured myself there was absolutely nothing to go on. I had to keep a pretty strict watch on my tongue as it was, perpetually biting back references to Rome, and remembering occasionally to refer to Australia.

"I won't say any more now," continued Ada briskly. "We'll have a nice tête-à-tête next week. I'll drop you a card." As she hung up I heard a very faint click and realized that someone had been listening on one of the extensions. I realized, too, that Ada, quicker than I, had also been aware of it.

I went up to Bianca's room. "That was Ada Holloway," I said, deliberately not watching her, because if it had been she who was eavesdropping I didn't want to catch her out. "We met at the hostel where I was living before I came here."

Bianca said languidly, "I thought you were in a clinic."

"The hostel followed the clinic. I ought to have written to her before. She wants me to meet her next week."

Bianca said in the same voice, "What an extraordinary name! Do you suppose her mother had a baby in Holloway Jail, or isn't that allowed any more?"

"I should think it's far more likely her mother married a man called Holloway," I said rather sharply.

"Why don't you ask her to come here?" Bianca inquired.

"It's a long way," I demurred.

"No further for her than for you. If the car's back by then, you could meet her at the station. Incidentally, do feel free to use the telephone whenever you like. Sometimes I wonder why we bother to have one, we use it so little."

I rang Ada the next day but not from the house. I walked down to the crossroads, where there was a telephone box on a little triangular green. "It's all right about next week," I said, and she named a place near Charing Cross Station and told me which train to catch.

"Who was our dear little eavesdropper?" she added. "Personally, when I want people to know my business I write a postcard. Now, Julie, do try and exercise a little sense. I know you have a romantic nature, but just remind yourself now and again that a girl like you, without connections and no regular home address, can vanish without trace and no questions asked—till it's too late."

"How melodramatic can you get?" I scoffed. "Why on earth should they want to get rid of me?"

"I don't know, but they seem to have kept you tied up pretty close for the past two months, and I don't approve of a household where the companion can't take a private call. But then I never wanted you to go there in the first place."

"No one's going to risk their neck for me," I expostulated.

"You don't risk your neck any more, a nice paternal government keeps you in bed and board and sees to your health requirements and your dependents go on National Assistance. If that isn't encouraging crime, I don't know what is."

She elaborated the point when we met the following week. Nothing of any interest had happened to me in the interim, except that I'd got the car back and persuaded Bianca to come out two or three times. Eventually I hoped she'd pluck up heart and take the wheel herself.

"Doesn't it strike you as odd that the Duncans took you on sight," she persisted. "No references, no previous experience, not in this kind of job anyway, no family backing. I wouldn't engage a junior clerk on those terms."

"I suppose they knew it wasn't everyone's job. What a suspicious mind you have."

"It's a pity there aren't a few more like it. In their shoes I'd have asked myself why a girl like you should jump at such a bargain basement job. After all, you have diplomas—at least I suppose they have those in Australia."

"It's not precisely the backwoods," I reminded her tartly. "And as for me vanishing suddenly, how could that advantage anyone? I've no knowledge of their guilty secrets . . ."

"There you are!" cried Ada triumphantly. "You feel the same as I do about them."

I was going to add, "So far as I know they haven't any." Only of course that wasn't quite true. There was the mystery of Evelyn Duncan in the background, a mystery that would now presumably never be solved. Ada could suspect them, Bianca could suspect Oliver, a lot of people in Rome had suspected me, but no one could prove anything.

Ada stuck to her point with tiresome pertinacity. "I meant what I told you. Suppose there are secrets and you stumble on them? Who would notice you'd gone? There's me, but I might get bowled over by a Green Line and then there'd be no one. If you've no family you ought to have some sort of representative . . . Being an anonymous atom in a big bloody universe is no joke."

"There are the locals," I protested. "And the doctor."

"Oh yes. What's he like?"

"The real one's on the Riviera. We're making do with the partner."

"And if the Duncans said there'd been a disagreement, you'd walked out, eloped, gone off with the family silver . . ."

"Wouldn't it be odd that no one actually saw me go?" I found to my surprise, rather to my chagrin, that I was taking all this seriously. I tried to turn it off with a laugh. "And all the while I'd be moldering under the privet bush by the gate? You can't ever have a dull moment, Ada."

"You have the look of a girl to whom things happen," said Ada bluntly. "Do you seriously tell me there isn't one other human being to whom you could drop a card or ring up on some pretext? Surely you have a bank or some place where you'd be recognized."

Suddenly I remembered the man on the train. It was absurd, he wouldn't remember my name by now; and yet I'd never been able to shake off the conviction that the card hadn't been left where I found it by accident.

"Well?" said Ada sharply. "Who is it?"

"There was a man on the plane, I met him by chance later, on a train journey; he told me I could always get in touch in an emergency."

"I suppose even you wouldn't be taken in by that."

"He gave me his card," I said. "He's a lawyer."

"Lawyers aren't allowed to advertise," Ada told me crisply. "What was he really like? One of these amiable paw-folders?"

I began to laugh. "Any paw-folding he did would probably break your wrist. He had an odd name for a man in his profession, though. Crook. There's a laugh for you."

"What did you say?" said Ada. She wasn't laughing.

"Crook. He . . ."

"Not *Arthur* Crook?"

"Well, yes, I think it was. Why?"

She stood up. We'd been drinking strong tea and eating soggy teacake. "Let's go for a walk along the embankment," she said, "and call in at The Pelican and Pie. We ought just to catch them at opening time. Well, really, Julie, I could have saved myself a number of sleepless hours if you'd had the *nous* to tell me that before. Why, with him behind you, you're safer than if you went round with a brigade of the Household Cavalry. Now, write to him at once—you haven't lost the card?"

"No. I haven't. But I can't write out of the blue."

"You poor nitwit!" She paid for the tea and was striding down Villiers Street toward the river. "Anyone can write to a lawyer who doesn't mind risking six-and-eightpence. At least, that's what it used to be. I expect it's gone up by now, but whatever it is it's a good investment when your lawyer's name is Arthur Crook."

"How do you know about him?" I asked curiously. I was half her age but it was all I could do to keep up with her.

"Every Londoner knows about him," returned Ada sweepingly. "How did you meet him, though?"

"I told you—he was one of the three survivors on the plane."

"He would be. The plane hasn't been built that would dare polish him off. The odd thing is that he should be on a plane at all. But I'll tell you this. If ever I'm accused of murder, and my life bristles with temptations, I'd make a beeline for his office. He can't only make black look like white, he can actually turn it into white. There was a case I recall . . ." She told me about it; it was very impressive. "And that boy hadn't got two half-crowns to rub together," she went on. "So—don't hesitate, and when you have written let the Duncans know. Now let's hear something about Mrs. D.? What's wrong with her?"

I knew it would happen like this. Before we'd even reached The Pelican and Pie she'd got the story out of me. "I told you you were the sort of girl to whom things happen. What's he like?"

"I don't see much of him. He's out a lot."

"Does his homework at his club, I suppose. You know, Julie, I have an idea. I think it might be a wise step for you to look for another job."

"I can't," I protested. "Bianca needs me."

She sighed. "Well, then, is there anyone you can take for an ally? That doctor?"

"He's an old cod," I said. "Still sunning himself on the Riviera."

"He's not getting much sun by all accounts," said Ada in satisfied tones. "Li'l ole London's getting most of that. I've got a friend flew to Sicily last week, rain's never stopped since she arrived. Same in Malaga and the Channel Islands. Well, we poor wage-slaves deserve a dividend now and again." We reached The Pelican and Pie and she marched in. After that she told me about the hostel and some of the people I remembered during my short stay there. Mrs. Stafford had wanted to be remembered to me. When we said good-bye she told me, "Ignorance isn't always bliss, whatever the poets tell you. Sometimes it's a through ticket to the cremation shed."

I suppose I should have come back trembling with apprehension, but I didn't. Meeting Ada stimulated me beyond anything I could have believed. I wondered where her secret lay, she wasn't young, she had never been good-looking, she looked rather like a camel and she dressed as far as possible to resemble one. Fawn-colored suit, fawn beret, fawn leather bag, sand-colored shoes—even her face had a camel hue. You couldn't imagine any man had ever given her a second glance.

When I got back I found Bianca rather bored. "You seem to have had a very amusing afternoon," she observed, "you've been grinning like a Cheshire cat ever since your return. Can't you tell me any of the funny bits? I could do with a little humor. Mrs. Dotrice" (she had agreed to exchange her late night on my account) "may have her place reserved in the hereafter, but to look at she's about as cheerful as a tombstone."

"Since you ask me, she doesn't seem to have told me anything very striking," I had to admit. "It must be the way she tells it."

The next morning I waited till Bianca had settled for a nap and got out my writing pad and pen and started my letter to Arthur Crook. I expected it to be easy, but it wasn't. I couldn't precisely say I was nursing a woman whose husband was going to murder her, at least who thought her husband was going to murder her, and I might conceivably be involved. ("Why not, sugar?" Crook asked me later. "That's the kind of letter I like best.") I tamely reminded him of our previous meeting on the train. I told him about my job, and said that in the near future I might need his advice in regard to my legacy. That wasn't straying far from the truth, if you agreed that to inherit a name and a past history can be as much of a legacy as a fortune. I reminded him of his promise to act for me if occasion arose. I didn't know him at that time, of course, how he could take any situation in his stride and that no maze of events could daunt him and no situation dismay. To him, I was to learn, the mysterious and the incalculable were the change of everyday life. If I'd believed in guardian angels I'd think mine stood at my elbow, prodding my reluctant pen.

"Writing your friend with the prison name?" inquired Bianca suddenly. I'd been so deep in thought I hadn't noticed she was awake.

"This is to my lawyer," I explained. "To do with my legacy. There seem to be some complications and I'm a bird-brain where business is concerned."

"Did Oliver recommend him?" she asked. "You've never mentioned him before."

"I knew him before I came here," I assured her. "But Ada did point out there was no harm giving him a jolt. These things do drag on so."

"Leave the letter in the hall and the postman will collect it when he brings the next delivery," suggested Bianca casually.

But I wasn't taking any chances. I ran down to the postbox by the crossroads after lunch and posted it myself. It was a drizzling sort of day and Bianca wouldn't leave the house in such weather. I had a sneaking suspicion she made it an excuse to stay rolled up in her blankets like a dormouse in its hole. I'd promised her I'd stay as long as I was needed, but my meeting with Ada had made me realize how cooped up I was here. I wanted to get out, spread my wings, meet some people—it was like living in a perpetual fog; you step carefully, you count twenty before you speak, and suddenly you're reminded of a world where it's normal for the sun to shine.

5

I HAD MY REPLY from Mr. Crook forty-eight hours after I'd posted my letter, three lines in a hand as rambunctious as his own personality. He said he'd been expecting to hear (why?) and the instant any cloud appeared on the horizon, though it was no larger than a baby's fist, I was to get in touch. He said I was to remember he was like that theater whose slogan was We Never Close, the only real difference being that he was still open. I carried that letter around with me like a mascot. I felt that with two allies like Ada Holloway and this unconventional man of law my luck was bound to hold.

I suppose I became too confident. Anyway, it was when everything seemed to be calming down that disaster struck from two directions.

It began with a thundering row between Bianca and Dr. Gregg. She had been bewailing the fact that it was impossible to get out in the wretched weather we were having just then.

"Some of us survive it," he said in his outspoken way. "No sense looking to me for sympathy, ma'am. If you took my advice, which incidentally you're paying for, and went away to a more seasonable climate, you could go out every day. You're luckier than a lot of my patients—a husband prepared to foot the bill and a girl like Julie for a companion. You should make the most of your chances," he went on, about as tender-hearted as a hickory nut, "you won't have her here forever."

Bianca sent me a darting glance. "What's she been saying to you?"

"It's what your own common sense should be saying. A

girl like that isn't going to spend the best years of her life dancing attendance on an imaginary illness."

Bianca reared up like an asp about to strike. "You must be out of your mind," she panted. "You, a doctor, dedicated, or so one's been led to suppose, to healing the sick . . ."

He interrupted her without a qualm. "Don't equate a doctor with a magician." I'd never seen him so worked up. He sounded as fierce and uncompromising as his namesake, the lion. "I need every waking minute I have for the really sick. Do you realize I open my surgery at nine in the morning, and I've dealt with my mail before that, and that I'm lucky if I can put up the shuters at eight p.m. And then there are the emergency calls and the inconsiderate kids who get themselves born in the small hours in their mother's homes or in taxicabs. I even had one start his life in a saloon bar."

"I can assure you I shall take up no more of your time," foamed Bianca. "Since this appears to be the hour of truth, let me tell you I don't require any more of your ministrations."

"Isn't that what I've been saying? But"—he grinned, shedding about five years—"if you think you're giving me the sack you're wrong. I've got to keep the bed warm for Dr. Mitchison. Come to that, I'm expecting him home any day now. He's getting the impression we're doing quite well without him, and that's bad for any doctor's financial blood pressure."

"I expect you can see yourself out," Bianca told him. "I need Julie here."

After he'd gone she said to me that if he ever had the nerve to show his face again, she was not at home.

"I suppose it's his version of shock treatment," I suggested.

"Whose side are you on?" she demanded.

"We're on the same side, all of us. We can't bear you to be cooped up here in one small room, with all life surging past the window."

I never met anyone, not excepting the Marchesa, so apt to get the last word.

"This may seem a very small room to you, Julie," she said, though actually it was palatial. "We know you're accustomed to wide-open spaces, but even this is more spacious than a coffin."

All the same, from that day she began to consider Dr.

Gregg's proposal. She asked me to write for holiday brochures. She said, "I'd forgotten how lovely Italy can be—the duomo at Florence—and the Uffizi. Though I've always thought Botticelli's "Venus" too good to be true. Surely she'd have looked a little more *surprised* . . ." She didn't talk about the mushroom affair any more. An unfortunate accident, Dr. Gregg had said. I hardly believed that Bianca agreed with him. And yet if it had been a deliberate attempt on Oliver's part, it was surely exceedingly chancy. Any one of us might have got the poisoned mushroom, and anyway, I told myself, all the mushrooms had come from the same field. Only, of course, I couldn't really swear to that. I had left Oliver alone picking the last few while I sped back to Bianca. I'd been out of the kitchen while I set the table; there could have been an opportunity for a fungus to be introduced. It's true I might have got it instead of Bianca, but I couldn't believe it was any part of his plan that I should stay on in the household indefinitely, not only a protection for Bianca, but a possible witness in case of tragedy.

Naturally, I encouraged her every way I knew. I did have a secret fear she would suggest visiting Rome, but luckily it was a city that didn't appeal to her.

"Why don't we go down and talk to the local travel agent?" I suggested one evening. "Tomorrow's going to be fine, according to the weather forecast, and there are some household things we need, anyway."

"We'll see what the weather's like," she said. Next day everything, even the weather, seemed to co-operate with my plan to get her out of the house and eventually overseas. The morning was so full of sun that the world glittered; skies, leaves, water, all seemed polished, throwing back the golden light. Bianca was up and dressed earlier than usual; she even spoke of getting back into the driver's seat in the near future. For once she didn't wait in the car while I did the shopping, but came with me; in fact, she seemed quite delighted to find herself inside a shop again. The local picture gallery was holding an exhibition of contemporary art, and we looked in there and she actually bought a picture. It represented a harbor, a matter of jagged lines and abrupt angles in dull blue and gold against a very dark background. It wasn't what I'd have expected her to choose, and it opened another facet of her nature to me. I suppose it doesn't sound much when you try to describe it, but the *effect* of the picture was quite startling. I felt I could hardly wait to pack a bag and go aboard any ship, sailing to any destination.

"What do you think of it?" Bianca said.

I came out of a sort of brown study. "It's like life, isn't it?" I told her "Waiting for you—me—anyone—to go on board, not knowing where the ship will take you."

"What I like about you, Julie, is your unexpectedness," said Bianca, smiling at my enthusiasm. But the man in charge of the gallery sent me a quite understanding look. I wondered if he was the artist.

From the gallery we went to the travel agency, where she made tentative arrangements for the two of us to go abroad next month. "I must talk to my husband," she explained. "He won't be coming, but I have to make sure it'll be quite convenient for him." I don't know what the clerk at the agency made of that, but Bianca was in tearing spirits. I secretly hoped it wasn't going to be a case of shine before seven, rain before eleven. She seemed keyed up to meet any event. And considering how the day was going to end, that was just as well.

We'd spent so much time in the gallery that it was too late for us to hope to get back to lunch, and Bianca decided. "We'll go to The Huntsman." I wondered if she secretly hoped to catch Oliver there with his beautiful girl—The Motive was how I thought of her—though I didn't see what she could do if she did. Even Bianca could hardly make a scene in public. However, the opportunity didn't arise. Oliver was nowhere to be seen, and when Bianca asked casually if he was expected that day the head waiter looked surprised and said he didn't often come in.

"I wonder where he does take her," Bianca said.

The lunch was very good, but we didn't wait for coffee. She didn't care for it midday, and though I could have done with a cup—standing around in shops can be very exhausting—she wouldn't wait.

"Get Mrs. Dotrice to give you some when we get back," she suggested. "She must swim in it, the amount she gets through."

On the way back she told me that the next time we came out she'd take the wheel herself. "I'm supposed to be a very good driver," she told me. "It's just that my nerves—but, thanks to you, Julie, I'm getting back to normal. You'll never know how grateful to you I am."

When we reached the house she took the picture in at the front, while I put the car in the garage and went around to the kitchen to give Mrs. Dotrice the things she'd asked for. There was the usual delicious coffee smell, and it was clear she had just made a fresh pot.

"Would there be a spare cup?" I asked.

Usually she was a smoldering sort of woman, not gracious, but today she actually smiled. She took a cup from the shelf, filled it and handed it to me.

"It wouldn't be as good as this at The Huntsman," I said.

While I was drinking the coffee she casually dropped her bombshell.

"I put the gentleman in the morning room," she said. "I told him I didn't know when you'd be back, but he said he'd come a long way and he'd wait."

"I wonder who he is," I murmured idly.

She sent me a sharp look. "He asked for you particularly."

"For me?" There was only one man I could think of who it might possibly be, and I felt sure that Mrs. Dotrice, with her British snobbery, would never describe him as a gentleman. A person, she would say, as if he'd called about a job, and he'd be lucky if he made the hall.

"He said his name's Hunter," said Mrs. Dotrice.

"He must have made a mistake," I murmured. "That was delicious coffee, Mrs. Dotrice." But I could hear the treacherous tremble of the cup against the saucer when I put it down.

"He's got a funny accent," Mrs. Dotrice went on. "Still, I suppose they're all like that in Australia."

"Julie," called Bianca. "What's happened to you? Where are you?"

"In the kitchen. I've been giving Mrs. Dotrice the stores." I was surprised how normal my voice sounded. "I'm just going to take your parcels upstairs."

"They can wait," said Bianca. "Come and see your wonderful surprise."

We went into what I'd been accustomed to call the breakfast room. A tall fairish man, thirty-ish, I suppose, with bright blue eyes, stood up as I came in—my visitor with the Aussie accent. Of course, I'd never set eyes on him before in my life.

"Here she comes," cried Bianca. "Here's Julie. Come and meet Charles Hunter—as if you didn't know."

I felt my legs turn to lead. I think I must have smiled, because I felt my lips stretching. I wondered how on earth I'd imagine I'd be able to carry this deception through. When

Julie had said there's no one in Australia now, I'd taken it literally. I should have known a radiant creature like that could never find herself isolated overnight, as it were. It was going to be odd if the frustrated romance I'd dreamed up for Bianca's benefit was going to be true. I thought all this while I waited for the fatal words—"What's the game? Who are you? That's not Julie Taylor." Even more frightful than the effect on my own career (if you could call it that) was the realization that this would put the final touch to Bianca's disillusion. "You're the one person I can trust," she used to say. For a moment I had a wild notion of somehow conveying the situation to this stranger, compelling him to play along with my story. I turned sharply as Charles Hunter took two swift steps forward and caught me by the arms.

"Julie!" he cried. "Where on earth have you been hiding all these weeks? Why did you vanish in that mysterious way? I've had the devil's own job tracking you down." For an astounded moment I wondered if he really knew I wasn't Julie, if he was a phony too; then he went on, "There was no need to cut and run like that just because of a legacy. There's always trouble over other people's money, and you had as much right to it as anyone."

I felt myself floating out to sea. From everything Julie had said, I had assumed there was no one left in Australia likely to ask questions. His hands tightened their grip; now they conveyed warning. Play up, play up and play the game, I thought idiotically. Some of my feeling must have showed in my face, because Bianca said, "You've given her a shock, Mr. Hunter, turning up like this out of the blue. All the same, Julie, you're a silly girl to keep his existence so dark. This isn't *Cranford.*"

I didn't get the allusion. I knew, of course, that *Cranford* was an English classic, but I had never read the book.

"No followers," amplified Bianca. "I've always wished you had a friend or two your own age, to supplement your mysterious Miss Holloway. Put it down to self-interest, if you like. You'd be more likely to stay with me if you had a little local romance. Well, you two must have a lot to say to each other. I'm going to my room. I'll take up my own picture, I think I'm strong enough for that."

Mr. Hunter closed the door behind her, and we waited a moment till the sound of her feet on the stairs had died away. Then I turned on him urgently.

"What's the big idea?" I said. "Letting her believe I really am Julie Taylor?"

His brows lifted. "Isn't that what you wanted? It's what you seem to have persuaded her to believe."

"You didn't have to go along with it, though. Why did you? I mean, what's in it for you?"

"What a commercial mind you have. Why did you do it? And what's your name really?"

"I'm Julie Taylor," I said in a stubborn voice. The odd thing was that now I felt like Julie Taylor, I could have described Aunt Marty and the house where they'd lived; it was Solange Peters who had become the stranger. They are all gone into the land of light—though how much light Solange merited I didn't care to speculate. "If you don't believe that, try and prove the contrary."

He rubbed his chin. "I might at that. In fact, I might even make a guess at your real identity."

"How did you find me at all?" I wanted to know.

"It seemed so odd you shouldn't write. Of course, the news of the plane crash reached us and it seemed probable you were one of the casualties. Only we had no notification, your name didn't appear in any list. Then I had this chance to come over, so I decided to make my inquiries in person. I saw the airline authorities, and they told me you'd taken quite a toss and had been in hospital, so gradually I traced you back to your hostel and they gave me your address here. I also saw a list of the passengers. There was a girl called Solange Peters, she was killed. You were identified, I heard, by a bracelet you were wearing."

"Julie gave it to me," I said quickly, as though he might suspect me of robbing a dead body. "She said it would bring me luck."

"It seems to have done so, doesn't it? You've quite fallen on your feet here. What was wrong with Solange Peters?"

"I didn't say . . ."

"My dear girl, you don't throw away your own name like last night's paper without some good reason. Coming from Rome, I heard."

"To make a fresh start. You must have ears like a bat's that can catch reverberations inaudible to the human race. Well, what do you do now? Tell Mrs. Duncan? Isn't that going to be a bit awkward when you've already greeted me as Julie?"

"Oh, I should explain that I wanted to hear your story before I lifted my executioner's ax. Of course, she'd throw you out at once, and without references—still, there's the legacy, isn't there? You can't have run through all that yet."

"I don't know about the legacy," I said painfully.

"Oh come, there are limits even to my credulity."

"When I said I didn't know anything about it, I meant I hadn't touched it. It's in the bank, or wherever it was lodged. All I had of Julie's was some Australian currency, and her insurance. I had to use that because I couldn't claim my own money."

"Travelers checks?" he murmured, and I told him, "Oh, I destroyed those."

"You did what?"

"I destroyed them. I couldn't have used them, and they were no use to her."

"Have you any notion what they were worth?"

"No," I said. "I didn't count them. Anyway, they were no good to me. I couldn't use them, it would have been forgery . . ."

"Every time you sign her name you commit forgery," he pointed out.

"But not for gain. And if the estate claims the money back, if this story becomes public property, I mean, then it can all be repaid out of Solange Peters' account."

"And how much is in that?"

"I don't know. Solange is dead, so there was no one to inquire."

"You really are the most extraordinary girl," he said. "I feel as though I'd stepped into a nest of snakes. You must know how much you possess."

"I was told to call at the bank and prove my identity and I'd be provided with a certain sum of money; the amount wasn't mentioned, or if it was, it didn't register."

Mr. Hunter pulled a packet of cigarettes out of his pocket and lighted one. He didn't offer me one. "Where did it come from, this anonymous sum of money?"

It didn't occur to me not to tell him. I felt he had all the aces in the pack, and if I refused, he could get everything he wanted to know from Rome. He didn't look the sort of person who'd give up easily.

"I see," he said after a minute. "A sort of bonus, because your patient died."

"After my patient died. It's not unusual to give a nurse a present."

"Coupled with the proviso that it shall be paid in another country. Perhaps you knew too much."

"I didn't know anything," I cried.

"And if the money's lodged in a bank and you've got to establish identity, it's more than a ten-pound note, isn't it? Why were you coming back to England? You told me a minute ago you'd lived in Rome most of your life."

"Perhaps I thought I'd like to see my father's country."

"And have a grand reunion with all your relatives?"

"So far as I know, I have none."

"Curiouser and curiouser. But perhaps there was a romantic reason?"

I didn't answer that.

He put another question. "How did your patient die?"

"She had a fall."

"While the nurse was off duty?"

"Yes."

"So you weren't responsible?"

"No, I wasn't responsible."

"And yet you left the country."

"If you think anyone accused me," I said, "you can make a few more of your searching inquiries. You'll find no one made an official charge, not even one of carelessness. Well, how could they, I wasn't even in the house."

"Which brings us back to romance. Did someone offer you a sizable sum to clear out? Was it perhaps because you suppressed a bit of evidence that could have involved someone else?"

"I tell you, I wasn't even in the house."

"But you wouldn't need to be," he pointed out gently. "It must be quite valuable evidence to merit an airfare and a lump sum. Perhaps there were documents you'd inconveniently come across and it was suggested you might, more conveniently, forget about them?"

"Must you be so crude?" I burst out.

"Anything to do with money is supposed to be crude, I never know why. Is that how it was?"

"No," I told him bluntly. "I wasn't exacting blackmail from anyone."

"All the same, it was worth somebody's while to pay you something, perhaps something handsome, to leave the country. Or perhaps you had something for sale or exchange, letters? No, I forgot, you have nothing to do with blackmail. Oh, Julie"—his voice changed, became impatient and human—"stop playing a tragic part. You had some very good reason for not minding saying good-bye to Solange Peters."

"Who on earth is Solange Peters?" Unheard by either of us Bianca had suddenly come into the room. She threw inquisitorial glances from one to the other.

"The girl who shared Julie's seat in the doomed plane," said Charles smoothly. "They had quite a lot in common, were much of an age and—didn't you tell me it was her first visit to England in years?"

"That's what she said."

"It was a frightful thing," said Bianca briskly, "but I'm sure if there was anything Julie could have done, she'd have done it. And—you're much too young to brood on the past."

"You talk as if you could wrap the past up in a paper bag and throw it out with the scraps," I protested. "It's not as simple as that."

"It can't do you any good to brood over her, and it certainly can't help her. You must learn to grow a shell, Julie, somewhere where you can retreat when you're angry or hurt. What was there so special about this Solange girl?"

"There was nothing special about her," I said. To my horror I found the tears were pouring down my cheeks. "She was just a girl, my age, who wanted to be allowed to run free."

"And someone wanted to shut her up?" Bianca looked puzzled.

"She'd had a bad break, it wasn't her fault; it's like the rain that falls on the just and the unjust."

"She seems to have made a great impression on you. I suppose it's the contrast, you safe and, I hope, with happiness just round the corner—but you know, Julie, she's safe, too, in a different way."

"Quite a different way," I agreed. I made a great effort, became calmer. "I'm sorry to make a scene. It was Charles, he brought it all back."

"I'm going to send him away now," said Bianca lightly. "There are some things we must get done. Come to dinner tonight," she added to Mr. Hunter. "You can meet Oliver and be reassured that we aren't slave-driving Julie. Where are you staying?" she added.

"I've got a room at The Fishermen's Arms, just for two or three days. I shall have to go up to London. I came over in connection with a job."

"What job?" asked Bianca.

"Well, as Julie could tell you, I'm an actor. No, don't look pained, there's no earthly reason why you should ever have heard of me—yet. I've been in a television series in Australia, and there seemed some chance of an English version. It was suggested that it might be worth my while to come over and see a man who's shown interest . . ."

"And take Julie in your stride?" Bianca was openly laughing.

"Julie will understand," he said. "Did you really mean it about coming to dinner? I should absolutely love it. The Fishermen's Arms has grand views, but you can't eat a view."

"Well, I simply don't understand the modern girl," Bianca said to me after Charles had gone. "Keeping so quiet. Still, you must feel complimented by a man crossing the world to find you."

"I'm the Also Ran," I reminded her. "And if you're staying up to dinner you really should rest now."

Dinner was an unqualified success. Oliver took to Charles Hunter at once, after Charles had told him he'd backed the winner in the Barleycorn Handicap.

"Moby Dick?" exclaimed Oliver. "Did you have a tip?"

Charles grinned. "Who hadn't? No, he was a gray horse, and I remembered something the Aga Khan is supposed to have said—always back a gray horse."

"He certainly ran some very successful ones himself," Oliver acknowledged.

"It was a pretty exciting race," Charles told us. "His jockey held him back almost to the end. Mind you, I'd been warned that's one of Harness' tricks, but this time I thought he was overdoing it. I didn't think Moby Dick could make it. And nor did the favorite. Dick Leslie was riding as gaily as if he were at a point-to-point. Then suddenly there was a sort of stir and Moby Dick got going. I understood for the first time what's meant by the expression went like the wind. You could almost feel the breath in your face as he flashed by. Even the bookies were grinning when they paid up. Not that that took them long. They must have netted a fortune."

He had a very lively turn of phrase, a prepossessing manner. Prejudiced against him as I was, I had to admit that. Bianca asked him about his job, and Oliver remarked that you must need a very elastic personality to be able to switch from one personality to another, overnight perhaps. To portray virtue, meanness, courage, treachery, dumbness . . .

"It's not so difficult as you suppose," returned Charles

eagerly. "Those are all qualities the average man possesses. It's like my mother and her housekeeping. She used to divide money up when my father gave it to her into a number of little bags labeled Gas, Butcher, Laundry, Wages, and so on. Then when an account was presented, all she had to do was find the appropriate bag and settle the bill."

"What happened if there was nothing in the bag?" Bianca asked.

"That was the one thing you had to avoid. Once you let one of the bags go derelict, you were sunk. And, in a sense—do I sound ridiculously picturesque?" (I thought he did but no one said anything) "—that's what we do."

"Like philosophers' theories about the world," contributed Bianca unexpectedly. "They say the energy that keeps the universe going will never be exhausted, because as one star dies another is born—or rather comes to light and begins to function."

"Or that bird," added Oliver. "The one that rises from its own ashes."

"The phoenix," I said, neatly fielding that one.

It was fantastic. Here we were, four apparently perfectly normal people with nothing but the normal cares that beset everyone, carrying on a pleasant not unintelligent conversation, the sort you might hear round a thousand dining-room tables. And no one seemed to realize that a bomb sparked at our feet and might explode at any moment. In fact, there was an instant when I might have exploded it myself. "Let's have done with this absurd play-acting," I might have cried. "This is more melodramatic than anything in Charles's TV series." And out would come the truth, bubbling and stinking like that hot mud you find in parts of New Zealand (I think), that is lethal and without pity for its victims. Of course, I said nothing. I told myself it was because Mrs. Dotrice came in at that moment to change the plates, but that wasn't why. The real reason was that my little bag marked courage was plumb empty.

"He seems very devoted," Bianca said after we'd left the men to their wine. (Charles had said, "I'd like to see the Aussie wife who'd leave her old man to get sozzled while she darned his socks in the parlor.")

"Ah, but you must remember he's an actor," I reminded her.

She sent me a shrewd, piercing glance. "That's the first heartless thing I've ever heard you say."

When the men came up, Oliver was saying that he and

Charles were going to the Dorbridge Races next week. Charles seemed like the sons of Belial flown with insolence and wine. He made airy references to "some pretty fine days we used to have on the race tracks, didn't we, Julie?" I really did think he had had rather too much to drink. Oliver was no fool, if he challenged Charles to name a winner, the odds are he would be completely taken off balance. As soon as I could I urged Bianca bedward.

"If you mean to go out again tomorrow," I suggested, and she said certainly she did, and she turned to Charles with a laugh and said, "You'd think she was a real nurse, wouldn't you? Any minute now I shall open my eyes and find her beside my bed wearing a starched uniform and flat shoes."

"I don't think you need be afraid of that," I said, coaxing her toward the door.

"Let Julie see him out," murmured Oliver benevolently, and we went into the hall.

"Don't push your luck," I warned Charles fiercely. "Oliver Duncan's no fool, and we're neither of us batting on a very reliable wicket."

"How quickly you've picked up the expressions," Charles teased me. "What do you know about wickets? Surely they don't play cricket in Rome?"

"It's like the nursery rhyme. If the baby comes down, the cradle comes down, too. You're playing with fire, you want to be careful."

"Hark who's talking," said Charles. "If anyone needs a good lawyer it's you, and it wouldn't do you any harm to look around and find one."

I said I'd certainly think about it. It was the only helpful thing I'd heard him say since his arrival.

"Take care of yourself," Charles said, grinning. "If there's anything I can do . . ."

Lying sleepless that night it occurred to me that the only useful thing he could do would be to crash his hired car into a tree on the way home or run off the road into the river. I realized with a shock that I really meant this, and was horrified to see how far I'd drifted. Six months ago such a thought would never have occurred to me.

6

NEXT MORNING I took Crook's letter out of my bag and read it again. A cloud no bigger than a baby's fist, he had said; this one threatened to turn into an atomic mushroom. Two days later was my free afternoon. Lately Oliver had insisted that I should have this and stick to it, unless Bianca was really seriously ill. "We don't want the neighborhood to think we're in slave trade," he'd said. Nurse Adams, of course, had insisted on her regular off-duty periods, but I wasn't on quite the same footing. Anyway, I didn't really know anyone thereabouts, and going to the cinema alone soon palls. When I told Bianca I'd be going to London but wouldn't be back late, she said, "Has Charles departed already?" and I said I wasn't going to see Charles, but he'd made me think about the future, and I was going to visit my lawyer.

"I suppose you're worried about your legacy," Bianca said. "Is that Charles's idea, too?"

"Well, in a way," I admitted.

She frowned. "I hope you're not making a mistake. Is it a large legacy?"

I said, evasively, it was all a matter of degree, so Bianca said, "He doesn't look like a fortune-hunter, though I suppose you never can tell."

"He won't get very rich on anything I can give him," I assured her.

"And I suppose you're going to see your funny friend," she went on. "I wish I could feel happy about her. You haven't known her long, have you? Yet she seems such an old friend—I mean, she is old enough to be your mother."

"Shall we say my maiden aunt?" I suggested. The very

thought of seeing these two champions gave me fresh heart. I had rung Ada from the callbox, not mentioning Mr. Crook, however. I didn't ring him; I didn't want him calling me back.

Bianca was suffering the inevitable reaction after her day of excitement. "Don't be persuaded to lend her money," she said.

"The boot would be far more likely to be on the other foot," I told her.

"I thought you said she worked in a shop."

"She's buyer for a multiple draper. I believe the shares stand very high."

"And she thinks it would be a good idea if you invested a bit in them."

"She's never mentioned money. I must go now," I added desperately, "or I shall miss my train."

"You've oceans of time," Bianca snapped. "Julie, if you should be near a grocer I wish you'd try and get some of those petit-fours—the shop in the village never has any choice."

"I'm not going shopping," I said.

"You're very disobliging all of a sudden. You're going to London, aren't you?" Even when I was at the door she called me back. "Julie, where's that book I was reading?"

"I think you left it in your room." She never stayed in bed when I went out. She said she felt so helpless without clothes.

"Just get it for me before you go."

I looked despairingly at my watch, and at that moment Mrs. Dotrice came in. "I'll get Madam's book," she said. "You'll miss your train, Miss Taylor, if you don't hurry."

The station was half a mile away, practically all uphill, and though I ran I knew I wouldn't catch the train. I was still two hundred yards away when it sailed into the station, and I was just in time to see the last carriage disappearing around the curve.

"Time and trains wait for no man," said the ticket collector pertly. He was a new man, young, with a pop non-haircut. "There'll be another at four," he added with a grin.

I turned and walked away, straight into Dr. Gregg's arms. "Hullo, Julie," he said, "you look like someone who's lost a rich patient and not been remembered in the will."

"Not a patient," I said politely. "Just the London train. I shall have to telephone . . ."

"Save your bawbees," said the doctor. "You're in luck.

I'm going up to London myself this afternoon, I'll give you a lift."

His manner didn't differ much from what it was in a sickroom, but there was something about him that proclaimed he was off duty. He looked as pleased as someone who's just won a Premium Bond prize, and no wonder, I thought, not having to listen to a trial of miseries, real or imagined, for the next few hours.

"Your patient's coming on," he said confidently as we streamed away under the eye of the ticket collector. "A month ago, even less, you wouldn't have suggested leaving her long enough to make a trip to town."

"Not my patient," I pointed out. "My employer. I'm not a nurse. And the housekeeper's there."

"I suppose you could say for this afternoon I'm not a doctor, but you can't shed your profession like that, any more than a parson can turn himself into a bookie by reversing his collar. I once had a disfranchised monk, he'd been dismissed from his order for misbehavior—but he told me he'd be a monk in his own heart till the end of time. The same with us."

"With you," I corrected him. "As a matter of fact, I may not be here much longer."

"Is that why you're going up to London—to see about another job? Not that I blame you, you know what I feel about your wasting yourself on the desert air."

"It's a private matter," I said briefly. A big furniture van came lumbering out of a side road and nearly ran us down. I thought the doctor would stamp on the brake, but he didn't. Instead, with remarkable coolness, he outpaced the van that missed us by a matter of inches. The driver yelled something incomprehensible and the doctor yelled back. Then he went on, "Who's kidding who? Do you suppose a doctor doesn't know the difference between a trained nurse and an amateur? It's a wonder to me that Mrs. Duncan hasn't rumbled you too. Or perhaps she has. She was a nurse herself before marriage, you know."

"She wouldn't think of such a thing," I said. "She wouldn't have a professional nurse in the house."

"She's got one just the same," the doctor said, taking a tricky corner on what appeared to be two wheels. "Mind you, it's smart business on her part. I bet she had to pay Adams twice what you're getting. What's behind it? Difference of opinion with the powers that be? Or a case of history repeating itself?"

"I don't know what you mean by that."

"Isn't your patient's neurotic condition due to the fact that one of her charges died on her? Is this your way of doing penance for a similar mishap? I must say, women are the most self-centered creatures in a self-centered universe. You've been hurt, and it isn't fair, so you're not going to play any more. Good God, girl, whoever gave you the impression that life was fair? Intolerable, indefensible things happen to the innocent every day of the week, and they can't all opt out. So instead of sulking in a corner at the mercy of a hypochondriac . . . get back, you fool." This was to a driver who was trying to overtake. "I've got some good news for your hypochondriac," he went on. "Dr. Mitchison really has uprooted himself and will be back on duty next week at latest. I didn't send for him, mark you, but there's nothing like trying to relieve your partner's mind to bring him flying home and rarin' to go. Anyway, it's rained most of the time."

"What made you become a doctor?" I asked. It's not the sort of question a nurse usually puts, not on our slight acquaintance, but we were both out of uniform this afternoon.

"I'll tell you," said Dr. Gregg promptly. "My father was a parson, all Christian love and no filthy lucre. He used to visit at the local hospital, and one day I had to stand in for him, take something he'd promised to an old woman who was dying by inches of an unmentionable disease. I didn't want to go, I didn't want to see her suffering, and I said as much. 'It'll give her pleasure,' my father said. 'It won't give me any pleasure,' I told him. And he stared. 'What's that got to do with it?' he said. She was a nice old girl and I suppose I wasn't very good at hiding my feelings—I was about sixteen at the time—for suddenly she caught my arm and said, 'Don't worry about me, I can stand the pain, because God sends it and He's my friend.' I stood up and told her, 'Well, you've just procured Him a lifelong enemy; because if he can visit this misery on you, then I'll spend the rest of my days finding ways to thwart Him.' I didn't believe then there was any such thing as an unanswerable problem. I got that from my father. When his parishioners asked him how God could allow this or that, he'd say, 'I don't know the answer, I only know there must be one, and one day we'll be clever enough or humble enough to know what it is.' Anyway, you'd sooner die in a ditch than ask advice. And don't tell me you don't need it, because I shan't believe it."

He had carried me away from the shores of discretion by his vigorous words, otherwise I wouldn't have made the answer I did.

"Of course I need it," I said. "I'm going to London to get it."

"Why didn't you say so right off instead of letting me shoot my mouth off?" But he didn't sound annoyed, though he changed the subject instantly. One thing, you couldn't be bored in his company, we were in London before I realized it.

"Do you want to be dropped in any special place?" he asked. "Do you know your way round the city?"

"I'll find it," I said. "It's somewhere near Bloomsbury."

He dropped me at Bloomsbury Square. "You'll have to make your own way home," he remarked lightly. "Well, good hunting."

He shot away, just dodging a red light, and I looked about me. "I feel as strange as if I were in a desert," I told myself. Whenever I thought of a city, Rome sprang to my mind. It occurred to me suddenly I'd thought of Rome less lately, and of Florian hardly at all. But if I had to revert to being Solange Peters, I'd be back where I started. I'd no doubt about that.

I walked round the square, looking at the big tranquil Victorian houses, with their gables and pillared doorways and cheerful cream-stucco trim. I felt I would hardly be surprised to see horse carriages drawing up and women in long skirts and big feathered hats alighting. All my ideas of Edwardian England had come from pictures in books and occasional Christmas cards the Marchesa had received from English acquaintances, showing women carrying muffs and leading little pug-dogs on strings. A clock striking nearby reminded me of the passage of time. I saw a taxi stop and put down a passenger, and I crossed and asked him the way to Bloomsbury Street.

"Which end?" he said. "It's a long street."

"Number 123."

I saw his face change. "Blimey, another for Mr. Crook," he said. "They come all shapes and sizes. Hop in and I'll drop you. Oh, come on, I owe Mr. Crook more than a free fare."

There was nothing particularly dignified or comfortable about Number 123. It was a tall house whose bricks were darkened with age and soot. I pushed open the door and went into a dark hall and up even darker stairs. There was no lift. Mr. Crook's office was at the very top of the building; the last flight of stairs wasn't even carpeted. I thought perhaps he wasn't so successful as I'd supposed, then I remembered Julie's instant confidence in him, the change in Ada's face, the respect, no other word for it, of the taxi driver. A tall thin man, the antithesis of Mr. Crook, let me in.

"Come in," he said. "Crook won't be long."

"I haven't an appointment," I stammered.

It didn't seem to bother him at all. "Crook doesn't go much for appointments," he said. "He's probably expecting you."

"But he can't know . . ."

"He expects everyone. Wait in here."

He opened an inner door, and I went into a big shabby room containing the sort of furniture you generally have to pay men to cart away. There were files and papers strewn everywhere. He didn't offer me a chair, let alone a newspaper, just shut the door and went back to whatever he'd been doing. I crossed to the window and looked out There was a wonderful vista of London. I could see the grotesque new post office building and miniature skyscrapers rising untidily in every direction.

"Nice, ain't it?" suggested a cheerful voice behind me, and I swung around to find Mr. Crook beaming on the threshold like some great furry bear. "You can't beat that view wherever you go," he continued, pulling off an appalling reddish-brown hat called a bowler. "Client of mine just back from Sicily. 'The views, Mr. Crook, you can't imagine. We could see Etna from our window all crowned with snow, and not a soul in sight.' If that's your fancy, I told her, why didn't you get yourself born a perishing seagull. Sit down, sugar. I was wondering how soon you'd turn up."

It occurred to me that neither man had asked my name. "Why should you think I'd come at all?" I countered, sitting in what must have been one of the most uncomfortable chairs in town.

"There's an old saying that you can fool all the people some of the time and some of the people all the time, but you can't fool all the people all the time, not even George Washington could have done that. What gives, sugar?"

"I'm in a fix," I said awkwardly, wondering how I was going to start explanations all over again. I should have had a record made on tape . . .

"That's nothing new," said Crook calmly. "You were in a fix the day I met you in a railway train. You knew it and so did I. Take your time, sugar, and just fill me in with what's happened in between."

So I told him about Bianca and the job. "And she's rumbled you? It was bound to happen sooner or later."

I repeated "Rumbled?" in a dazed sort of way, and Crook said kindly, "No-spika-da-English? I mean, she knows you ain't Julie Taylor. It wouldn't surprise me if dear Oliver knew it, too. Then there's the doctor—I don't suppose you had him fooled any longer than you had me."

"So you did know that day on the train?"

He looked incredulous. "Sugar, I'd met the lady."

"Still, there'd been the accident and the surgery, it could have made a difference."

"You can dye your hair and have your face lifted and change the shape of your nose, but you can't change yourself. I didn't notice specially what she looked like, but if I'd been blindfolded that day in the train I'd have known you wasn't her."

"And that's why you left the card where I was bound to pick it up? I did wonder, only you never said."

"I told you silence was golden and gold's the best there is and the best is good enough for me. What more do you want? And I couldn't exactly hand you the card, not without you asked. I ain't allowed to tout for clients"—he didn't say it in so many words but his whole manner proclaimed he didn't need to—"but it did go through my mind that one of these days you might be needing a legal beagle and I might suit your book better than some who put their immortal soul—professional reputation to you—above their clients' interest. Now stop looking shocked, sugar. If anyone should be shocked about this it should be me, and any man who's capable of being shocked after the age of forty should be on a psychiatrist's couch. I didn't ask you why you'd switched monikers with the real Julie, because it was no business of mine, only I was pretty sure it wouldn't work out, not for long. You must be brighter than most to keep it up the time you have. And when the day of doom dawned, that's when you'd need allies, and so far as I could see, you didn't have any."

"And yet you were the one to identify me," I protested.

"I identified a bracelet I'd seen on the wrist of a girl called Julie Taylor; and that's all I told them. Not my fault if they jump to conclusions, and I didn't notice you putting 'em right when you had the chance."

"I did try," I protested weakly.

"Only not very hard. A girl like you could find some way of persuading them, if your mind was on it, only it wasn't. So why? And remember," he added quickly, "I charge by the hour, so keep it as short as you can. Julie gave you the bracelet—that about the size of it?"

"She said it would bring me luck."

"It seems to have done that."

"I wouldn't be too sure," I murmured.

"Well, I would. Take the word of the man who knows, sugar, being alive is the luckiest thing that ever happened to any of us. Now, start at the beginning."

So I told him about Solange Peters and the debacle in Rome. I repeated that I had tried to persuade the authorities I wasn't Julie Taylor.

"More to the point," remarked Crook shrewdly, "did you ever try and tell 'em you were Solange Peters? Think before you answer. Did you ever mention her name?"

"I don't remember very well, everything was so confused," I pleaded.

"You'd remember that."

"All right," I said. "I don't think I did. And by the time I was more normal, everyone was accepting me as Julie Taylor—Solange Peters had been buried, I daresay the people in Rome had been informed, I don't know about that—and it seemed a wonderful opportunity to make a fresh start. Julie had told me there was no one who'd be inquiring for her, so what harm could I do?"

"I wish I had a sovereign for every time I've heard that one about shedding your past," said Crook. "Don't you realize you're attempting the impossible? At best, you're only putting it into hiding, and there's always the chance someone's going to surprise your little secret. Anyway, it's part of the human story, you can't blot it out and pretend it never happened. Because life doesn't just happen to an individual, it's like a stone, all the ripples fan out—listen to Arthur Crook, the philosopher. I shall have to have that put on my cards. Philosopher and Metaphysician."

"It sounds good," I congratulated him drily.

"Trouble is it 'ud scare off ninety percent of my clients, who ain't specially interested in the good. Now listen, sugar, an ostrich is a valuable bird to trappers, or used to be when ladies decked themselves in ostrich plumes to visit the palace and give a free show to all the down-and-outs on the embankment, but if it had had a bit more sense it might have kept some of those plumes for itself against the cold weather. You've had your head in the sand long enough, it's time you pulled it out and had a good look round. Tell me some more about Lady Clara. What's she threatening to do? Go to the police?"

"I don't think she knows," I explained. "Not unless Charles has told her."

"You keep pulling rabbits out of hats," Crook complained. "His name was Oliver just now."

"Didn't I explain about Charles?" I told him. "I don't see why he should tell Bianca," I went on. "She's virtually a stranger, and . . ."

"Why indeed?" agreed Crook cordially. "Seeing, as I've just said, silence is golden."

"But that would be blackmail," I cried, shocked.

"Any reason to suppose he wouldn't stoop to blackmail? You haven't known him long, have you?"

"And anyway, I'd be a pretty poor prospect. I spent Julie's Australian pounds—there was the insurance, of course—"

"Hey, you never told me about the insurance. Tell me now."

So I did and he pulled his long chin. "You don't believe in doing things by halves, do you, sugar? Still, that's the way I like my clients to be. Whatsoever ye do, do it with all thy might. All the same, they could get you for fraud, you know. I mean, you ain't going to get them to believe you didn't know who you really were."

"But the insurance had been paid for," I argued. "Someone had a right to it."

"But not a young woman called Solange Peters. And I daresay dear Charles recognizes that, too. I mean, if he comes looking for a girl for whom he had a yearn and finds another girl he never saw before, wouldn't you expect him to blow up on the spot?"

"He said he was naturally curious."

"I daresay that's as good an answer as any."

"And he hasn't made any demands."

"Give him time. It's not a week since you met. He knows about Solange?"

"Yes. He'd made inquiries and he put two and two together."

"A mathematician," said Crook respectfully. "Don't look

so surprised, sugar, they're rarer than you suppose. Plenty of chaps can add two and two and make them twenty-four or eighty-four or a hundred-and-four, but just plain four is too simple for most. This chap needs watching. Unless there's something else you haven't mentioned. I mean—no question of love at first sight, anything like that?"

"Of course not."

"Take a deep breath, sugar, and tell me all you know about him."

"It isn't much. He came over on the Hillbilly Jet, that's supposed to be the most modern plane in existence. There was a famous film actress on board, he said a lot of the passengers thought she was Princess Margaret."

"I read that in the press," agreed Crook. "Not that I believe everything I read."

"He's an actor . . ."

"Aren't we all?"

"He's trying to fix up a television show over here. That's really why he came."

"Not to track you down?"

"Well, I suppose it was a case of killing two birds with one stone."

"I'm no sportsman, but it always surprised me that the sporting English should think that a matter for congratulation. Anything else? Hasn't mentioned a wife or anything?"

"I get the impression he was in love with Julie, and there was a row about money."

"Most rows are about money. Must be a singe-minded chap if he came half across the world to claim his share. Can't have been much in her confidence, though, or he'd have known it wasn't really worth dividing."

"How do you know that?" I asked, startled.

"Little lady told me. She was going to stretch it as far as she could, see as much of the world as possible and then go home. His half wouldn't pay his return fare. I don't think your Charles is as clever as I supposed, unless he's got another ace up his sleeve. Now, tell me something more. When Mrs. D. had left you together, who spoke first? Take your time, we've got all day."

I counted up to fifty. Then I said, "I did. I asked him what his game was, letting Bianca go on believing I was Julie Taylor."

"You're sure about that?" said Crook.

"Of course I'm sure. I asked him why he hadn't given me away."

"And he said because he was curious. Doesn't occur to you there could have been another reason—that he accepted you as Julie Taylor, because he thought you were Julie Taylor?"

"But he must have known I wasn't. If they knew each other in Australia."

"Who says?"

"He did, of course." I was all at sea now.

"What the soldier said ain't evidence. You've been telling people for months you're Julie Taylor, but that don't alter facts. It wouldn't surprise me to know he really did think you were her, and then you rush in where any self-respectin' angel would fear to tread and make him a present of the situation on a plate."

This solution nearly took my breath away. "But if he hadn't known Julie Taylor, how did he even know she'd existed?"

"That's a point. You see, if he didn't know, someone must have told him."

"But no one knew."

"What you mean is that so far as you know no one knew. But we don't know a lot ourselves yet, do we? What else did he say on his own account? Mention any special part he'd ever played? Talk about Stratford-on-Avon? They always do. Call everybody darling? No?"

"He's great on horse-racing," I said. "He's one of the few people who backed Moby Dick for the Barleycorn Handicap. Oliver was quite envious. He said he'd dropped quite a packet."

"So he backed Moby Dick, did he? Who put him on to that?"

"I don't know, but it must be true. He couldn't have described the race as he did if he hadn't been there. And he said the bookie actually grinned when he handed him his winnings."

"Could afford to, I daresay," agreed Crook. He lifted up his voice and shouted, "Bill!" The door opened and the man I'd seen before came in.

"What was the day the Hillbilly Jet made her maiden flight?" Crook asked him.

Bill supplied a date without an instant's hesitation.

"And what was the date of the Barleycorn Handicap?"

"Same day," said Bill. "Flight was delayed twenty-four hours, if you remember, because of some fault in the engine. They couldn't risk an unholy crash when they were trying to sell the line to the world."

"Thanks a million," said Crook, and Bill slouched out again.

"Bill Parsons," Crook explained. "My right hand, the human encyclopedia. And if the Lord God had someone like that on His right hand he wouldn't need any Recording Angel, Bill would have it all pat. Well, you see what that adds up to, sugar?"

"That he couldn't have been in two places at the same time. But he did see that race, Mr. Crook, I swear."

"I believe you," said Crook heartily. "What I don't believe is that he ever came over on the Hillbilly Jet. He could get all that stuff about the actress and Princess Margaret out of the papers, and they've advertised the line so much I could shut my eyes and believe I'd traveled on it. Well, there's the clue I was looking for. I will give you the end of a golden string and wind it into a ball; it will lead you straight into heaven's gate, set in Jerusalem's wall. That's something I learned in Sunday school when I was a boy. Only heaven's gate ain't precisely Charles's destination. Know what brings down eighty percent of these con men? Eighty? Ninety 'ud be nearer the mark. Just old human vanity, they can't leave well alone, like those dames that keep adding a flower here and a furbelow there till they look like something out of a market garden. If he'd kept his big mouth shut about the Hillbilly—safer to stick to racing if you can't have both—he'd be riding pretty. As it is, he opens his big mouth and puts his foot right in. Lucky for him, I daresay, he ain't a centipede. Point is, what's his game?"

"The money?" I hesitated.

"If he never knew Julie Taylor and you ain't opened your trap outside the house, how come he knows there ever was any money? Don't tell me because he knew Aunt Marty, because my guess is he was never much nearer Australia than Brighton Pier. Any chance of getting a peep at his passport?"

"I shouldn't think so. He isn't staying in the house."

"Ninety to one it's British, the blue-coated variety. Well, then, someone told him. To whose interest is it that he should be in the house at all? I mean, who's going to need an alibi when the balloon goes up?"

It never seemed to occur to him that it wasn't going up. I hadn't many doubts either. I'd read enough to know that when you commit a crime it's always as well to have someone to confirm your story. And I'd thought all along it was queer the way Oliver had taken to him from that first night. Already they'd gone racing together and they were planning another excursion. And rather more than excursions, I thought. And I'd left Bianca at their mercy. I half rose, then I remembered this was one of the days they were going racing and Mrs. Dotrice would be there to take care of Bianca. All the same, I decided the sooner I got back the better.

"Sit down, sugar," said Crook, as I came to my feet. "I know what's in your mind, but nothing's likely to happen while you're away from the house."

"You mean, I'm to be involved?"

"Why do you think you're bein' allowed to sit so pretty? Christian charity? They wouldn't know how to spell the word. Anyway, you're the one I'm acting for, you're the one I'm concerned with. And I don't think they'd play their trump card—Charles, that is—if they weren't getting ready for the Grand Slam. Got any chums anywhere, sugar? Come on now, you've been here several months . . ."

"Only Ada Holloway," I told him. "I don't quite see how she can help."

"Tell me about her. What age?"

"Oh—around fifty."

"My favorite age for a dame—no offense meant, sugar, but they don't get their sense much younger, and sense is what I'm lookin' for now. A sensitive plant?"

"She'd tell you she can't afford to be sensitive in a job like hers. She's a buyer for a multiple draper."

"She'd need all her wits in a job like that. No point taking a load of bust bodices and then finding the hooks and eyes have got fastened on the wrong way round. That happened once in a case I was interested in, and believe it or not we only escaped a murder charge by a thread. She sounds just my cup of tea."

"A dose of arsenic might be more apposite." I didn't know I was going to say the words until they came out. They didn't surprise Mr. Crook nearly so much as they surprised me.

"There's times when a dose of arsenic is the most handy thing on earth," he said serenely. "Know my favorite character, sugar? Queen Boadicea. Now there was a dame knew her own mind, which was to save her kingdom. So what did she do? Tied scythes to the wheels of her chariots and rode in among the foe. No love your enemies about her, and that's the way I like 'em."

I was finding it difficult to follow his darts of fancy; it was like trying to track the movements of a dragonfly in brilliant sunlight, which is as tricky as anything I know. Its very radiance and swiftness blind the eye.

"I don't see what Ada can do," I said. "And I think I should go back. Bianca and Charles—oh, there's no one I can really trust, no one who'd be likely to believe my version, even if I could tell."

"Which at the moment you wouldn't want to do," capped Crook. "When you're as far in Dutch as you are, sugar, silence isn't just golden, it's pure diamond-studded uranium. We've got to establish our facts."

"They are established," I told him desperately. I could see it all so clearly now. The only bit about Charles's story I could still believe was that he was an actor—look at the way he'd walked into the house and into Bianca's confidence. Whoever disbelieved his story about coming over from Australia, Bianca took it all for gospel. And every move she made increased her danger. Because who was going to suspect Charles, the casual visitor, who'd used me—me—as a means of entrance into the house? Oh, it had all been very cleverly fixed. I saw why Oliver had been so anxious for me to stay on, going out of his way to ease things for me, being so sympathetic and congratulatory.

"Must be fun being a dame," said Crook unemotionally, breaking in on my thoughts. "No proof, no heed of road signs: Go Slow—Major Road Ahead—no nothing, just one wild leap and there you are. And what have you got to support your version? No, don't tell me. Feminine Intuition. What you don't seem to understand is you're like St. Paul, in jeopardy every hour. This Ada Holloway may be Boadicea up to date, but she's a long way off. No one else?"

"No one else ever comes to the house except the doctor."

"What's he like?"

"The real one has been away, we've been having the partner, a much younger man Bianca has taken a dislike to. Dr. Mitchison's no good, he's soft as a pillow."

"Don't decry pillows," said Crook. "They serve their purpose. How about the locum? No signs of little Dan Cupid in that direction, I take it?"

I laughed. I couldn't help it.

"The strong silent type. Well, you can say as much of a tombstone."

"Anyway, he's already suspicious," I blurted out. "He thinks I'm a trained nurse, I don't know why."

"Probably because you told him."

"I never said a word."

"He's a doctor, that 'ud be enough. Well, we're back with Ada Holloway. You might as well let me have her address. I know these old girls, if they're put to it they can move swifter than light. Not hampered by any silly ideas about fair play or the old school tie, either. Anyone in the household ever seen her?"

"Bianca did say I could ask her down, but she never came. I don't think she takes her seriously, she's always making jokes about her name."

"It's her error. I don't like the situation, sugar. You might have been tailored for the job. Young girl, just over from the other side of the world, no connections, no private means—no references?" I shook my head. "It didn't seem to you odd they took you without?"

"I think Oliver was so anxious to get anyone Bianca took to, and she was so relieved not to have a trained nurse . . ."

"It's all about as lucid as a ball of wool after a kitten's been at it, isn't it?" suggested Crook amiably. "Well, we shall have to rely on Ada. An old maid, you said, wearing last year's titfer and shoes like canoes?"

"That's a very good description."

"It's the best disguise there is. Makes 'em more or less invisible. No cash, no influence, no connections, that's what the criminal thinks. Oh, she could be mighty useful."

"But I can't be any danger," I burst out. "I don't know anything."

"All possible witnesses are dangerous; the only safe witness is the silent witness. Now there's two ways of silencing 'em. One's blackmail and the other's the chopper."

"Blackmail?"

"Say you thought of going to the police—who's going to believe your yarn. A girl impersonating a dead woman, using her documents, *her* ready cash, havin' been pushed out of Italy under a cloud. Truth is what people can be persuaded to believe, and I daresay there are plenty who'd believe you knew more about the Marchesa's death" (he pronounced it Markeeser) "than ever you said. I don't say you wouldn't get the benefit of the doubt here, but that wouldn't do you much good on the mortuary slab. Of course, the sensible thing 'ud be to pull out . . ."

"I can't do that," I said.

"The police ought to love you, if it was a just world, risking your own life in the interests of law and order. Only we know it ain't just. Say someone suggests you're there for your own reasons, that it was you brought Charles into the picture—any proof that you didn't? See? And you didn't denounce him nor him you. Still sure you're going to stay? Could this Ada friend of yours give you a bed for the night?"

"Would you run out on a client?" I asked. "Of course I'm going back, and I'm going now."

Crook put up a huge hand and thoughtfully caressed the back of his head. "Believe it or not, sugar, I've got a scar there a veteran might envy. But then I'm used to it. I've had chaps gunning for me since 1916, that's the way to learn about self-preservation. You don't sound to me you'd got beyond Lesson One."

"I must get back," I insisted. "If anything should happen . . ."

"You get on the blower and I'll be down faster than light. And remember, you don't have to answer any questions or make any statement without your lawyer's standing by. Where to now?"

"I was going to meet Ada near Charing Cross, but I haven't the time."

"You haven't the time to give her the go-by," agreed Crook grimly. "You can't afford to shed any outside contacts. You might tell her I'm in the picture . . ."

"She knows about you," I said.

Crook beamed. "Old customer? Funny, I don't recall the name."

"She knew someone whose life you saved."

"Could be. And don't forget, sugar, history has a way of repeating itself."

"I know," I said tensely. "That's what I have in mind. Bianca takes pills, too. Just as Evelyn did."

Crook scowled. "These doctors have a lot to answer for," he said, "distributing the means of death left, right and center. You confided in the Iron Maiden, by the way?"

"About Solange Peters? No. And I'm not going to. There's no sense involving her to that extent. Besides, she may have a conscience."

" 'Tain't likely," said Crook comfortably. "I don't mean she don't have a conscience, may have a cast-iron one, for all I know, but it don't necessarily have to work along conventional lines. I had a client once, told me she didn't give a flip of the fingers for the law, what was it but a lot of rules made by men for their own convenience. One of these days, she said to me, women 'ull run the world, and then we'll see some changes. Makes my blood run cold just to think of it," he added frankly. "You can learn to dodge the way of man like the wireworm that dodged through the three-pronged fork, but God help us when we have to contend with the official devious female mind. We'll never know an instant's peace. Oh, and let her know I'm at her service as much as yours."

I was just flying out of the room when I remembered something else. "I don't know about your fee," I said. "I didn't think . . ."

"That's what I like about women, they do put first things first. I'll collect later, sugar, on the basis of work done. Well, I don't know how much of my time you're buying, do I? I ain't one of these private dicks working for forty quid a day and expenses, I'm just a man of law."

"So you are," I agreed. "That's something else I'd forgotten."

I saw a cruising taxi as I came running down the steps into the street and asked the driver to take me to The Golden Owlet, near the Charing Cross station. I was afraid he mightn't have heard of it, but he took it in his stride. I was out of the cab almost before he'd stopped, and pushed the fare into his hand. He grinned reassuringly. "No need to get cold feet," he said. "Crook's clients always win."

That man certainly got about. I found Ada sitting at a table near the door, eating an ice. "I can't stop," I told her. "I must get back immediately. I oughtn't really to have come."

"There isn't a train for twenty-five minutes," she told me briskly. "I checked. So sit down and have a cup of tea. And don't ask for coffee, because in this place they're the same thing." She caught a waitress's eye—a lot of other people were doing the same—but it was to our table that the girl came. "Tea and hot buttered scones, and we've a train to catch," she said. "Now, Julie, what's the trouble? I can't think how you suppose you can stick your head in the lion's mouth and not get it snapped off."

I gave her an expurgated version of the situation. "And of course you never did meet Charles in Australia? No, how should you? You were never there yourself."

"Why should you say that?" I asked feebly.

"Because I have been there. Never mind, don't tell me, it's your life. And if I should have to go into the witness box I could swear on oath you hadn't told me a thing. If it should come to that," she added thoughtfully, "I shall wear one of these nylon fur caps that are all the rage this year. Softening to the aging face, and Fishers do a very good line for thirty-nine-and-six. Why are you really in London this afternoon?" she went on, pouring out tea as dark as the famous little red hen. "Not that Crook man, by any chance?"

"Do you have second sight all along the line?"

"It was obvious something was in the wind when you rang up, the telephone wires shook like aspens. And I didn't know who else a lone orphan could be coming to see on business, you said. I've always wanted to meet that man . . ."

"You may have a chance sooner than you imagine," I told her, and I gave her Crook's message. I hadn't realized till I'd finished that I'd cleared a whole plate of toasted scones and there was a bit of Bath bun on my plate that I never remembered seeing in its entirety.

"I knew you had a lucky face the first time I clapped eyes on you," continued Ada buoyantly. "Lucky for me, I mean." I could see the struggle going on in her mind. She genuinely didn't want anything bad to happen to me, but on the other hand anything that gave her an excuse to meet Crook would get her vote.

I wouldn't let her come and see me off. "Stop here and have another ice," I said. "Have another pot of tea." I didn't suppose there was anyone trailing me, but I didn't altogether rule out the possibility, and accidents happen so easily.

7

IT WAS A QUICK TRAIN and there was a bus waiting at the station to meet it, the commuters' bus, it was called. The train had been pretty full, and though a good many travelers had parked their cars at the station that morning, there were still enough left to crowd the bus to standing point. Just as it started, someone jumped onto the step and pushed down to where I was sitting, swinging on a strap.

"Have a nice time in town?" he said. I nearly jumped out of my skin; it was Charles Hunter, who should have been at the race course.

"What happened to the horses?" I asked. "Did they all drop dead?"

"Racing was canceled because of the weather."

I looked out of the bus window and realized for the first time that it was drizzling.

"It was fine in London," I said.

"What's the good of being a capital city if you can't hog the best weather?"

At the first stop a woman got out and another, sitting beside me, obligingly moved so that Charles and I could sit together.

"Thought any more about what we were discussing?" Charles inquired.

"Why did you really come?" I asked in what I hoped was a casual voice. "Who tipped you off?"

For an instant he looked startled. "Did your spinster friend put that idea into your mind?"

"She knows nothing," I told him. "Nothing at all. You can leave her out of this."

"She doesn't sound precisely my cup of tea. By the way, did you see in the court column that the Marchese Polli is to wed his cousin, Perdita?"

"That was to be expected," I said. "It doesn't surprise me." What did surprise me was that my coolness wasn't assumed. At one time, to hear the name Florian would have set my heart beating like a drum, now I could say it and feel I wasn't even changing color. It occurred to me that the real Julie Taylor would never have made my mistake: she was free of trouble forever and ever. But even so I couldn't envy her. I knew Crook was right when he said it must always be better to be living than dead.

Back at the house I had a crushing sense of anticlimax. Everything looked so orderly, the picture of a happy couple waiting tea for their guests. Bianca was carefully made up and had taken a lot of trouble with her hair, Oliver looked as though he hadn't a care in the world.

"How was London?" Bianca asked.

"No rain," said Charles.

"One of these days I shall surprise you and make the trip myself," Bianca threatened. "Did you meet your friend with the funny name?" She always referred to Ada like that. "How was she?"

"Going great guns," I said, realizing as I spoke that this was an expression I had picked up from her.

"Did you go to a show? Oliver, I think sherry all round would be a delightful idea. I'm sure Charles and Julie could do with a glass. You came back early, didn't you?" Bianca went on to me.

"I said I shouldn't be late. Ada couldn't stay and have dinner, but we had tea together."

"Going to a buyers' conference, I suppose. And Oliver and Charles deprived of their racing by bad weather, and Mrs. Dotrice's daughter suddenly taken ill."

"I didn't know she had a daughter," I said.

"She lays claim to one and she should know. She said she'd had a message. This was just after you left. I suppose it was by telephone, though I didn't hear it ring."

Oliver came back, carrying an unopened bottle of sherry and four glasses. "I really must get one of these things that open a bottle by suction," he murmured. "Or change to a brand that has a simple stopper." He gave the corkscrew a deft twist and the cork came out as clean as a whistle. I watched him carefully as he poured the sherry. He handed the first glass to Bianca, but she said she only wanted half a glass and passed hers to Charles. Charles handed it on to me. I drank it without a qualm. I was quite sure that Oliver wouldn't take any chances with so many witnesses.

"We were wondering if Mrs. Dotrice really has a daughter," murmured Bianca lazily. "Personally, I think it's far more likely she has a sultry private life. I never knew anyone who gave out such an effect of smoldering. What did she tell you when you engaged her, Oliver?"

"That she was such an exceptional housekeeper she was justified in asking about fifty percent more than the normal rate, and for a further consideration would consent occasionally to stay and cook dinner for us. As we were desperate, of course she could dictate her own terms, but I agree with Bianca, there's something sinister about the woman. I feel as if she were my conscience following me wherever I go."

"Have you any reason to fear your conscience?" Bianca demanded, and he laughed and said, "Who hasn't?"

"I've got some news for you," I announced. "Dr. Mitchison's coming back next week."

"Who told you that?" Bianca wanted to know.

"I met Dr. Gregg up by the station. I think he's rather relieved, at being able to shunt some responsibility, I mean."

"That answers one thing that's puzzled me," said Charles. "Why a pushing chap like that hasn't got his sights on Harley Street, but of course if he's afraid of responsibility . . ."

"I didn't say he was afraid of it," I snapped. "It's just a question of there only being twenty-four hours in the day."

"How the profession hangs together!" teased Charles, and Bianca put in, "You're wrong about Julie, she's not a nurse; after Adams I swore I'd never have another one on the premises."

"I must say Julie's a very refreshing substitute," Oliver conceded. "I'm glad about Mitchison, though, he may be able to persuade you to follow Gregg's advice and take a holiday in the sun."

"There hasn't been much sun, according to what I hear," I said.

"Dear me, Oliver, how anxious you are to see the back of me. Still, for your information, Julie and I probably will be taking a trip in the very near future."

Later, when we were in her room, she told me, "I can't tell you how thankful I was when you and Charles came in together. I hope you won't go to London too often, Julie, I do worry so. If you want to see your friend, surely she could make the effort to come down here. I'd have thought she'd want to reassure herself that you were getting a square deal."

"I had to see my lawyer as well," I reminded her. "I could hardly ask him to come down here."

"If he's anything like Oliver's Mr. Marsden you've plenty of time," Bianca warned me. "I know Oliver despaired of ever getting Evelyn's affairs settled up."

"Oh, Mr. Crook's not like that," I told her proudly. "Definitely on the ball." That was another of Ada's expressions.

When we came downstairs Charles and Oliver were checking a crossword clue in the library. "Very educational, these crosswords," Oliver said, coming to join us. "Until tonight axis to me meant something on which the world revolved."

"And what does it mean from now on?" Bianca inquired.

"You see? Even you don't know. It's a small Indian deer."

"Very educational," Bianca agreed. She looked at me and grinned.

"That's a funny thing about women," said Oliver, "they don't seem to care about information for information's sake."

Bianca turned to ask Charles if his dealings with the television authority had reached a further stage, and he said, "Oh, they like to think they have you dangling on a string," and that got them started on a conversation about power complexes. I left them to it and went along to the kitchen. It was one of Mrs. Dotrice's early days and I had the responsibility of preparing the meal. One advantage about having a companion who isn't officially a trained nurse is that she can be asked to do practically anything. Not that I minded. I was glad of a chance to be alone, and think, but I wasn't alone for long. Charles came breezing in to say he'd come to lend a hand, but I knew that was only an excuse.

"What is it now?" I asked, not very graciously. I knew, of course, he wouldn't be going back to Australia. I didn't really care where he went, so long as he left me alone. And not just for the future, but also for the moment.

"Can you do with a vegetable hand?" he suggested. "By the way, if it's not too personal a question, does the worthy doctor have the facts?"

"Facts?" I repeated in an absorbed voice.

"Wake up, darling. The facts about Solange Peters."

"Why should you suppose he'd be interested."

Charles's eyebrows flew up. "He is Bianca's doctor."

"A stand-in," I corrected.

Charles sat on the edge of the table where I was preparing food, an unhygienic habit that always annoys me. "This lawyer you went to see—didn't he advise you to come clean?"

"Surely you know that conversations between a lawyer and his client are confidential?" I said.

"I can't make up my mind about you," Charles confessed. "It's hard to believe anyone could be as innocent as you appear. Ergo, you're as deep as a well."

"And what's that supposed to mean?" I said.

"You told me you weren't going to touch Julie Taylor's legacy. Doesn't it occur to you that sooner or later someone's going to think that odd? She was listed as a survivor."

"You talk as though it were a fortune," I said, "instead of just a little nest egg that would cover her fare and a few months traveling around on a shoestring."

"Who told you that?" His voice sharpened.

"I got it from the horse's mouth." Well, if Crook wasn't actually the horse, he was the next best thing. "Now," I went on, "can I ask you something?"

"Speech is not yet taxed."

"All right. Here goes. Were you ever in Australia?"

"If I wasn't, how should I ever have heard of Julie Taylor?"

"I don't think you really expect me to answer that. You're quite sharp enough—and of course you were never engaged to her."

"What are you trying to prove, Solange?"

"I can't prove anything, can I?" I said. "And that goes for you, too. I'm just reminding you as nicely as I know how that those who live in glass houses shouldn't throw stones. And now, if you don't mind, I'd like to get on with the dinner."

After he'd gone I wondered if I'd been a bit too free in my speech. I didn't need Crook to warn me of the unwisdom of making enemies when you yourself are virtually unarmed.

In spite of my anxiety the dinner was a great success.

Oliver helped to carry the dishes back to the kitchen and stayed to wipe, as he often did. But tonight it seemed he had an ulterior motive.

"Bianca tells me you've been to London to see a lawyer," he said.

I couldn't see that it was anyone's affair but mine. "He's looking after my affairs," I pointed out. "There isn't anyone else."

"I'd like to think you thought of us as your friends," Oliver said.

"This is a business relationship. Aunt Marty," I improvised glibly, "instilled in me the fact that the laborer is worthy of his hire, and it's usually good sense to employ the expert in the field. I don't mean to sound offensive or ungrateful," I added, "but this way he carries the responsibility."

Oliver smiled. "You're very independent, aren't you, Julie? Whatever we were able to do for you would never repay you for all you've done for Bianca. She's a different woman since your arrival. Tell me, does she really mean to go abroad?"

"Unless Dr. Mitchison unsettles her," I said. "I do hope not, it's taken such a lot of work on Dr. Gregg's part, to say nothing of mine, to encourage her to—to start living again as a responsible person. She's like those people in the hymn who start and shrink to cross the narrow sea, they just want a little push . . ."

"And you're the well-meaning citizen eager to do the pushing. Well, you have my blessing, Julie, for what it's worth."

It didn't seem to me it was worth very much.

In spite of his encouragement my spirits were still under a cloud. I put that down to Charles, though he'd done no more than point out and emphasize the facts of the case. It was going to be very awkward if I didn't eventually come clean, as Ada would have said, and each day I postponed it made the situation more difficult. If I wanted to marry I couldn't marry under Julie's name—at least, it would be a lie if I did; I wasn't even sure about the legal position, whether you were expected to produce some evidence of identity, though I thought most likely not. But I didn't want my children to discover I was living a double life—and I wasn't a second Ada Holloway, single bliss held no attractions for me. And any time I came out of the shadows I was going to brand myself as a liar and a deceiver, and I couldn't suppose that would endear a possible husband to me. Men like to think of themselves as subtle and of their wives as being clear glass.

Coming along the passage from the kitchen I heard the voices of the others, laughing, debating, sounding so intimate, so secure. I supposed Charles really might be an actor, he didn't show a trace of unease. Oliver came into the hall enroute for the study—another clue, I wondered?—caught sight of me and said, "Come on, Cinderella, the ball's nearly over." I remembered that when midnight struck, poor Cinderella went back to the ashes and the rags. The simplest word seemed to hold a threat tonight.

"I'm going up to put Bianca's electric blanket on," I called. "I'll be down in a minute." I reminded myself of that splendid pair, Crook and Ada Holloway, but tonight all I could think of was that they were a long way off.

Coming up the stairs the house seemed cold. I stopped on the landing, what Bianca called the entresol. One thing about these rather old-fashioned houses is the amount of space they can afford to squander. I liked that, I liked the feeling you didn't have to make every inch pay its way. There was an immense window here, with a cushioned window seat, and the best view in the house. I used to sit there sometimes; it was near enough Bianca's room for me to hear if she called or rang her bell. In the early morning you could sometimes see a heron fishing in the distant river, and once I'd caught sight of a kingfisher, a flash of emerald and vivid blue, making for the insanitary hole it called its nest.

I pulled back the long curtains and to my surprise found the window was open. In the dark sky a little new moon lay on a cushion of cloud, and automatically I bowed to her. I couldn't turn the money in my pocket, as I wasn't carrying any. I realized what had happened. Mrs. Dotrice had all a countrywoman's respect for superstition, and her own experience of seeing a new moon through glass would strengthen this. She must have opened the window, knowing how often I paused here, to preserve me from ill luck. I was rather touched by her thought. The window, which was a heavy one, was open and closed by cords, operated by light boxwood handles. I caught the handles but stood for a minute looking out at the huge tranquil immensity of the night. It was always very still on this side of the house. Below me the world was dark, mysterious, but never, never asleep. An owl called from a tree and I softly called back. I was grateful to that owl, it made me feel I was still part of the living world. Kneeling on the window seat, still grasping the window cords, I found myself envying any girl, no matter how plain, how undistinguished, who could come out into the daylight and say, without fear of contradiction, "I'm Mary Smith, this is my background." I remembered Florian, but no longer with pain. I thought of a dream lover—I might deceive the rest of the world, but what chance of happiness would there be for either of us if I tried to deceive him?

I leaned forward, pulling gently on the cords—and something struck me violently between the shoulder blades, thrusting me forward into the dark. Only the cords saved me, it was fortunate they were strong. All the same I had a terrible falling sensation. The next blow, I thought, would fall on my wrists. I'd be compelled to loosen my hold—one hand would be enough. I tried to lean backward, to cry out. Then the hand on my back went away and I slipped down onto the floor, my eyes hidden in the crook of my arm.

"Very natural but not too bright," Crook was to say later. "That way you made sure you wouldn't catch sight of whoever it was."

The carpets on the stairs were very thick, I'd been deep in my dream, I'd heard no one approach. The attack was rash, because I might suddenly have turned, but it would have been simplicity itself for my assailant to pretend to look at the new moon or even ask what the hell I thought I was doing, did I want to commit suicide? Whichever way you looked at it, I couldn't win.

I became aware of Oliver's arm around my shoulders, of Charles bounding up the stairs carrying a glass of something; and then of Bianca's voice calling to know what was happening.

"That's what we want Julie to tell us," Oliver said. "Drink up, Julie."

Sentences and odd words blew about in the air like leaves from a tree.

"Did she get giddy? What on earth made you open . . . ? Don't understand. She can't have meant . . . Don't be absurd." That was Oliver's voice, rough with confidence. I drank the brandy Charles gave me and leaned back. I was on the carpet, I found, I'd let go of the cords. Someone had closed the window.

"Pull the curtains," said Bianca's voice abruptly.

"Don't look at the new moon," I said in the idiotic way people do when they're coming out of shock.

"So that's it," said Oliver. "She didn't want to see the new moon through glass. And overbalanced."

"I always said that window was dangerous," Bianca declared. "There's a story about a woman who lived here a hundred years ago . . ."

"What happened?" asked Charles. "Did she fling herself . . . ?"

"No," said Oliver, and his voice was almost a shout. "And there never was any such story. You're worse than Mrs. Dotrice, Bianca. This house isn't a hundred years old. Anyway, there's a ledge above the window seat to prevent accidents."

"What are you saying?" asked Charles. "That it wasn't an accident?"

"Of course it was an accident," said Oliver. "Can't either of you use a little imagination? Having opened the window, she was trying to shut it, leaned out too far, it's pretty heavy . . . Now, Julie, everything's going to be all right. Your guardian angel was on sentry duty. All the same, don't try going to sleep again or falling into a reverie, whichever it was, when balanced on the window seat."

"Who pulled the curtains back?" Bianca said, and Oliver told her, "Julie, I suppose."

I looked across and saw Bianca's face, strained, apprehensive, and snapped back into my usual role like a joint being returned to its socket. There's an instant of agony and then all's well.

"I'm sorry I've given everyone such a fright," I said. "I gave myself one, too. Next time Mrs. Dotrice tells me it's unlucky to see the new moon through glass, I shall have an answer for her. It's a good thing I'm not a real nurse," I added, meeting Charles's eye without a tremor, "you'd probably give me the sack, alarming my patient. Bianca, your room's all ready."

She let me lead her upstairs. I was back where I'd started, nurse and guardian.

"What really happened?" she asked me when the door was closed.

"I was looking at the new moon," I told her steadily, "and I suppose I leaned out too far, there was a little owl calling . . ."

"Providence seems to have been on your side," Bianca told me. She was still rather shaky. How much she believed of what I'd said I couldn't be sure.

"Will you tell me something?" she said. "This lawyer of

yours, I know you told me you had to consult him about your legacy, though how he can do much on the other side of the world—" She let that drop. "Did you go for any other reason?"

"What other reason could there be?" I asked.

"I couldn't blame you if you wanted to get into a less melodramatic household. Or if he advised you to do it."

"Mr. Crook would never advise that," I said. "If he knew what was going on he'd be thrilled. Not that he's a monster, but he does like things to happen."

"Where did you meet him?" Bianca asked, and I said he was on the plane, and we'd encountered one another again by chance when I was coming back from the clinic.

"He told me if ever I needed help . . ."

"Are you sure he is a lawyer?" interrupted Bianca sharply. "They're not supposed to tout for clients. They can be disbarred, or whatever the word is."

"He didn't tout," I said. "At that stage he didn't know I had a legacy, at least I don't recall mentioning it."

Bianca managed a rather uneasy laugh. "The fact is," she acknowledged, "I suspect everyone. It even seems to me strange that Oliver should be the first person at your side tonight. Now that you've produced a lawyer you've become a source of potential danger. I think, Julie, we'll arrange to go abroad as soon as Dr. Mitchison gives me the word."

Dr. Mitchison proceeded to throw a spanner into the works as soon as he got back. He made it clear he'd had a disappointing convalescence himself—shocking weather, hordes of undesirable tourists, numbers of them British, high costs and none of the respect he still believed Europe should accord to a man of his race.

"I really couldn't recommend a change at this precise moment," he said. "The weather forecasts are anything but promising, we all know what foreign doctors are like . . ." It didn't seem to occur to him he was light-heartedly maligning a whole body of men.

And Bianca listened to him. "He is my doctor," she reminded me rather acidly. "And Europe will still be there next month."

I could hardly point out that the question was whether she (and possibly I) would be equally available.

The next morning I slipped out and rang Crook's number from the phone box on the Green. A voice that certainly wasn't his answered me. I realized it was the man I had seen when I called at the office.

"Crook's up north for a couple of days," he told me. I wondered if anything would make him change his unemphatic manner; all humanity might be a set of puppets, for all the interest he seemed to take. "I can't give you an address because he hasn't phoned. That means he's on the trail."

I wasn't really surprised that Bianca thought him a queer sort of lawyer; he seemed to be his own private eye as well.

I hung up and asked the operator for Ada Holloway's place of business. I knew she didn't like being called there, but this was an emergency, I had to have some help. If anything happened to Bianca now, I'd feel a murderess for the rest of my days. It had been bad enough being labeled one when I knew I was innocent. This would be far worse.

Ada came to the phone at once. "Am I glad to hear your voice?" she said. "I thought they must have cut your tongue out or bound your hands behind your back—or have you taken a vow not to answer letters?"

"What letters?" I said.

"My last, you dope. Don't tell me they forgot to give it to you."

"I haven't had it," I said.

"They're a forgetful crowd, aren't they? Or could it be that they remember too well? You know, I wouldn't have them on my list, not for free. I suppose they didn't give you my message either."

"What message was that?" I felt as stupid as the notorious barn owl. But I could feel the sweat breaking out on my forehead. All this time my sole consolation had been the thought that I had two allies who wouldn't easily let themselves be silenced. Now I felt bereft of both. I only had to be out of the way when the postman called, or out of the house when the phone rang, to be washed up utterly. Why, Crook might have tried to get in touch, but I didn't think so, because Bill Parsons would have told me.

"I tried to get in touch with Crook," I said, "but he's gone north."

"Something fresh?" asked Ada, in a voice as sparkling as the dew.

"Did I tell you about the mushrooms? Oh well, there's been another attempt since then, though they're both tactfully labeled accident."

"What does your employer do to make herself so unpopular?"

"Oh, the second attempt wasn't against her, or at least

only indirectly. I sort of slipped when I was closing a window. Oh, and one more thing. If you should be in touch with Mr. Crook before I am, you might just mention I think we're being followed. I've noticed a dark car two or three times when I've been out." I wondered if that, too, was part of the Oliver-Charles plan.

"You can't ever have a dull moment," said Ada enviously. "You and Mr. Crook are a pair. He's a card, isn't he? His wife would never have a dull moment, either."

"Has he got one?" I asked.

"What do you think? No woman would allow him to go round in that fancy dress. You know, it might be worthwhile checking up on this follower of yours. Do you know where he hangs out? After all, you can't expect Mr. Crook to do all the work."

She rang off and I came out of the phone box. If the little dark car was really on my trail, it had hidden itself very conveniently. Positively no expense spared, I reflected, making for home.

Charles cleared up one part of the mystery that night. "Did you know you had an admirer at The Fishermen's Arms?" he asked me. "Very interested in you, he is. Chap of the name of Penrose." And he laughed. "Julie Taylor, the Human Magnet." His eyes taunted me. I understood how it was that people who'd always appeared normal could suddenly pick up a bread knife and go to work on a tormentor. If the man in the little dark car wanted to run anyone down, I couldn't think of a better choice than Charles.

I never thought the day would come when I should be grateful for his presence. I had been out doing some shopping on a rather chilly day, when Bianca had elected to stay behind. I'd got some parcels in the trunk and they rattled like chains, so, stopping near a cluster of cottages, I got out. To my surprise the world was instantly alive with women. They seemed to me to come out like the rats after the Pied Piper. I'd always realized there was an immense body of gossip always on the boil, like a stockpot, with fresh tidbits thrown in from time to time. They gossiped about Bianca, of course. I daresay they'd unearthed the fact that she'd married her late patient's husband. Their voices came clearly to my ears. It was the usual boring tittle-tattle of small communities confined within their own limited activities.

"You'd wonder how she could," said the first. "That brown, the color of weak gravy, all over the house."

"And those pink bricks, I never saw the like. Shows us all up."

"They could do a bit with their garden. Nothing touched for years and then dashing round and digging here and planting there, makes the place look as though it had the mange."

"Or as if they were looking for something," chimed in a third voice.

"Or hiding something." They all chuckled. "You do read such awful things in the paper. Let's see, who was there before the Havelocks?"

"Mrs. Cherry—you remember."

"What—the one whose husband disappeared overnight?"

"If he was a husband."

"She had her lines," said Number Three in the authoritative voice of one who can't be mistaken. "Did anyone ever hear what happened to him?"

I discovered the trouble in the trunk and rectified it. As I came back to the side of the car, the first woman stared at me insolently and asked, "You want anything, young woman?"

"I found out what was wrong," I said. "There was a knocking."

The woman nodded grudgingly. "How's Mrs. Duncan then?"

"She's improving," I said vaguely.

The second woman leaned over her gate and they both broke into shrill laughter. "That'll never do, will it? Find yourself out of a job, won't you, lass, and there's not so many soft jobs going."

The first began to tell the world what a hard time she'd had as a girl, no one offered you a packet of notes in those days on the end of a stick for nothing.

"I didn't know they did now," I told her.

"That Nurse Adams," said the first, and the second chimed in, "Soon sent her about her business, poor worm. Couldn't wonder really . . ."

I had been listening in a state of more or less suspended animation (there's no one to equal village women when it comes to spiteful gossip, Bianca had said once) but now I began to see the trend of their words.

"What are you driving at?" I demanded.

"My frying pan 'ud take a beauty prize before her," one said. I realized they were referring to Nurse Adams.

"I'm afraid I can't continue this conversation," I said

lightly, getting back into the driving seat. "Mr. Duncan doesn't like me to leave her alone too long. She has been quite ill, you know."

"Some of us wouldn't mind that sort of illness," said the second woman.

It was sheer female nastiness. I couldn't help wondering what Bianca had said to make them so malicious. I wondered, too, if they were hinting that Oliver had dispensed with a plain middle-aged woman in order to have something fresher and more amenable on the premises. But that didn't bother me, they could never have seen us together because we'd never been together, alone, I mean. And though he was attractive to look at he'd never been anything to me but my patient's husband, and now I thought of him as something considerably more sinister. There was the sound of wheels behind us and a small dark car drew up and a man's head poked out of the window.

"Having trouble?" he asked. "Can I help?"

"Got 'em all round her, like pies round a honey pot." One of the women grinned.

"Pistols for two and coffee for one," said another. I supposed she was quoting from a television script.

"You girls on strike from the washtub?" asked the stranger genially.

They went up in smoke. "Never heard of washing machines?" shouted one.

"There was a knocking in the boot," I explained. "It was only some of the parcels, though."

"You're from the Manor House, aren't you?" the man went on. "I thought I'd seen you around."

"I'll bet," said one of the women.

"I'm staying at The Fishermen's Arms," the stranger continued. "Any time you want help—either of you ladies want me to come and turn the mangle?"

It was the day after that that it happened. Whoever was after Bianca and possibly after me was certainly a trier.

Since she decided to follow Dr. Mitchison's advice and vegetate some more in her own home, Bianca had become more jumpy, more impatient, went back to her old hobby of brooding over her health. I had persuaded her to drive her own car on two or three occasions, and I realized she spoke the truth when she said she was a natural driver. Nothing disturbed her, not even when a van came hooting out of a side road. But the last time we went out she made me take the wheel again. I found myself wishing that Dr. Mitchison had died on the Riviera. Dr. Gregg and I had worked hard on Bianca and she'd come quite a way, and now, more or less overnight, that old phony had pushed her back to Square One. He was a menace in disguise, like a box of poisoned chocolates done up with pretty pink ribbon.

Bianca had started complaining of nervous headaches again, and because the little car skidded once on a bad place in the road she made me take it out for a few minutes each time before she got into the passenger seat, just to make certain it hadn't been tampered with. She called it warming the car up. I honestly don't think it occurred to her she was buying her safety at my expense. Kings of old had their official tasters, without whom they wouldn't touch a mouthful or drink a sip of wine. The tasters, of course, were expendable. I supposed I was expendable, too. Another thing —Dr. Gregg had tried to get Bianca off the drugs she took for these headaches, but when Dr. Mitchison came back he said, with that silly smile, "We have to please the patient," and one morning gave me a prescription on the old lines. "On second thoughts," he added, "I'll drop it in myself, and you can pick it up later in the day."

I went up to urge Bianca to come out with me; I thought even an excursion into the town might do her good. I remembered the day we bought the picture; it seemed to belong to a different age. She wasn't keen at first, then she said, "Who's that walking about downstairs?"

"Oliver," I told her. "He's waiting for an important phone call."

Perhaps Bianca didn't like the notion of being left alone with Oliver; anyway, she decided to come. The day, which had dawned brightly, began to cloud over and I tried to hurry her a bit to get her out of the house before the inevitable rain. Oliver was still hanging about waiting for his call; he went to the garage and brought out his car and then he fetched the little Parker. Bianca decided that if she made the effort she might as well try and get her hair set; she hadn't made an appointment but she said confidently that they'd fit her in. By the time she came down, the sky was quite gray, and she hesitated.

"I don't believe it's going to stay fine," she said. "I hate being out in wet weather. By the way, did you check that the pills will be ready?"

"No," I said, "but Dr. Mitchison will have told them it's urgent."

"Urgent's a matter of degree. Ring up and find out, there's a dear."

I came in. Oliver was in the morning room, which he used as a sort of office when he was at home. I picked up the phone and got through to find a moron of the first water on the line.

"Mrs. Duncan?" she said. "Well, I don't know, the dispenser's very busy this morning."

"Perhaps you could find out," I suggested. "Dr. Mitchison brought it in himself."

"I didn't know he'd been in this morning," the girl said.

I suggested again she might inquire, so rather reluctantly she put down her phone and went away. She seemed to be a long time. Oliver popped out of the morning room to say in irritable tones, "Is that a very important call, Julie? I particularly wanted the line kept clear."

I explained about Bianca's pills. Oliver's frown deepened. "She's going back on those?" he said glumly. I pointed out it was important for her to get her sleep. I didn't add that mine depended on it, too.

"I suppose so," he said. "How much longer is that girl going to be?"

His irritation was infectious. I found myself calling, "Come on! Come on!" into the phone. She did come back at last and say they were ready and to remember they closed at one. And then as I released the phone, the rain started. It was like a football crowd that has waited too long for the gates to open; it simply pelted down. Oliver shot out to put his precious car under cover and nearly collided with Bianca dashing in.

"I told you it wasn't going to hold up," she said. "I can't go out in this."

"The girl took ages to find out."

Oliver came back, sweeping raindrops from his coat sleeve. "I only had her washed yesterday," he said. "Bianca, hadn't you better change your shoes? Julie will get your prescription for you, won't you, Julie?"

Bianca looked sullen. "I need her, there's something . . ." She was deliberately vague. "Oliver, couldn't you get them for me?"

"Oh, for heaven's sake! You know I'm waiting for this call."

"Well, Julie can take a message, I suppose."

"I don't want to keep this chap waiting. Tycoons don't like it."

"I thought you were in the tycoon class," returned Bianca, rather spitefully. "You don't want to give the impression you're the office boy. Anyway, he may not ring for another hour."

"It won't last, this sort of rain never does. This afternoon . . ."

"The shop will be shut. Really, Oliver, I don't often ask you . . ." I thought she was making it pretty clear she didn't want to be left in the house with him.

"All right," said Oliver ungraciously. "Julie, just sit by the phone. I know you think me unreasonable, Bianca, but this contract could mean a good deal."

"I'll get the message," I promised.

"Get a number where I can ring him. Or if he suggests a rendezvous, make a note of the address and say I'll be there."

"It's not like Oliver to be so worked up," Bianca murmured. She paused at the foot of the stairs. "Tell Mrs. Dotrice we shall be in to lunch, after all, and then come up."

Mrs. Dotrice took the change of plan without any change of face. "It looks as though we may get thunder," I suggested. I was always trying to establish a cordial relationship with this extraordinary woman, but she never displayed any more feeling than a robot.

"It's to be hoped not. Madam doesn't like thunder. Turns her right up. I couldn't say why. She says it was the war, the guns, you know."

"But that's twenty-five years ago," I protested. "She could only have been a little girl."

"My sister's the same," said Mrs. Dotrice, getting out a vegetable chopper and preparing to make celery soup. She never used tinned soups. "Of course, she was buried for two days. I suppose it makes a difference."

As I came out of the kitchen the telephone began to ring. Oliver came sprinting back into the hall. I heard him say, "Yes, yes, it is. Of course. Certainly. I'll be there." He hung up.

"I'm sorry, Julie," he said. "You'll have to go after all. My contact has arrived and wants me to meet him immediately. Mrs. Dotrice can explain to Bianca. As she says, it won't take long, if you go straight there and back."

I thought if Oliver was out of the house, too, she need have no fears, but I loitered at the corner until I saw his car disappear. I thought it was a pity Bianca had been so precipitate. Already ahead the sky was clearing; probably it would turn out to be quite a fine afternoon. She was always less restless when she'd been out, and if a plan of hers was thwarted she seemed to think it was part of a wholesale conspiracy to deprive her of some pleasure she'd anticipated. Five minutes later though I was thankful she wasn't in the car.

The Manor House stood rather high, which accounted for the magnificence of its views. To reach the town you came down a long, spiraling hill that got very steep near the bottom. There were hedges on both sides, and incautious motorists were inclined to open the throttle and let their cars rip. Bianca always came down carefully, braking as we reached the steep lower half. I did the same; there was a wide curve ahead and this was the most dangerous part of the road, because if a lorry or a tractor was coming up and you were making an unreasonable pace, there might be a crash. I applied the brake, as usual, but it didn't seem to hold. I started with the hand brake, stamped on the foot brake, and nothing happened. Neither of them gripped, and the car began to rock slightly from side to side. I knew that if I couldn't get it under control before we reached the turn, we should probably add one more to the list of fatalities—it was known as Dead Man's Hill locally, though it had a perfectly sedate name on the maps. I heard a car coming up behind me, and desperately I pulled in.

There was a terific hooting and a voice yelled, "Turn her into the hedge, you fool, it's your only chance."

The hedges were tall and thorny. Even a small car would probably plow through and hurtle the occupants down a slope that ran plumb to the lower road.

The car came nearer, forcing me off the road, taking a pretty good chance of crashing itself, and giving me no choice at all. I charged the hedge, and it seemed as if the skies were falling. My head banged violently against the windscreen; I thought it must have cracked in two. I suppose I blacked out for a minute, and when I came around I decided I was in a hospital or something, because Dr. Gregg was staring furiously at me. I giggled fatuously.

"It's becoming quite a habit," I said.

"Have you been drinking?" Gregg asked. "If not, what the hell do you think you're playing at? If you're tired of life, what's wrong with a bottle of aspirin? You don't even need a prescription."

I noticed he was pretty white himself. "You always seem

to come to my aid when I'm in trouble," I murmured. I had realized by now I was still in the car, and, amazingly, still in one piece. My head seemed stabbed and I felt sick, but I could move my arms and legs. "I'm alive," I said encouragingly.

"Which is a damn sight more than you deserve. What was the object of the exercise? Thank heaven you hadn't got your patient with you. Is that what happened last time?"

"Last time?" I said, fogged again.

"Well, you've got some reason for passing yourself off as a companion to a chronic neurotic. And I suppose it would be too much to expect you to consider anyone else's feelings. Whose car is that?"

"Mrs. Duncan's."

"Did she ask you to wreck it?"

"Of course not. It was an accident. The brakes went on strike." That seemed to me suddenly awfully funny and I began to giggle again.

Dr. Gregg slapped my face. "Keep your jokes till you get back," he stormed. "I'm on the way to deliver a premature child and you're holding me up. You'd better stay where you are, or no—I'll take you in with me, and the garage can send a breakdown gang for the car. You should know better than to drive an unserviceable machine."

"It wasn't unserviceable yesterday," I insisted.

"Well, you're not likely to have a closer handshake with death than you had this morning," he grumbled.

"What a lot one seems to hear about death these days," I mused. I actually seemed to see my words going up in a little cloud, like midges. I thought of William Tyrell, the English archer, who shot at a deer and killed a king. "Some people think it wasn't an accident," I said aloud.

"What wasn't an accident? Oh come, you're not suggesting someone's trying to rub you out? What's wrong with the car anyway?"

"I told you—the brakes." I managed to extricate myself and got out to examine the damage. I had shot into the hedge almost at right angles from the road. It was impossible to tell how much damage there had been. "I wonder if I could back her," I said aloud. "I don't want to leave her here, I have my reasons."

"If you imagine anyone can drive *that*—"

"They might. And if they didn't know about the brakes." It was perfectly obvious what had happened. Oliver had brought the car around practically for the first time, knowing that Bianca was going to drive into town. I thought her reaction would be the same as mine, to try and keep the car on the road around the dangerous bend, after which the slope decreased. It was one chance in a hundred, but she would have taken it and so would I, and with ninety-nine chances against us, it would be bad luck for Oliver if we survived. I recalled his distracted expression when Bianca asked him to fetch the pills. Of course, he'd use his own car, but somehow the damaged brakes would have to be explained away. The telephone call coming in the nick of time must have sounded like the heavenly choir. And now he'd got to start all over again.

"Life's very frustrating, isn't it?" I remarked in conversational tones. I still wasn't quite sure I had my feet on the ground. "Whoever planned this has got to think up something else."

"So we're on to murder now, are we?" Lionel Gregg suggested. "Any proof?"

"You don't suppose brakes put themselves out of action."

"It's no use giving me that mechanical talk," he warned me. "I can find my way more or less blindfold through the human diaphragm, but when it comes to an engine, I pay the expert. You've probably got it wrong," he added casually. "How could you be a danger to anyone?"

"You'd be surprised," I told him.

A lorry came crashing gaily around the corner and stopped in its own length.

"Want a hand, mate?" the driver offered. He was a fair young man with close curls and a cap pushed on the back of his head. "What were you thinking of, girl, when you ran her into the hedge? It could have been the end of love's young dream for you."

The doctor said frostily, "The brakes failed."

"When did you last have her overhauled?" asked the driver. He produced a cigarette and stuck it in his mouth.

"A month, give or take a day," I said.

"That garage should be strung up. Here. Maybe we could back her a bit."

"If you back her and the brakes aren't working and we're still on a hill, doesn't it occur to you what'll happen?" Gregg demanded.

"She won't run sideways, mate," said the lorry driver, who told us his name was Ted. "Here, can you move yours a bit?" He yanked open the door of Bianca's car and got into the driving seat. Dr. Gregg shifted a couple of yards.

"When I was a boy," the doctor said, "I had a private terror, induced by one of my father's sermons, that it might be my Godgiven vocation to end up in a madhouse. He was preaching on the necessity of being prepared to give all. I've steered clear of them to date, but I do begin to wonder now . . ."

"You want to watch out for that religion, mate," said Ted, treating the stricken car as if she were a girl he loved and was afraid of hurting. "It can get you worse than the drink."

From my position on the road I could see the havoc that sturdy hedge had wrought on the Parker. Great slashes of paint had been scraped off, a mudguard had assumed a shape a machine shop had never intended and the windscreen was badly cracked.

"You handled her nice," said Ted approvingly. "She could be in a lot worse shape. It's like cutting your hand, you bleed like a pig and wish you'd remembered to make your will, but when your mum's got to work with a bucket and cloth the damage doesn't look much, after all."

"Of course, there is the chance you could cut an artery," said Gregg encouragingly.

"In your hand? They never told me that at the practice."

The doctor and I both fell silent. The car heaved a little, shuddered, a bit of glass fell out of the windscreen. She was straddled across the ditch, and it seemed to me that even if Ted could extricate her, she'd only plunge nose-down with her bottom in the air. However, I underrated him. I don't know how he did it, but he appeared to take such a contingency in his stride. There was a roar as the engine came to life, then he spoke to it in a succession of affectionate four-letter words; she trembled, lurched, for one instant I thought she'd turn on her side, then he had her back on the road, her front wheels dangerously overhanging. I saw Dr. Gregg glance at his watch. "Don't you wait," I said quickly. "That baby won't."

"I've got this baby's measure," said Ted in muffled tones. "This your car, miss?"

"Well, I drive her. She belongs to a friend."

"Nice friends you've got." His head bobbed up. "Funny what a lot of mischief you can do by tinkering with a bit of wire and a nut."

"You mean it was deliberate?" ejaculated Gregg.

"I don't think she did that by herself." Ted got back into the driving seat and performed another miracle. "May as well take a look-see in case there's any other damage," he remarked coolly. He went back to his lorry and hauled out a big spanner. "Changed the wheel lately?" he suggested.

"No."

"Well, someone did. Or started and changed his mind." He was tightening the wheel as he spoke. "If the brake had held, which isn't likely, that wheel would have come off round the last bend. Now you take her into the garridge directly you get into town, tell the old man any yarn you like, but you have her investigated from top to toe. You got a jealous boy friend?"

Gregg turned to me. "Have you any explanation?"

I said, "Mrs. Duncan should have been in that car."

Unexpectedly the doctor jumped back into his own machine. "Perhaps this 'ull persuade her to take my advice and go abroad for a bit. I'll tell the garage to send their tackle . . ."

"No need," said Ted calmly. "She'll make it to the garridge under her own steam, and I'll stand by to make certain. You game, love?"

"Of course," I said.

"Don't be absurd," stormed the doctor.

"If Ted says it's all right, I believe him."

"That's the ticket," said Ted. "I like to see a bit of spirit myself. Not thinking of applying for a job on the lorries, I suppose? Come to that, the last mate they offered me had hair longer than yours. When I start riding round with a poof, that'll be the day, I told them." He pulled out his packet of cigarettes and thrust them at me. "Have one of these, love, good for the nerves and death to the lungs, isn't that right, Doctor?"

"I shan't sign a certificate," said Dr. Gregg fiercely. "It's suicide."

"What's eating him?" asked Ted, cool and friendly as ever.

"He's a doctor," I explained.

"So what? Diddled him out of a job by not breaking your perishing neck? I didn't know they got paid on piecework. Now take the wheel and go slow, very, very slow. If anything doesn't seem kosher, just stand on the brake."

I put the car into gear and we started. I half expected her to stand up on her tail, but she didn't. She went smoothly around the corner—I almost stalled her, I was so scared of another runaway—and made the rest of the journey, which fortunately wasn't far, under her own steam. Ted chugged patiently alongside, infuriating the driver of a van who wanted to pass. Ted opened his window and stuck out his head.

"Patience is a virtue," he chanted.

At the garage I saw Mr. Leverson, who was the proprietor, and explained what had happened.

"What have you been doing to her?" Mr. Leverson asked. "You're not going to get that job done overnight."

"Well, how soon?" I said. Mr. Leverson hummed and ha'd and talked about the great body of work and chaps not liking to do overtime, until Ted, who'd been standing by, said, "Look, mate, I'll be coming through myself a bit later, and I'll lend a hand. Can't you see the young lady's in a hurry?"

"I didn't say it couldn't be done, I said it would take time."

"That'll be all right," I assured him. "Mr. Duncan . . ."

"He's not going to like having another bill on top of the last." Mr. Leverson still sounded huffy.

"He might be glad his wife wasn't aboard," suggested Ted. "Or did he set up the job himself?"

Mr. Leverson looked so outraged I thought he was going to explode. "What are you hanging about for?" he demanded.

"Petrol, mate," said Ted. "You sell it, don't you? And don't forget my green stamps." He drove the lorry into the appropriate bay and walked across the road. He was back a minute later carrying two big china mugs.

"Tea, love?" he said, handing me one. "Ever heard of a chair; the lady's had a shock. That's better. Plenty of sugar," he went on encouragingly. "Hope that doctor got there in time. If it's a first the mum's generally having fits . . ."

"Are you married?" I asked, and he said, "Too right I am. Got two kids. Like to see their photo?" He pulled them out of his pocket. "Little Eddie. And Lou. That's my missus." He showed me a dark, laughing girl. "That's the life," he went on, putting the pictures away. "You should try it sometime. You often on this road? Ah well, see you—maybe." He paid for his petrol and got his stamps and had his book signed and then he was off.

"Cheeky beggars," muttered Mr. Leverson. "Think they're as good as you."

I was surprised to hear myself say, "I shouldn't think they come any better." He hadn't even let me pay for the tea.

"Have you got a phone?" I went on, knowing, of course, that he must have. "If so, I'd like to use it."

When Bianca answered the phone she sounded puzzled. "Where on earth are you speaking from?"

"Leverson's Garage. There was a slight hitch with the car, nothing to worry about, but I'm afraid I've scratched the paint a bit."

"Nothing to worry about?" Bianca repeated.

"Mr. Leverson's going to make a rush job of it."

"But—what happened?"

"I'll tell you when I get back. I skidded or something coming down Dead Man's Hill. I'll be back as soon as I can. Mrs. Dotrice is there, isn't she?"

"She's here, Oliver's out, but I'm not alone. Charles turned up . . ."

"Oh no!"

"Why not? Now don't be absurd, Julie." Her voice sharpened. "If he came to see you and you weren't here, obviously I should entertain him, so no sulks, please."

For a minute I didn't get her meaning. Then I thought, She really thinks I'm jealous—of her and Charles. But I couldn't tell her just what I did think, not there, not on the phone. And as I moved toward the bus station I didn't see how I was going to tell her, anyway, not without selling myself short down the river. It began to look as if that was going to be the only solution. Five minutes before the bus was due I remembered the pills I'd come to collect and rushed into the chemist to fetch them. The young woman behind the counter said, "Wait a minute, please," but I said, "I can't, the bus is going, and Mrs. Duncan's had a shock," so hardly knowing what they were doing, they gave them to me.

"What sort of a shock?" one of the women asked, but I'd no time to answer her. Anyway, if Bianca hadn't already had a shock, she was going to make up for lost time in the course of the next hour.

8

I LEFT THE BUS at the crossroads, though it would have taken me another two hundred yards nearer the house. I had never dared use the house telephone for fear of eavesdroppers, and now with Charles on the premises I had to be more particular than ever. I shuffled some coins into the box and dialed Crook's number. It was a relief to hear his voice at the end of the line.

"How come, sugar?" he hailed me. "I was thinking of paying you a little visit. I thought we were going to keep in touch, then I heard from Ada that something was screwy your end. How's tricks now?"

"I've got a lot to tell you," I said. "There was another attempt today." I told him about the car. "And something else. Charles has turned up, and it could have been his work."

"Who else was in the car?" Crook demanded.

"Only me. Bianca was coming, but the rain started."

"How come you ain't hearing holier songs than the larks?"

I told him about the doctor's intervention.

"Very co-operative of him," said Crook, "but then life-saving is his job. Still sure there's no sign of little Dan Cupid around? Well, you should know. I must meet him sometime. Ada's been on at me like a wife, nag and worry, worry and nag, steps not clean or vegetables late. Never mind, sugar, that's an allusion from the Dark Ages before your time. But we really did get worried, specially when we phoned and were told you weren't available. I mean, an expression like that's like charity, it covers a multitude of sins."

"Who said I wasn't available?"

Crook shrugged huge shoulders.

"Some female."

That confirmed me in a suspicion that had been growing steadily, that Mrs. Dotrice was also in on the plot. I don't say she realized how far Oliver was prepared to go, but it was he who had engaged her, paying her top-scale wages—and what inducement was there to come to this very unromantic household unless it was being made well worth her while? One thing, I felt pretty sure she knew how to look after herself. When the chips started falling she'd be on the right side of the fence.

"And Ada's letter never reached me. One thing, I think this may wind Bianca up to agreeing to a holiday."

"It wouldn't surprise me one little bit, but it wouldn't surprise me either if what the press calls a Domestic Tragedy didn't happen just in time to prevent your departure. And the only thing I hate worse than having no client is having a dead client."

"Did you really think I was dead?"

"My voices told me to the contrary. But, of course, the luck's like the weather, it can change any minute. Now you'll have to play it by ear, sugar, and I hope yours is a musical one. I have a notion we're pretty near the end, that's what my watchdog thinks, anyway."

"Your . . ."

"Your time is up, subscriber," said a voice, "and there are two calls waiting to come on the line."

"Let 'em wait," said Crook, but she was standing no nonsense. She cut us off ruthlessly, and I came out into what was once more a rainy afternoon. On the way back I wondered if I'd get the chance to see Oliver's face when he walked into the room and found I wasn't dead.

The first thing Bianca said to me when I walked in was, "Did you remember my prescription? Thank goodness for that. I was afraid in all this excitement—where is the car now?"

"At the garage, naturally. It wants a good deal done to it, including respraying. It practically went through the hedge."

"Oliver isn't going to like that," opined Bianca. "He's only just paid a big bill."

All this seemed such anticlimax after my near-death, I could only stare.

"Things do happen wherever you are, don't they?" said Charles.

"You didn't tell us you were coming back." I accused him. "Didn't London play up this time either?" I felt quite venomous.

"Believe it or not," said Charles, "I'm practically in. A television serial." He began to outline the plot. They didn't have a television in this house, but when I'd been in the clinic it was turned on for every program, and I knew the story Charles was telling us was a series that had been playing twelve months ago.

"What part are you taking?" I said, astounded at his carelessness. Or did he know that come what may I wouldn't dare sell him short?

"Oh, I'm to play Bernard," he said cheerfully, and I felt a stab of scorn. Because he hadn't even bothered to do his homework. Bernard was a character who died in the second or third episode.

"I'm going upstairs to put my things away," I said abruptly. "I didn't know you were coming."

"According to Bianca, I only missed you by inches. I didn't know you were going to have this encounter with a hedge. Well, having fulfilled my job of stopgap . . ." He stood up.

"But you'll come back to dinner?" urged Bianca. "Oliver will be most disappointed to miss you."

"Since you're so pressing. Anyway, I've got a tip for Oliver ought to be worth something."

"What's the matter, Julie?" Bianca asked me when Charles was gone. "I thought he was a friend of yours."

"Let's say I don't like attempts at murder," I retorted. "Do you realize that but for the storm, you'd have been in that car, too?"

Bianca turned quite pale. "You're saying it was deliberate? I thought . . . couldn't it have been accidental?"

"I don't think so. I think this was meant to be the final addition."

"But to choose such a time—when Charles—but he didn't know Charles was coming."

"Are you sure? Bianca, there's something I must tell you. I've wanted to for some time, but I was in a cleft stick."

"About Charles?" She seemed rather on the defensive.

"Yes. You don't really know anything about him."

"I know he was a friend of yours in Australia."

"I was never in Australia. And I wouldn't be at all surprised to know Charles never was either."

There was a long pause. Then Bianca said, "Who are you then, if you're not Julie Taylor?"

"I'm Solange Peters."

"The girl who was killed in the plane crash?"

"The girl who wasn't killed in the plane crash."

"But what was the point—this isn't some macabre sort of joke, I suppose?"

"I only wish it were. It's an extraordinary experience to be knocked out in an accident as one person and come round a fortnight later—I was concussed for a fortnight—and find you're someone else. It was a perfectly simple case of mistaken identity, you see. Someone had seen her wearing that snake bracelet and identified me by that, not knowing she had given me the bracelet. I was pretty well knocked about and bandaged; anyone who'd only just seen me on that plane could have made the same mistake."

"I see that," said Bianca. "But why did you let them go on with it?"

"It sounds easy to say, Oh, you've got it wrong, I'm really Solange Peters, and that's what I did say—at least I said I wasn't Julie Taylor, but they thought I was still wandering, and I'd had a lot of dope and drugs, and I thought, I'll feel fresher tomorrow, I'll tell them then. And the days went on—oh, it was inexcusable, but—well, Julie was a so much nicer person than Solange . . ."

"But you couldn't think you'd get away with it forever."

"When you're in the state I was in then, you don't look more than a day ahead. I suppose at the back of my mind I knew I was going to try and carry it off, but in the front I persuaded myself that it would be best to wait till I was clear of the hospital and then go to the authorities and make a clean breast of things. It never occurred to me I mightn't be believed."

"And that's what happened? No one believed you?"

"No," I said. "I didn't try. By the time I'd been patched up by the clinic I even began to feel like Julie Taylor."

"But why?" demanded Bianca. "What was there about Solange Peters—you're keeping something back, aren't you?"

"If I hadn't had something to hide, I'd never have started on this—impersonation," I said. And I told her about the

Marchesa. "Now do you understand? Would you have given me this job—would Oliver have employed me—if you'd known who I really was?"

"I should think Oliver would have regarded you as a heaven-sent gift. I take it he didn't know?"

"Of course he didn't know. If you want me to leave now," I added desperately, "I can go and pack my things. I'd quite appreciate your position."

"What are you going to do now? Are you going to the police?"

I hadn't thought, but "I suppose it will come to that in the long run," I said.

She thought back. "But Charles said he recognized you."

"How could he, when he'd never seen the real Julie Taylor? If he had, he'd have given himself away at once, I don't care how good an actor he is."

Bianca shook her head. "It still doesn't make sense. Why should he turn up here at all, asking for you?"

"Perhaps someone put him wise," I said. "Well, it was a way of getting a footing in the house, wasn't it?"

"I'll make you a confidence now," said Bianca. "I knew all along there was something you weren't telling, though I never dreamed it was anything as melodramatic as this. You see, you're not like Charles, you haven't been on the stage, and though you might cover up in a general way, you betrayed yourself again and again in the sickroom. I'm a nurse myself, you know, it was a case of birds of a feather."

"You mean—you knew, and never said a word?" It was what Crook and Dr. Gregg had both suspected.

"I thought it might be part of a plot hatched up by Oliver, but I tested you out in a dozen ways, and I became convinced you were genuinely on my side. In the end, I came to the conclusion you'd been in some sort of trouble and wanted to avoid the police. And if it's any consolation to you, I don't believe you had any hand in that Italian woman's death. You may have been deceiving me ever since your arrival, but I'd stake my life—in fact, it's just what I have been doing—on your professional integrity. It's a wonder to me Dr. Mitchison didn't spot you."

"Perhaps he did," I murmured. "Or perhaps Dr. Gregg told him."

"You mean, he knew?"

"He was convinced I'd been a nurse and there'd been some—blockage."

"Did you tell him what it was?"

"And chance his going to the police? I haven't told anyone in this house."

"Have you told anyone at all?"

"My friend in London." For some reason I suppressed Crook's name.

"She sounds just the sort of fuddy-duddy who'd love this cloak-and-dagger business."

"I'd have told you before," I said, "but I was afraid you'd send me packing at once, and—you do need someone to look after you. Today proves that."

"How annoyed Oliver will be!" Bianca murmured. "He'll know you'll put two and two together. Tomorrow, Julie—I shall go on calling you that, I couldn't confide in a stranger called Solange Peters—we'll go into Wister, to the big travel agency there and arrange for a continental trip. For both our sakes," she added emphatically. "You're in nearly as much danger now as I am. You've seen through Oliver, and he's bound to realize that. Even if you hadn't suspected foul play, the garage mechanics would know—wouldn't they? —that nuts and wires don't work themselves loose?"

"You mean, you still want me to come?"

"I've got to have one person I can trust," said Bianca simply. "You've got a passport, I suppose?"

"Julie Taylor's passport."

"That got you into the country, it must be sufficient to get you out. When we're safely abroad we can start making plans. I'd ask you to stay on with me indefinitely," she added in a rush, "but it wouldn't be a practicable suggestion. You'll want to do something more than that with your life."

"My life," I repeated. "Not Julie Taylor's. I've been a long time seeing this, but—well, I'm twenty-five. I could live another fifty years, if I don't push my luck too hard. I can't go on skulking in shadows in case someone recognizes me. I don't suppose I could be legally married under another name—don't you have to produce a birth certificate or something?"

"Has it occurred to you to wonder how you're going to prove you're Solange Peters?" Bianca asked.

I hadn't thought. "There'll be witnesses enough in Rome," I said. "Florian and Perdita and the servants; the police out there, they'll have my fingerprints—and then how do I know so much about Solange Peters unless I am her?"

"You're not going to have much fun either before or after," Bianca told me shrewdly. "I don't know much about the law, can't they have you on false pretenses?"

"Only if you get money that way. There are the Australian pounds in Julie's purse and the insurance—that's the only crime I committed, and I could repay that, if there's anyone to repay it to. No, what I really dread is raking up the Solange Peters story, but at least . . ." I stopped. It occurred to me for the first time that it might bring a lot of what are called old-fashioned looks if two women I'd been nursing died in suspicious circumstances.

"You did mean it, about getting out, I mean," I urged.

"The sooner the better," Bianca agreed. "Don't mention our plan to Oliver, will you? I'll present him with a *fait accompli.* And never let down your guard."

"I'll be like the beasts in the Revelations," I promised soberly, "that had eyes before and behind."

She was an amazing woman. You might have expected her to be on the verge of collapse after learning of a plot against her life that so nearly came off, but she not only insisted on coming down to dinner, she was the life and soul of the party, teasing Charles and mimicking Oliver, who was more silent than usual.

"I hope nothing's wrong," she said solicitously. "You look like a man who's just had a big diasppointment."

"How very perspicacious of you!" congratulated Oliver. "It's quite true. I thought I was being very subtle and pulling a plum out of a golden pie, but it didn't work out quite as I expected. Now I shall have to try a more direct approach."

Was that meant to be a hint that he knew we were on to him? Or did he really mean that the offer he'd put up to his nameless correspondent hadn't come off? It didn't matter, because a minute later Charles changed the subject.

"Did you hear of Julie's accident with the car?" he asked. "Ran her into a hedge and was rescued by—who did rescue you, Julie?"

I told them Dr. Gregg and a lorry driver.

"Gets 'em in droves, doesn't she?" said Charles, looking fascinated.

"What was wrong with the car?" Oliver wanted to know.

"The brakes wouldn't function when I was on Dead Man's Hill. I drove straight into the hedge, it was my only chance."

Oliver said smoothly, "What a mercy Bianca wasn't with you." Charles wasn't the only actor of the party. "I hope you're having it repaired. It's enough to shake your nerve."

I muttered something about the wet roads. "They're going on being wet for some time according to the long-range weather forecast," observed Charles.

"Why don't you change your mind," Oliver urged, "and take that holiday the doctor was so keen on? It would do Julie good, too. You know I can't come."

"It's just as wet everywhere else," objected Bianca casually.

Oliver hunted out the Times and looked at the weather reports. Rome cloudy, Florence rain, Athens fair, Balearics cloudy—Lisbon sunny. "You've never been to Portugal, have you? I believe it's an admirable winter climate."

"Go to Cascais," cried Charles. "Perfect little place near Estoril where all the deposed kings retire—Estoril, I mean, not Cascais. Lovely bathing, a palace by the sea, one of those gorgeous continental markets where you can buy all the exotic fruits, and lovely striped blankets in the most vivid colors for about a third of their price in England."

Oliver said quickly, "I thought this was your first visit to Europe," and Charles equally quickly took the hint. "Oh no. I've been over three or four times. I might even fly out for a weekend," he added. "Give Julie a whirl."

"You should be working for a travel agency," Bianca taunted him. "I must say the thought of bathing—I grew up by a river, I and my friends were in and out like otters. Is the sea warm at this time of year?"

"It was the year I was there. We used to sit in the sun in T-shirts, drinking coffee and making our fortune on paper. And when you're bored you can always do the excursions, Sintra, Pena Palace, you know; there's a most alarming little monastery where the ceilings are so low all the tall monks had to walk with bent heads, and all the rooms are just excavations of natural stone."

"It does sound beguiling," Bianca agreed. "We might write for a few brochures, anyway. When I was a nurse and had to have holidays on a small budget I used to write to every travel bureau I saw advertised, and I went half round the world before I joined a friend for an economical holiday at Boulogne or Jersey."

"We could plan clothes, too," I said in hopeful tones.

"Then, if we like the sound of any of them, we can go into Wister next week, we shan't have the car back till then, and make inquiries in person."

"I could drive you in my car," Charles offered.

"It won't be any use till we've got the brochures," Bianca pointed out. "We'll fly—unless, Julie, you have some inhibition . . ."

"No," I said. "None. Accidents can happen to anyone."

"You never said a truer word," Charles agreed.

No one showed any sense of strain, though it must have been in every heart. When I went into my room that night I had a sense of relief such as I hadn't known since my arrival in England. I still thought it possible Oliver would make one more attempt, but we were all on our guard now. I thought in the morning I'd telephone Crook and let him know what was afoot. Then he could come down quite openly. It wouldn't occur to anyone as strange that I should need a lawyer to help me to re-establish my own identity. Officially, only Bianca knew my secret, but Charles had known all along, and I couldn't believe he hadn't shared his knowledge with Oliver. My creeping fear now was that Bianca would try and hang on to me—as she said herself, she needed someone she could trust—and when my life as Julie Taylor was over I wanted to shed all my connections with her, too.

That night I saw my future as radiant as the day. I sidestepped thoughts of the unpleasant interlude when I would be trying to get back into my own skin. I didn't feel, however unpleasant the experience, Crook would let anyone defeat me. One day, I thought, I should love again, marry, bear children. There was no reason why my husband should know anything about Julie Taylor. I'd lived in such a backwater since I took over her identity that my fears of recognition were virtually nil. Or I could imagine Crook saying, "Tell the truth and shame the devil." Things lose interest when they lose mystery. Men coming out of prison are daunted sometimes by their own liberty, even think nostalgically of the world they knew where all their companions were their equals—so I'd been told. I could sympathize with their sense of strangeness at having to reorient themselves, but I didn't share it. It was only the weaklings, I decided, who ever went back.

I woke next morning to one of those perfect days you sometimes get at the end of September. The trees were bannered in gold, the leaves varnished by sun. Bianca seemed to feel the magic of the day as much as I. And my confession of the night before seemed to have established a relationship between us that hadn't existed till today.

"I feel restless," she told me. "Let's go out somewhere. We could hire a car from Leverson, that has to be safe, and you could drive. If we're really going abroad in the course of the next week or so, I must get accustomed to dashing around a bit."

I told myself she looked better, more relaxed and at the same time more full of spirit than I'd seen her hitherto.

"Why shouldn't we take a picnic?" I said. At least, that would keep us safe from any plans Oliver and Charles might be cooking up, for one day at least. And I was still only taking the days one at a time. "We could get a cooked chicken from Anderston" (no one could have tampered with that, I reflected) "and salad. His are authentic farm birds, not these old broilers."

"A long French loaf slit up the middle and buttered," murmured Bianca. "Fruit. We might get a melon and eat it from the hand as we did as children when my mother didn't stop us. We could go to Heathcote Bay. You've never been there, have you? I have a yearning to see the sea again."

"Anywhere you like," I said. "I might get a camera and some color film. I used to be rather handy at that."

"When you were in Rome?"

Five small words and they hummed like a bar of music. The fact that she could say them and I could accept them was like a miracle.

"Yes," I said, "when I was in Rome."

Now it even seemed possible that I could go back one day. Bianca seemed like myself, something that had burst overnight from its cocoon. I wondered if she had been racked by secret suspicions about me all this time, guessing I wasn't the person I was pretending to be, and never absolutely sure I wasn't on Oliver's side.

Our first rebuff was when Mr. Leverson said he didn't have a car available. He only kept three as a sideline, two were out on self-drive hire (I supposed Charles had one of them), the third was engaged for that day. He was sorry he couldn't help.

"There must be someone," Bianca insisted. "That woman at the Corner grocers—the Woodland Stores, they call themselves—advertises a car, but I think you have to take the driver along as well, and I so much wanted us to be on our own."

I didn't think it likely that Oliver could have got the whole place in his pay, but I also would have preferred us to go under our own steam.

"What can we do?" Bianca wondered, and like an answer to prayer, though surely not mine and not hers, Charles's car drew up at the gate. He came striding up the path.

"I know it's early," he called as he came in. "But I felt I must ask after Julie. I was in at Leverson's Garage this morning, and he showed me the car. You took a beating all right. I suppose you could say you're lucky to be alive."

"Very lucky," I agreed. So that's why Leverson couldn't rent us a car, I reflected. For one thing, seeing the Parker, he mightn't be keen—he probably didn't believe my story about the brakes, just thought I'd lost control on the hill, and naturally wouldn't want that to happen to one of his own machines—but it was more probable that Charles had talked him around. I had to admit that was rather a far-fetched theory, but supposed Leverson had said—no, that didn't work either. I had reached the stage where I suspected everyone and everything. The first reason was probably the true one. And he might have told Charles I'd been on the phone, and that would send him hotfoot up to the Manor House.

"It's very tiresome of Leverson," Bianca said. "We wanted to hire a car, but he hasn't got one free."

I looked at her in horror; she had spoken without thought, she didn't seem to realize she was playing straight into Charles's hands.

"It doesn't matter," I said quickly. "I was just going to ring the Woodland Stores. They have a car for hire, and it's not likely that'll be engaged, too."

"But there's no need," protested Charles, as I knew he would. "I'm entirely at your service. My car is at the gate."

"But you'll be wanting that yourself, won't you?" I said, before Bianca could speak. "We wouldn't want to put you out."

Charles smiled in what he'd call a rueful manner. "I was going to offer myself as chauffeur."

"That's very kind," said Bianca uncertainly, looking at me as if she expected me to get us out of this impasse. "Only we shall be out all day."

"And I'm free all day. I shan't be here much longer. That's another thing I came to tell you. I've got a firm offer from London at last, they want me to go there tomorrow, and this time I think something really may come of it. I thought we might celebrate."

"Aren't you counting your chickens?" I asked desperately, racking my brains to find some good excuse. I even wondered if I could manage to disable Bianca in some quite small way, injure her ankle or something, only that's easier to think about than to accomplish. Before any sound idea occurred to me the door of the morning room opened and Oliver joined us.

"Hullo!" he said to Charles. "I thought I heard your voice."

"Charles came to tell us he's got an offer at last, he has to go to London."

"You don't have to dot all the i's and cross all the t's," said Charles, smiling in the same way as before. "I don't have to go till tomorrow and I was offering to drive your wife and Julie out wherever they planned to go, but I don't think they trust my driving."

"Julie and I thought we'd take some food and go for a picnic," Bianca explained. "We don't want to interfere with anyone else's plans."

"A picnic!" exclaimed Oliver. "What a splendid idea! Why don't we all go? The office can carry on without me for one day. We can take my car."

Bianca did the only thing possible. She said, "That solves all our problems, doesn't it?"

I thought they wouldn't try any tricks with Oliver and Charles in the car; anyway, two car accidents in two consecutive days might arouse the suspicions of a far more trusting heart than Ada Holloway's or Mr. Crook's. I wondered if I could somehow get a message through to him. I'd have to get out of the car to get the food.

"Where did you think of going?" Oliver asked.

"We thought of Heathcote Bay, but perhaps that's rather far."

"Oh, nonsense," said Oliver. "It's a wonderful idea."

"We could bathe," offered Charles. "I'm sure Julie swims like a seal."

"I haven't got a costume," I said hurriedly. I'd no intention of leaving Bianca with Oliver, while Charles and I frolicked about in the ocean.

"Couldn't you buy one in the town?" Charles urged. "There's a very snazzy shop there."

"You could get a camera, too," agreed Bianca, giving me a meaning look. I wondered if she expected me to snap Oliver and Charles working out their murder plot, imagined me taking the undeveloped film to the police. One thing, if anything happened to Bianca, I was pretty sure I wouldn't get off scot-free either. All the same, I agreed about the camera. I thought it might give me an excuse for not going into the water.

"You'll need one for Cascais, anyway," Oliver encouraged me.

It was at that moment that I was absolutely certain we should never go to Cascais together, Bianca and I.

And how right I was!

"I'll ring my office," Oliver said, and Bianca chimed in, "Julie can fetch the car for you, we don't want to miss all the good weather. I'll tell Mrs. Dotrice."

Charles came with me to roll back the garage doors. "What have you been saying to Bianca about me?" he asked. "Why was she so dead set against going in my car?"

"You'd better ask her, hadn't you?" I said.

"I'm asking you."

"Well." Crook was right, I had to play this by ear, and I only hoped my ear was true. "It could be because I've told her the truth about Solange Peters."

Charles was so much taken aback that his mouth fell open. "Are you out of your tiny mind?" he gasped. "Or did she guess?"

"She guessed I was a nurse who had somehow stepped out of line. She didn't know I was Solange Peters. She'd probably never heard of Solange Peters."

"But why, Julie? Why?"

"Because so many people are getting suspicious—the doctor, Ada Holloway, Mrs. Dotrice, for all I know."

"Who's going to tell Oliver, or is he to be kept in the dark?"

"That'll rather depend on you, won't it?"

Charles looked disturbed. "You're making a monkey of the man who pays your wages. He's going to feel no end of a fool when he finds out."

"Perhaps Bianca doesn't tell him because she's afraid he might think me unsuitable, and she really does rely on me. I shan't let her down, you know."

"No," said Charles thoughtfully, "I don't believe you will. Only your position's going to be a bit unenviable if trouble blows up."

"Why should it?"

"You do realize she has this persecution mania?"

"You mean, she's talked to you about it?"

"I'd have to be blind not to recognize it," Charles told me

soberly. "Still, I won't give you away. We'd better take the car round, hadn't we, or they'll suspect we're putting on a Romeo-and-Juliet act in the garage."

He grinned, but I wasn't amused. I couldn't make up my mind whether he'd told Oliver about me or if Oliver had worked it out for himself. Because by now I was convinced that Charles hadn't expected to see the real Julie Taylor, and no one could have suggested the substitution to him except Oliver.

"I was beginning to think Oliver's car had broken down, too," said Bianca briskly. "We'll let the men sit in front, Julie. They always hate taking a back seat, and when you're a driver yourself" (as I am, she meant) "it's really torture to watch someone else at the wheel."

I was remembering I'd heard the phone in use earlier in the day. I wondered if it had been Oliver telephoning to Charles. I'd heard his voice through the closed door. That would certainly account for Charles's prompt appearance, an appearance too pat, to my way of thinking, to be a coincidence. I decided that even if I bought a bathing suit I would discover, when I got to the beach, it was too cold to go in. If I stayed beside Bianca the whole time, surely nothing could go wrong for her.

We drew up at the garage for petrol and oil. Oliver said, "While I'm here I may as well take a look and see how much damage Julie has managed to do to your car, Bianca."

Charles said, "What about a bottle of wine?" and got out to cross to the wineshop.

"We'll want some of those plastic beakers to drink from," Bianca told him. "You can get them at the stationer's on the corner."

"Will do," promised Charles, swinging away. I ran a few doors down the street to the delicatessen and said I wanted a chicken for Mrs. Duncan. Bianca had an account here and was an excellent customer, so a fine chicken was instantly produced. I asked Mr. Lamblett, the proprietor, to cut it up for me, and also butter half a dozen rolls. He had some covered dishes of salad in cellophane packets and I ordered four of those, too. While he prepared the bird and the rolls I said I was just going over the road to get something for Mrs. Duncan. I would only be about five minutes. Coming out of the shop I saw Charles emerge from the wine merchant, with bottles, wrapped in brown paper, under his arm. He waved to me and dived into the stationer's. Bianca was leaning forward in her seat talking to Mr. Leverson. I didn't see any sign of Oliver.

There was a better choice of bathing suits than I'd anticipated. I particularly liked two, and couldn't make up my mind which to have. The girl suggested I should try them on in the dressing room. One was a dark red wool, made in Switzerland, with a border of white flowers, and was quite superb, the other a more ordinary but exquisitely cut white sharkskin, which would be just right for Portugal, though I'd never dare wear it here.

"Aren't you lucky?" said the salesgirl with a sigh. "Anything looks like the Queen of Sheba on you. Though it's a shame really you have to wear a costume at all."

I laughed with pure pleasure. "I'll tell you what," I said in a sudden, rather high voice. "I'll have them both. I'm going to Portugal next week and I shall need two there."

"Lucky you!" said the girl. "Going with a friend?" Her grin was unmistakable. And it had the oddest effect. Suddenly a knowledge of my responsibility for Bianca swept back over me. I remembered that I'd intended to try and ring Mr. Crook. I wondered if this girl would let me use her phone while she tied up my parcel. I went to the door and looked out. Bianca was watching the shop, and when she caught my eye she beckoned rather impatiently. I suppose I had been longer than I realized. All the same, I felt I must somehow get in touch. When the girl brought me my change—lucky, I thought, I'd had money enough to pay for the two—I told her, "Keep that and do something for me, if you will. I wouldn't ask if it wasn't extremely urgent, you could almost say a matter of life and death. Would you ring a London number and give a message? I'd do it myself but Mrs. Duncan's waiting, I daren't stop. I promised to get in touch," I added desperately. "Going to Portugal's all very fine, but I don't get a lot of time for my private life."

I gave her Crook's two telephone numbers. "You're bound to get him at one or the other," I said. "Keep on trying. Here's the message, and say it's from Julie. 'Picnicking at Heathcote Bay, why not join us?' "

"You've got him on the hook all right, haven't you?" said the girl in admiring tones. "Just calling him up like that. Some people seem to have the lot." But she said it without envy. She was a nice girl, with a face as plain as a bar of salt. "It's too much, though." She meant the money I'd left. "You may have to try both numbers," I said. "If there is any change, keep it to drink to my luck."

She laughed. "I'll do that, then. Not that anyone with your looks should need it."

I hurried back to the delicatessen, where the parcel was waiting for me. The other three were all set to go.

"I'm sorry," I panted, "I couldn't make up my mind." I remembered too late I hadn't bought the camera, but I didn't suppose I could have used it, anyway. As we drew away, another customer went into the draper's: I hoped the girl had got her connection first. This woman looked as though she might spend half the morning choosing a couple of vests. Conversation on the way to the Bay was easy and general. Charles had an amusing story to tell about a couple who'd stopped at The Fishermen's Arms the night before and asked for dinner. Oliver capped it. Bianca brought the talk round to Portugal. "Luckily I have a passport," she said.

At the Bay we found we weren't alone in thinking this a good day for an excursion. A number of cars were parked on the promenade above the beach, and the seats set at regular intervals facing the sea each had one or more occupants. Women had brought their knitting, men their newspapers. Someone remarked in our hearing that this was St. Luke's summer and no mistake.

"Who was St. Luke?" murmured Charles, loading himself with rugs and the bottles of wine.

"He was a doctor," I said.

"She knows all the answers, doesn't she? Look, Julie, there really are people bathing. I take my hat off to St. Luke if he can produce this kind of weather in an English autumn."

For the moment he seemed to have forgotten the part he was playing and spoke with a markedly English accent, but no one else seemed to notice. We made our way down the beach to a fairly secluded spot. A man was renting out motorboats at an outrageous charge per hour, but Bianca said peaceably that it hadn't been much of a summer, and you had to make hay while the sun shone. On the further side there were rowboats drawn up on the beach for hire. Oliver looked at these wistfully. "That's my idea of an afternoon's pleasure," he said. "Fishing from a boat."

"Bathing from a boat's hard to beat, too," Charles supplemented.

"Aren't we going to have any lunch?" Bianca inquired plaintively.

We spread a rug for a tablecloth and another for her to

sit on. Despite the lateness of the season the stones were quite hot to the touch. I unwrapped the chicken and put the rolls on a napkin we had brought with us. Charles said proudly "I didn't forget the corkscrew when I was in the wineshop," and produced it; it was the kind that screws up into a little cylinder.

"Shall I open them both?" he said.

"One at a time," Bianca told him firmly. "Oliver, do you remember when we were on our honeymoon and we took a picnic from the hotel to Isola Bella, and as we got out of the boat you dropped one of the two bottles the hotel had given us? One was wine and one was beer . . ."

"And which was broken?" Charles inquired.

"Need you ask? The wine, of course. I don't like beer." She laughed. The sun and the excitement had brought color into her face; she looked handsome and gay. I could discern now the Bianca Oliver had married and lost within the year.

The chicken tasted as good as it looked, and it was obvious that Charles had a very acceptable knowledge of wine. This is the best day yet, I thought. I didn't even worry any more about Crook getting my message; somehow I thought today nothing could go wrong. It wasn't just the sun, the openness of everything, the casual lightness of heart of my companions, there seemed a positive promise in the air. Though it was the wrong time of year I thought of the words of the prophet: Rise up my love, my fair one, rise and come away, for the winter is over and past, the time of the singing of birds is come . . . I wasn't sure I'd got all the words in the right order, but the sense remained. One of the little boats bobbing near the shore was for sale. "Ninety pounds, is that a fair price?" Bianca said. Oliver told her it 'ud depend on the boat's condition, but it was about right. Charles opened the second bottle of wine, which was golden and not too dry. Oliver produced a melon with the air of a conjuror bringing a colored handkerchief from nowhere. Melons were Bianca's favorite fruit and this one was perfect, the flesh pale near the rind, a ripe gold where the seeds grew.

"All we need now is a cup of coffee," sighed Bianca as we wrapped the melon rinds in a sheet of paper. "Why didn't we bring a Thermos?"

"There's a coffee stall up aloft," said Charles lazily. "Wouldn't like to vouch for the coffee, though."

"It's probably all right," Bianca said.

"I wonder what they charge for those rowboats," speculated Oliver.

"You haven't got any fishing tackle," Bianca reminded him.

"I don't know why I never thought of going out before," Oliver said.

I unrolled my two bathing suits and Charles whistled. "When you're in your Gorgeous Gussie outfit you must let me take a snap," he said.

"I forgot the camera," I explained.

"I've got one," said Charles. "The foolproof variety that you can load even in sunlight."

We must have presented a very harmonious appearance, because there came through a moment of silence a woman's voice, indignant, rather whining, saying, "They seem to be enjoying it all right. I don't know why you always . . ." The voice died away again. "Blessed matrimony," said Charles. "Bianca, you don't really want that ghastly coffee, do you?"

"I really think I'll just ask about that boat," said Oliver softly.

"Come on, girl," Charles told me. He sprang to his feet and pulled me to mine. "We'll go and treat for four cups of poison."

Bianca's head turned sharply. "What made you say that?"

Charles looked confused. "Just a joke. What's biting her?" he asked as we made our way up the beach, the stones scuffing away from our shoes and falling in a series of little plops onto the slope below.

"Didn't you really know?" I asked. "About the first Mrs. Duncan? She died of an overdose of sleeping stuff—didn't Oliver tell you?"

He shook his head. "He's never mentioned his first wife. Why, did Bianca know her?"

"She was the nurse," I said briefly.

"Oh God!" said Charles. If he was acting, he was putting it over very well. He offered me his hand and drew me up the last steepest part of the beach. On the top the sun was even hotter than by the water side. There were more people on the benches than there had been. Charles nudged me. "He's there," he said. "Your conquest, I mean."

I turned, thinking he must be mistaken. But no, Mr. Penrose, his face buried in a newspaper, was sitting on a bench two or three yards from the coffee stall. An old, old woman in a long black dress, such as they must have worn in the days of Queen Alexandra, came mousing along the promenade and stopped nearby; she had a huge black hat trimmed with roses, and a parasol.

"I wonder what she's advertising," Charles murmured. "Or do you suppose she's expecting the Day of Judgment and wants to be first in the queue?" I don't think she could possibly have heard him but she turned and stared.

"If you want coffee," she said in a voice as rusty as a key that hasn't been turned for years, "there isn't any."

"It'll be ready in a few minutes," said the girl behind the stall. "I told you, there's been such a rush . . ."

"Is it good coffee?" the old witch asked, and the girl said tossing her head, "It all depends what you're used to."

"When I was your age I used to be offered champagne," announced the old woman. "Did you ever taste pink champagne? But no, of course you didn't. It's all that stuff they call Coke nowadays, and who wants to be offered that?"

Charles turned with a little bow. He'd been so charming and natural all day I had to keep reminding myself that he was only playing a part. He didn't bother to play it when we were alone together; there wasn't a trace of accent in his voice as he turned to the old woman, saying, "I can't offer you champagne, but I'd be honored if you'd have a cup of coffee with me."

"Very civil," said the shaking old voice, though it was remarkably deep for a woman's. "I wouldn't care to deny you an honor so easy to bestow."

While we waited for the coffee I saw Bianca resting tranquilly on the stones; Oliver was still talking to the boat man. When the coffee came the girl gave us our four cups on a tray. Charles paid for them and put down a shilling for the old woman.

"She looks half starved," he confessed as we moved away. "But there wasn't so much as a sandwich in that bar."

"She'd probably have felt insulted at that," I said.

"They've got some bathing huts here," said Charles. "Why don't you change into one of those?"

"I'll have my coffee first," I told him. "Anyway, I haven't brought my suit up."

Charles set the tray down beside Bianca and started to tell her about the old woman. "This is the day for turning up flat stones," he said, and immediately my mistrust revived itself.

"It's not so warm as I thought," declared Bianca. "I tried to signal to you when you were up there, but you were so deep in conversation—I wanted that fisherman's knit coat you put in the car for me."

"Can't I . . . ?" began Charles, but she said sharply, "No, Julie knows just where it is." I hurried up the beach and found the coat and stopped an instant to inquire about bathing huts on the way back. Oliver was returning from his conversation and said he hoped Bianca wouldn't mind, he'd hired a boat; if we liked we could bathe from it.

"Have your coffee hot," murmured Bianca. "Well, why not? The way the beach slopes must make it quite dangerous for bathing, but out there . . ."

"There could be currents," I suggested, and even Bianca looked startled.

"Not on this coast, surely. There's a coast guard or whatever they're called, we might ask him."

Charles strolled over, and a minute later we saw the man's face split with laughter. He asked me who'd been pulling my leg, Charles reported on his return. He says a kitten couldn't drown here, not if it knew how to swim.

Bianca was tasting the coffee critically. "I can't think what people put into cups to make a simple drink like coffee taste of absolutely nothing."

"There's your answer," said Charles. "They put in absolutely nothing."

"During the Boer War," contributed Oliver, "they learned to make a substitute coffee with eggshells."

This was so unexpected and sounded so absurd, we all began to laugh. Bianca said, "Lucky to have the eggs, it wasn't like that in the last war."

"Does anyone say they were hens' eggs?" asked Charles, and we speculated on the sort of coffee an ostrich egg, for instance, could be expected to produce.

"How many for the boat?" asked Oliver, laying his cup aside.

"I shall stay where I am," said Bianca at once. "Leave me your camera, Charles, and I'll take pictures of you all, swimming back like seals."

"Not me," said Oliver, "I shall be in the boat."

"I think I shall lie on the beach and sunbathe," I murmured. "It seems a shame to get that lovely suit wet."

Both the men went into fits of laughter. "I can't see how husbands can ever find marriage monotonous," said Charles, "You never know what's going to come next."

"Of course you must bathe, Julie," Bianca said. "What do you think is going to happen to me while you're all in the sea. The Loch Ness monster doesn't inhabit these waters, you know."

It made sense. Nothing could happen to her with both Oliver and Charles at a safe distance. I decided to swim shoreward as soon as I dived from the boat. I was a strong swimmer, and it should be easy for me to reach the stones before Oliver had a chance, though it was difficult to see what even a determined killer could do in such a public place. The nearest group to us was only a few paces away. I suppose I might have thought that they'd considered pulling off their plan by two stages, I mean, with me out of the way, Bianca would be the more defenseless.

"I'd come with you in the boat," Bianca said, "but who would look after all our gear. Besides, this is meant to be a holiday and rowing two females is quite hard work."

In the end she had her own way. Charles and Oliver rowed and I steered. The sea was calm as a millpond and blue as a jewel. I did look over my shoulder as we pulled away, in case Crook had put in a miraculous appearance, but there was no sign of him. We were some way from the shore when I remembered Penrose, that man of mystery, sitting on his bench on the promenade. I couldn't imagine how I could have forgotten, yet surely even he couldn't launch an attack in broad daylight. I was glad to remember we'd drunk the coffee before we set out in the boat. It seemed to me we were going a very long way from the shore. "Surely we're far enough?" I suggested. "If we're going to swim in—I'm a bit out of practice."

"I'll life-save you, darling," said Charles. "I've got a medal somewhere." All the same, Oliver stopped rowing and I slipped off the coat I was wearing over my suit and looked over the side. The sea was unbelievably blue and clear. I stared into the depths. There wasn't a wave or a movement.

"You ought to be able to see the bottom of the sea," I suggested. "Coral castles and fish never yet glimpsed by the eye of man."

"There's precious little never yet glimpsed by the eye of man," Charles assured me prosaically. "Who's that chap who's got a house on the sea bed? As for coral castles . . ."

"All right, all right," I said. "Didn't your mother ever read fairy tales to you?"

There was a sudden hard look on Charles's face. "Darling," he murmured, "how romantic can you get."

I felt rather foolish. For a moment I forgot I'd been

regarding him as a partner in a nameless crime, even felt compassion for him. An instant later I'd dived over the side into that blue world. The water was a little colder than I'd anticipated, but had a buoyancy I hadn't expected either. I remembered hearing that in the Dead Sea it's impossible to submerge because it's full of salt. Perhaps there was some peculiar quality about this water, too. After a minute or so I turned on my back and floated. There were no other boats very near, and the people on the shore seemed very far away. Sometimes I'd tried to imagine what eternity might be like—impossible, of course, the finite mind couldn't hope to grasp it. Ever and ever and ever forever—no time, no future, only a perpetual present, the eternal day that never becomes tomorrow. Floating there, under that bright shadowless sky, blue water as far as I could see, a heaven filled with light over my head, I thought perhaps this—this—might be a foretaste. For that short moment I was freed from fear for myself, for Bianca, for the whole tormented uncertain world. A long way off I heard a motorboat, a voice far away as a gnat's traveled across the water, but too far away to disturb my sense of enclosed peace.

There was a violent splash behind me and I thought, Well, Charles isn't such a performer as he lets on, because a good diver cleaves the water, and it closes up behind him silently. A good dive is one of the most beautiful sights imaginable. I flapped my arms to turn myself where I could see him surface, offer him a word of demure congratulation, only that word was never spoken. Because it wasn't Charles in the water, but Oliver. He wasn't bathing, either. He must have tipped out of the boat, though it wasn't very easy to see how this could happen on so calm a day. He didn't seem a very expert swimmer either, but Charles was there, leaning down, an oar in his hand. I saw Oliver put out his hand to grip the blade of the oar, and what I saw next was unbelievable. I saw the blunt end of the oar pressed against Oliver's throat, and Charles deliberately pushing him under the water! I said it was unbelievable. They mightn't be estimable characters, and I didn't trust either of them an inch, but they were partners. I turned over and swam a few strokes. Charles was down on his knees in the boat, leaning out. Anyone from the shore or from any distance would suppose he was trying to rescue his friend. But I saw Oliver's head slowly submerge.

"Stop!" I shouted. "You're drowning him."

I thought perhaps someone would hear, would come up

to help, but all the other boats were too far away. Besides, when you're enjoying yourself, making holiday, you don't really notice anyone else, and screams like mine were all part of the picture. "Ow, you're killing me!" I'd heard a girl shout that while we were having our picnic, but she didn't want any assistance. It was all part of the game. I was wondering when this situation stopped being a game and turned into black earnest. The coast guard might say there was insufficient current to deter a kitten, but it seemed to be pulling pretty hard now. I was thrashing through the water, making practically no progress. I thought I had the picture in my mind. Charles was the double agent, playing at being Oliver's ally, but actually with an eye on the unshared spoils. As Oliver's widow, Bianca would be a comparatively rich woman, eminently marriageable to an adventurer like Charles Hunter. No one knew better than I how he could deploy his charm. I hadn't a doubt that he saw himself in Oliver's shoes within the year. And after that? It was like the famous stone sending out ripple after ripple till they lap the shore. I wondered if there had been a Mrs. Charles Hunter who had died rather unexpectedly . . .

At this stage I realized that if I continued to try and assist Oliver I should simply be playing into Charles's hands. There might be a few acid comments when it became known that of the three of us only Charles had survived, but he'd soon live that down. And if there should be any bruising on Oliver's body, well, that had occurred while he struggled and Charles went into his life-saving act. Before I'd reached this conclusion I had turned and was making for the shore that seemed further away than ever. I knew that unless Oliver could save himself, he was doomed. My intervention couldn't help him now. And my job was to get back to Bianca. Going through that calm sea was like trying to swim through treacle. I can't explain it, but every ounce of energy seemed to have deserted me. I once saw a famous runner within a hundred yards of completing the course, well in the lead, suddenly come to a dead stop, just moving his legs as you might see an up-ended beetle do, only with less energy. He knew his rival was coming up behind him, the goal was within easy distance, and he struggled and strained and couldn't move. It was one of the most painful things I ever saw.

I remembered him now. Every time I lifted my arms the water washed them down again. I knew I wasn't progressing at all; at one time I wondered if I was even facing in the right direction. Then I heard the sound of someone coming up behind me and I turned my head to say, "Get me ashore," and it was Charles. I couldn't believe it was going to end like this, because naturally I realized he couldn't afford to let me return and say what I'd seen. It seemed such a waste, though, when I'd survived so much—the Marchesa's death, Florian's defection, the plane crash, the damaged car.

"Take it easy," said Charles's voice in my ear. "Just relax, and I'll get us both back. I promised I'd life-save you, remember?"

"Oliver," I said, and he told me soothingly, "He's okay, you don't have to worry about him. Leaned too far over the side and went in with a plop."

But of course I knew that wasn't true, because why hadn't the boat capsized? And why hadn't Charles saved him by grabbing at his shoulder or arm? "Relax, I said," repeated Charles's voice in my ear. "Don't struggle, you'll only make things harder."

"He's dead," I whispered.

"He's okay," said Charles.

But I twisted my head and I could see the boat now, floating upside down, and no sign of Oliver anywhere.

"They've got him, he's all right," insisted Charles in the same patient voice.

"You mean, the fishes have," I said, and I began to laugh. The water came into my mouth and I choked instead.

"I can see you mean to give the fishes a field day," muttered Charles, and now his voice was grim. "Lie still or I'll have to knock you over the head."

My pet devil wouldn't let me keep quiet. "Like you did Oliver?" I said. "Only you haven't got the oar now, have you?"

Charles was a magnificent swimmer; I'm not bad myself in the ordinary way, but he cleft the water as easily as an oar blade. The odd thing was that though he swam so strongly we didn't seem to be getting any nearer the shore. I saw a spot in the distance, a motorboat, I thought and opened my mouth to hail it. In an instant Charles's hand came over my lips; I felt my head sinking into the water. It rushed into my eyes, into my nose, then I came up again. Charles said, "Don't do that again, it'll be the end if you do." I thought it was going to be the end, anyway. They say drowning people see their past lives flash in front of them, but mine didn't. I thought about Bianca—I'd failed her as I'd failed everyone else—the Marchesa, Ada, Mr. Crook—because naturally they'd expect me to behave with a little sense—myself. I didn't count Oliver. Whatever came to him he'd asked for it.

The roar that had been increasing during the past minute or so, or however long it took me to think all this up, time seemed to have stopped, became louder. It was like a motorcycle; quite soon the noise would deafen me, only it wasn't the noise that would be responsible for my death, but the sea—the sea and Charles. I wasn't struggling any more; it wasn't that my will acquiesced, as they say the wills of the dying often do, but I simply had no more strength left in me. At any instant I knew my head would go under, but actually it seemed to lift a little. I opened my eyes—I suppose I'd shut them without realizing it—and a great wash of water came over my face. And that was the last thing I saw. Except for that minute or so of panic, when I'd struggled to survive, dying had proved a very peaceful affair.

9

IN ROMANTIC NOVELS when the heroine comes around from a swoon her first words always are: Where am I? I was no heroine and I didn't ask that question, because to a nurse's eye there could be no doubt at all where I was. I was in a hospital or nursing home, and it occurred to me vaguely that something of the same kind had happened to me before. I turned my head, wondering if I were alone, and "Praise the pigs!" said a voice as loud as a booming clock, and there was the most comforting face in the world, better at that moment than a mother, a lover or even one's own child, a great round face like the westering sun. Then a voice which didn't belong to the face said briskly, "She's coming round." And Crook's voice, unmistakable this time, observed, "About time, too, seeing I charge by the hour. Now, sugar, take it easy, and don't let anyone hustle you. Chaps going up a mountain have to take time out for training and that's what you're going to do, go right up a mountain. Now, Sister . . ."

I thought at first he was speaking to me, but it appeared he was addressing someone on the further side of the bed. I moved my eyes languidly.

"You have a visitor," said Sister, crisp as a goffered shirt.

"She can see that," Crook pointed out.

"I mean, in the corridor."

I supposed it was Bianca, but for the moment I didn't want to see anyone—except Crook, of course. I was busy chasing memory; it was like running after a dog in a wood, where the dog goes at twice your pace. If I didn't actually catch up with it, at least I came within shouting distance.

"Bianca," I recalled. "I sent you a message."

"And I came like the wind. Mind you, I had my watchdog on the trail."

"Another dog?" I felt puzzled.

"Name of Penrose."

"Was he *yours?*"

"That's right."

"Did Charles know?"

"He thought he was a D.O.M. with a lech for you."

"He was on the promenade when we went for the coffee."

"He saw you."

I let Penrose go. "Bianca," I whispered again.

"She's being looked after," said Crook. "You don't have to worry about her any more."

"And Charles? He . . ."

"Fit as a flea," said Crook. "And about as welcome."

I thought again. "Oliver Duncan?"

Crook's big face clouded. "You can't win 'em all, sugar," he said.

I took a tremendous stride and practically came up with my quarry.

"It was Charles," I proclaimed. "He drowned him."

"That was the object of the exercise," said Crook.

"Oliver and me—both?"

"That's right."

"Wouldn't he be afraid of what Bianca would think?"

Crook shook his big head. "Sugar," he told me gently, "it was her idea."

I looked across the room to where Sister was listening, with ears as flapping as an elephant's on the other side of the bed.

"I'm not the only one who's confused," I told her. "Bianca was the one who was threatened—her husband—"

"You'd better tell that to the police, hadn't you?" suggested Sister. "He's waiting outside."

The very mention of the police brought back other memories, the days at the palazzo while we were waiting to know whether the Marchesa would live or die, and afterward whether a charge would be brought, "No," I said, "no. I can't see the police."

"Not till the doctor gives the say-so," said Mr. Crook soothingly. "And he ain't here yet."

I supposed I was in a private room; perhaps the police had insisted on that, because somehow I was going to be involved in Oliver's death, and you can't have a criminal mixing with decent citizens.

"What is this place?"

"The Dovercrest Nursing Home. We live and learn, don't we? First time I ever knew a dove had a crest. And the doctor's on his way."

"What am I doing here?"

"You gave us quite a turn," Crook said. "Baby, you sure do like water. You soaked it up like an aspidistra. That was what Lady Macbeth was counting on, of course."

I shook my head. I might be snugged up in a nursing home, but to all intents and purposes I was still at sea.

"Comprenez?" Crook inquired of Sister, but Sister simply said, "I want that policeman out of my corridor and I want this bed for a post-operation case, and I don't mind how soon."

"You'd make Florence Nightingale turn in her grave," Crook reproved her. "Give the policeman a nice cup of tea and tell him to come back in the morning."

"He wants to see Miss Taylor tonight."

"He's got a long wait coming," said Crook outrageously. "Miss Taylor's been underground these six months past."

"Now you're getting me confused," said Sister.

"That makes two of you, and if we let the rozzer in now it'll make three. The young lady can't answer any questions till she knows the answers."

"She's only got to tell him the facts."

"She don't know the facts."

(At this point I began to go off, and although I heard the words, they didn't register until much later.)

"You mean, you're going to instruct her?"

"I represent her. You can hear for yourself how muddled she is. She actually believes she's been defendin' a victimized wife from a murderous spouse all these months, whereas actually it's been the other way round. Like looking in a glass, if you get me. Come outside a minute, Sister, there's something I want to say to you and I don't want the patient to hear."

I don't know what he said to her, but next time she came in she was positively smiling.

"Where on earth did you meet a man like that?" she asked me, but quite pleasantly, and I said, "He was on the plane and then on the train and then, I suppose, in the boat. I'm not quite sure about that, though."

"He's quite right, you're not yourself yet," Sister said, not realizing I hadn't been myself for the past six months. "Drink this, and Mr. Crook will be back in the morning."

"And the doctor?" I hazarded.

"There won't be any need to see him tonight."

"What time is it?" I asked, and with that fatuousness too often employed by those in charge of the helpless she answered, "Time for you to go to sleep."

I suppose my training made me react automatically. Anyway, the next time I opened my eyes the room was full of sun. Crook came in like an actor on his cue.

"If you want to do any primping, sugar," he said, "now's the time, because that rozzer's back kicking his heels outside, and he'll get more than his heels kicked if he loiters much longer. Remember, he ain't asking for theories, and you never want to give the police more than they demand and sometimes not all of that. I'm stopping, because I'm your lawyer, but I'm not prompting you. I wasn't there at the time, not till just before the fall of the curtain, that is, and so I can't give him the facts."

"I'm not any too sure of them myself," I confessed. "Last night you said . . ."

"Never mind what I said last night. He ain't going to ask you about that. That comes under the heading of theory. There's only three answers—Yes. No. And I don't remember. Stick to those and you'll do fine."

The policeman was a sober middle-aged man who looked like a stage parson.

He asked me if I was Julie Taylor and I caught Crook's eye and said yes. He asked me if I remembered what happened on the afternoon in question and I said well, some of it, anyhow. He asked if I would tell him in my own words, and reminded me I might well be giving the same evidence on oath in due course. Crook said, "Oliver came in this morning on the early tide. There's bound to be an inquest, and seeing you were one of the last to see him alive . . ." The policeman said, "I'll ask the questions, sir, if you don't mind," so I told him about the picnic and he asked me what we'd had to eat. That was easy, too. I added that we'd had wine that Charles bought at Hotham St. Michael, which is the market town of Hotham St. Mary, and coffee from the kiosk. Then the three of us had gone out, leaving Bianca on the beach. I had been the first to leave the boat, and quite soon afterward I heard a splash and saw Oliver in the water. I hadn't worried at first, because I thought Charles would pull him back into the boat, and then I'd realized that he was doing just the opposite.

The policeman said, "Do you mean he was trying to prevent his regaining the boat?" and I said, "He was trying to push him under water."

He asked me how near I was and how good my sight was and was I certain, and then could I suggest any reason why . . . Crook interrupted to say that wasn't a proper question. I was only there to answer statements of fact, and not to theorize. He said it wasn't the duty of the public to try and do the police out of their pensions by solving their cases for them. Then I told him that though I hadn't a witness, I was prepared to state under oath that Charles had also tried to drown me, and told him about Charles putting his hand over my mouth. The policeman didn't look shocked or startled; he said that tied up with the eivdence this gentleman gave. I said, "What gentleman?" and Crook broke into a roar of laughter that must have been heard in the street outside.

"A very good question, sugar. What he means is me and my watchdog, we were in the lifeboat."

The policeman said, "What lifeboat?" and Crook told him it was a case of angels unawares, and just as some chaps didn't look like angels, so some lifeboats looked like motor launches.

I had a sudden moment of revelation, and exclaimed, "Was that the noise I heard—the boat zooming up? I thought it was the end of the world."

"I wouldn't be surprised," said Crook. "Damn near cut Charles's head off. He had to go underwater to save himself, and you'd wonder he thought it was worth the effort."

At this stage the door opened and someone came in. The policeman said, "Do you mind, sir?" and a voice I'd heard before retorted, "I'm Miss Taylor's doctor, I can't have my patient upset. Are you nearly through?"

I was surprised to see that it was Dr. Gregg. I exclaimed, before I could stop myself, "What on earth are you doing here?" and he said, "I happen to be a doctor, this is a nursing home and you are my patient." He felt my pulse and told the policeman, "I can't risk another rise in temperature. Are you nearly through?"

The policeman looked through his notes and asked me if I had anything to add, and I thought and said well, I remembered asking Charles what about Oliver, and he had said he was all right, but when I looked back I could see the boat capsized. Then Charles had said relax, I've got to get us both back.

The policeman asked if I would call myself a strong swimmer, and I said yes, but I supposed I was out of practice, because I seemed to have no power at all. Crook said even a denizen of the deep might have his work cut out to make his finny nest with all that dope inside him, and I gaped and asked him what he was talking about.

Dr. Gregg said sharply, "You can see she can't tell you any more," and I said were they sure Bianca was being properly looked after, because with Charles still at large and me in the hospital—and Crook said that was okay, he wasn't, Charles, he meant, and at large. At the moment he was being held on a murder charge. The policeman said this was very improper, and Crook said, "You leave that to the man who brought the charge." I didn't know until he told me that a private citizen can bring a murder charge against another private citizen. Then he turned back to the policeman and said, "You can see she's in no state even to add two and two at the moment. I'll guarantee to produce her when she's sent for, meantime she'll be staying here."

All this had taken much longer than I realized and Crook said he'd leave me for a while to sort things out. I had a wonderful sense of relaxation. Sister came in to ask how I was while I had my lunch. She said, "It makes a change, doesn't it, having a character like that about the place?" By which I knew she meant Crook. Doctors and patients are three-a-penny, but Crook was in a class all by himself.

They held the inquest the following day; all I had to do was repeat the statement I'd made in the nursing home. When I went into the witness box I was startled to see Ada Holloway in the court, and then wondered why I should be surprised. It was so obviously the place one would have expected to find her. What surprised me more was that Bianca didn't show up; I supposed she was medically unfit. It wasn't till we were well on in the inquiry that I realized she was being accused with Charles of Oliver Duncan's murder.

Ada Holloway was worth her weight in gold then. "She's going to take you under her wing," Crook said, "and she's got a wing a fighter bomber might envy."

It was she and Crook who later put me in the picture, as they say. He'd prevailed on Sister to let me occupy my room at the nursing home for one more night. "No sense us rescuing her from a watery grave if she's to be submerged by the press," Crook pointed out.

"What difference is one night going to make?" Sister demanded, but Crook said she'd be surprised.

"It's like I've always told you," Crook explained. "It ain't just the facts that matter, it's how you arrange them. You had your facts right, sugar, there was a would-be murderer at large in that house, only it wasn't Oliver Duncan."

"You mean it was Bianca? I still find that difficult to accept. I mean, what made you . . . ?"

"I'm a reasonable chap," said Crook modestly, "and I like things according to nature. I mean, to my mind it ain't according to nature if it rains when the sun's shining. I know the answer to that is it's April weather, but it still ain't reasonable. Here you had a dame who was so much afraid her ever-loving was going to drive her underground, she had to have a paid guard—you, sugar—to stand between her and her fate. But when she's given the go-ahead sign, told to get out, go south, find the sun, put a couple of hundred miles between her and murder, what does she do? She hums and ha's and says no, she won't be druv out. Now most people wouldn't need driving, they'd jump at the chance."

"She said it was her house and why should she be chased out of it."

"According to her she was expecting to be chased into the grave seven days out of seven. That's Point One. Point Two—what did Oliver stand to gain by her dyin' on him in mysterious circumstances? A chap has a job to live that kind of thing down the first time, and we know he crossed two counties to escape the gossip. Just what was said I suppose we'll never know. But twice in a matter of—what?—three, four?—years, that's a mug's game. He'd need a pretty strong motive . . ."

"There was Fiona Lane."

"I've never been a young girl," acknowledged Crook handsomely, "but I don't know that I'd go for a chap who's already scored a couple of ducks in the Matrimonial Test. You don't have to stick out for a century, but you do like to see a few runs on the board. Anyway, he was a lot too old for her. And there's another thing. Here's this chap, not quite in the tycoon class maybe, but not too far off, put quite a lot of his competitors out of the running from all accounts, yet when it comes to a simple job like shoving a woman off a cliff or under a bus, he makes a hash of it each time. You know, I knew from the start this case reminded me of something. It happened on the Continong, five, six, years ago?—I don't remember. I was bein' a tourist, fact, me, one of these coach trips, rush in from A to B, and before you've had time to down a pint you set off for C. There was this dame, rushed at me, caught my arm. Oh, Mr. Crook, I don't know what to do, my husband means to murder me. Found him through a matrimonial ad. made over her little bit to him—oh, she told it very nice. She had the cliff walk, too, the mixed medicine bottles—did Bianca have them?"

"Hers were mushrooms," I reminded him.

"Yes, well, that showed a bit of originality."

"She really did have a poisoned one."

"I'll say. But darling Oliver didn't give it to her."

I thought for a minute. "You mean, she did it herself? That was taking a terrific risk."

"Nothing is for free," quoted Crook. "And having been a nurse, and knowing she had another nurse on the premises, she probably realized just how far she could go. Now use your thinking-piece, sugar. You knew you hadn't picked a deathly nightcap—is that what you called them?—and nor didn't Oliver, but she had plenty of time while you were out of sight . . ."

I remembered I'd found her walking up and down the road, and I remembered, too, the clump of deadly nightcaps Oliver had shown me before we started to pick. She'd have to show some subtlety first to get the poisonous fungus cooked and, second, to make sure it got onto the right plate, but the chance would be there. I was setting the table, Oliver was opening the wine—I remembered how she'd fixed on a particular plate—and I remembered, too, how quickly she'd recovered. I think that piece of acting shocked me more even than her attempts on my life. Because I didn't doubt now that my near-fall from the window was her work. Charles would be told to occupy Oliver while she came up the stairs, quick as a cat, ruthless as a cat, too. She had a certain harsh courage, you had to admit that. She took chances.

"Suppose I hadn't been able to get a doctor right away?" I asked. "Suppose I hadn't waked . . ."

Crook shrugged his big shoulders. "Then it 'ud be a case of 'The angels in Heaven are singing today, Here's Johnny, here's Johnny, here's Johnny.' Bianca 'ud give them a bit of trouble, wouldn't it? It don't scan. Of course it was her opened the window on the—what's that fancy word you used?"

"Entresol," I said.

Crook snorted. "I can't see why the English language ain't good enough for English men and women. You played right into her hands by kneeling up on the seat, but if you hadn't she'd have managed to give you a shove, wouldn't have been above suggesting you took a floater all on your owney-oh, if she was pushed. Charles 'ud back her up, Charles knew your guilty secret."

"I wonder what saved me," I said.

"I'd say you had Oliver to thank, that poor decent chap. Came out of the library a thought too soon, saw the pair and thought Bianca was tryin' to save you. What's known as doin' good unawares. Well, let's hope it's counted to him for righteousness wherever he may be."

"But even if she had been sucuessful, there'd still be you to cope with, and Ada. She knew about both of you."

"You mention my name?"

I thought back. Had I? "Yes, I think so."

"Oh, mate," Crook sighed, "you do like taking chances. She mightn't have heard it before, but an out-and-out no-good like Charles 'ud know it at once. As for Ada, dames like your Mrs. Duncan are inclined to underrate these old warhorses. They may not win any beauty competitions, but they still have hooves and teeth and they don't scruple to make use of them. Any other little point you want clearing up?"

"I still don't quite get the motive," I said. "All that risk, two deaths, no." I looked at him. "You think she had something to do with the first Mrs. Duncan dying when she did?"

"I'm darned tooting she did," said Crook. "If Oliver had given her the overdose the whole lot would have been in the milk. There was always the chance dear Nurse would come back so late her patient 'ud be asleep and a shame to wake her, and next day she'd have to start all over again. No, she put a normal dose in the milk, knowing he'd be the one to give it, and when she came back it 'ud be, Oh, darling, how awful of me, have you waited up, did you have your pills? No? Take them now. Positively no deception, help yourself, here's the water, drink it down, there's a love, night-night—and good-bye, Evelyn D. Mind you, she must have put the wind up darling Oliver just a leetle to get that European vacation out of him directly after the funeral. Probably thought it cheap at the price to have her out of the road, and then back she comes and—he'd have no more chance against a pro like that than a baby rabbit against a full-grown anaconda. Does it occur to you that before he'd start thinking of murder he'd suggest a divorce? She could have taken him for half his kingdom, if he was really as sold as Julie here says. But no, never a whisper."

"And she took that risk on the chance of marrying Oliver, say, a year hence?"

"She'd framed him very nice, remember. Maybe she hinted that day at Salisbury—and that meeting was no accident—that there was talk and what would happen if the case was reopened, she didn't wish him anything but good, of course—or it could have happened the way Sugar heard, she pulled out the soft stops and his soft heart did the rest."

"And if her plan had worked?" I insisted. "Did she really mean to marry Charles?"

"I'd say Charles really meant to marry her. In my job you meet all kinds and you get to recognize certain types, and the minute I heard about Charles I thought he sounded like a professional widower. Mind you, I daresay he is a widower—does anyone know? Only if he suggested puttin' up the banns, after a decent interval, that is, she don't have much choice."

"But she hardly knew him," I protested.

"Who says?"

"He came to the house looking for Julie Taylor."

"How come he'd ever heard of Julie Taylor? No, sugar, we know she'd rumbled you. She knew you weren't a little schoolmarm from the other side of the world, talking English as good as me and nursing like a pro. She puts her boyfriend on to asking a few questions. After all, if you ain't J.T., you know a lot about her, got her passport, her photos. So—you met up with her somewhere."

"And she—or Charles—followed up inquiries and found that there had been two girls on the plane that crashed —yes, I see. If I wasn't Julie I had to be Solange Peters."

"Which was jam for her, because it meant you'd fight shy of the police, even if you did get a bit suspicious."

"I'm still not sure where Charles comes in, though."

"No. How about the buddy she went to London to meet the night Evelyn Duncan got her quietus?"

"But that was a woman," I protested.

"Who says?"

"She always spoke as if it were." Only it was true, Bianca had never actually said she and I or Joyce and I, or . . . "I suppose I just took it for granted."

"Didn't stop to wonder where Bianca got the extra dope for Evelyn? Well, maybe it did come out of her own store, but it's interesting to know that Charles works with a pharmaceutical firm. Getting a little bit extra 'ud be child's play to him."

"All the same, it was pretty crazy. Suppose Oliver had struggled more, he was quite a vigorous man, they couldn't have known he'd go under so easily."

"No?" said Crook. "How much did you struggle?"

I remembered my sense of extraordinary lassitude as I tried to swim for shore.

"It was something about the tides," I said vaguely.

"Oh, come to the point," cried Ada, speaking for the first time. "Why not tell the girl the facts, instead of spinning them out like some old spinster describing a love affair she never had? Not in the tides, not in the water at all, in the coffee. You and Oliver were both doped to the eyelids, and clever Mr. Crook is going to be able to prove that in court."

"The coffee!" I exclaimed. It couldn't be anything else.

"That's right. Now, you'll be asked about this, and don't tell them anything you don't remember."

"But I do remember," I said. "Charles and I fetched the coffee and he said why didn't I stop on the way back and get into a suit in one of the bathing huts. But I hadn't brought the suit with me. And as soon as we reached Bianca she sent me to fetch her coat from the car."

"And you went?"

"Oliver was still chaffering about the boat. I didn't see how Charles could do anything with so many people around . . ."

"And when you came back Bianca gave you your coffee—right?"

"That's right. She and Charles had started on theirs."

"Well, naturally, it would never do to get the cups mixed. They must have planned something of this kind when they prepared the picnic. Of course, Oliver played right into their hands, first by offering to come and then by hiring the boat and offering to take you both out. But even if he hadn't they'd have found some way. Bianca would have suggested the boat herself. When Oliver started getting drowsy she'd have sent you two to swim—that was the way Maudie worked it—my continental line-up, remember? She'd have managed to tip the boat, she'd have screamed for help, you'd both have come back—they hadn't a scruple between them. By the time the bodies were washed ashore there'd be precious little trace of drugs, and of course the coffee cups would have been collected and washed."

"And, of course," said Ada, "they couldn't guess Mr. Crook would be around."

"Thank Sugar for that," said Mr. Crook. "Minute I got

your message you couldn't see me and the Superb for dust. By the time I arrived, my watchdog was down on the beach; he'd seen the party setting out and he didn't like the look of it at all. Trouble was the last motorboat had just been snapped up by some tourist, and of course he wouldn't have stood an earthly in a rowboat, specially on his own. This chap wouldn't yield to him—very ladidah he was, till I came storming down and told him if he didn't let us have preference I'd have him cited as accessory for murder."

"You really told him that?" I gasped.

"It has happened and I was not there," Ada mourned. And Crook grinned.

Only none of it seemed amusing to me.

"There's times when truth is your only hope," Crook said. "Well, he was fascinated, of course. I mean, it's not much of a lark for a chap to sit around on a beach with his missus, and everyone likes the sound of murder. I told him if he could swim he could come, too. His wife's face would have made the Medusa look like a sucking dove. Never any harm having an extra witness, and off we pushed. Mind you, we were too late to do anything for Oliver, and, anyway, he wasn't my client. By the time we were near enough to go into our Grace Darling act, Charles was onto Corpse Number Two. You can't really blame Charles, though I'm sure Bianca does, for letting go. A charging motorboat would test anyone's spirit. Anyway, we got you out and came hell for leather back to shore. Cream of the joke is I heard our third passenger say to Charles, 'If you're going in for life-saving, you should learn the art. You could have drowned that girl.' We found a real reception committee waiting for us on the beach. Everything was laid on. Ambulance came at the double. Fourteen people all wanting to practice their first aid on you, sugar, and finish what Charles had begun. Our passenger's wife dashed up to say, 'What about me and the children?' and if he could have sent her to join Oliver at that moment I don't believe he'd have hesitated. And of course Bianca going into an act that wouldn't have shamed Mrs. Pat Campbell."

"You'd remember her, of course," said Ada maliciously.

" 'Where's my husband? He must have got cramp? Is Charles . . . ?' And running down to the water's edge to greet Charles—we hadn't stopped to bring him back. She wanted a word with him, of course, but Penrose stopped that. He was waiting, too, and all Charles could say was, 'I'm sorry, Bianca, I did my best, I swear I did,' and she kept saying, 'I'm sure you did, Charles, I'm sure you did . . .' Only she seemed a bit calm for someone who'd just seen her ever-loving flounder to a watery grave."

"I suppose you heard this from about fifty yards away?" suggested Ada.

"I told you, Penrose never left his side, and in the general tamarsha, Penrose slipped back and secured the four cups and popped them into his little Gladstone bag. He takes it everywhere, you'd be surprised some of the things that bag's contained. Those cups have been through the mincer . . ."

"Don't tell me," I said. "Of course they found traces of dope in two . . ."

"The ones you and Oliver had handled. And they found the rest of the stuff in a little bottle marked aspirin in Bianca's bag. It's hard to see how even she's going to talk her way out of that."

"What'll happen to them?" I said.

Crook looked surprised. "Not my worry, sugar. They ain't my clients. Interesting to know who gets Oliver's estate, though, seeing murderers can't inherit."

A small silence fell. Then I said. "There's still one thing you haven't quite cleared up. The car whose brakes failed—who was responsible for that? I thought Charles or Oliver, most likely Charles."

Crook pulled his long chin. "We-ell, I don't know. I like the evidence of my eyes myself. Didn't notice his car anywhere around? No? Then I'd say that was Bianca. She'd tailored the situation to suit herself. Oliver brings out the car, you go in to phone the chemist—she probably knew that's generally a lengthy affair. Oliver's prowling like a leopard waiting for his call— And she'd been a nurse accustomed to taking a car around at all hours, probably knew as much about its entrails as she did about the human variety."

"And she meant me . . . ?" I couldn't accept it.

"Not you, sugar. Oliver. She can't go because of the rain, you can't go because you're needed in the sickroom, but Oliver's there, his car's under cover, take mine, there's a dear, won't take you above twenty minutes, stuff's all ready and waiting . . . Must have given her a nasty shock when she learned you were at the wheel. Must have hoped, too, it 'ud be curtains for car and driver. Not that she didn't like you, Julie, in her Cynara fashion, but you have to look after Number One. And then the interfering doctor spikes her guns. I'd have given a golden sovereign to see her face when you came through on the blower—must have wondered if you were in touch from another world."

"She meant me to drown, though," I said.

"Well, sugar, you cant make an omelette without breakin' eggs and she was an ambitious kind of a cook. A sticker, too; you have to hand it to her, she knew her own mind. She meant to get Oliver both ways, first in church and then in the churchyard. It's all in the Good Book, sugar, 'whatsoever thou doest, that do with all thy might.' "

The door suddenly burst open and Dr. Gregg came storming in. "Sister said I'd find you here," he said. He looked at me, but he spoke to Crook. "This may be a picnic for you," he began, "but Julie happens to be my patient, and we've had enough funeral processions in this affair as it is. Can't you give the girl a break? She looks dead to the world." He glared at Ada, as if he thought she was some bird of prey. "Gab, gab, gab," he said. "Very amusing story for you, I daresay. How I nailed another murder by Arthur G. Crook. Does it occur to you this girl's flesh and blood?"

"She's going to have quite a job persuading the authorities of that," Crook told him, completely unmoved. "According to them, Solange Peters stopped bein' flesh and blood six months ago."

"You're her lawyer, aren't you?" Gregg snapped. "Right then. It's up to you to straighten things out. You can't expect everything that comes your way to be fun."

"It's going to cost you plenty," Ada assured me in sympathetic tones. "If you've got to bring your witnesses from Rome. No one in England can speak for you."

"I should koko," said Crook. "Let the taxpayer foot the bill. He'll get his money's worth out of the press. What do you bet those two tear each other to shreds in the witness book?"

"When it's all over," I suggested to Ada, "perhaps you could find me a job in your drapery business. No one will want me for a nurse after this. Two spectacular deaths . . ."

"What use 'ud you be to me?" asked Ada, honestly amazed.

"Ask the doctor," suggested Crook.

"Thanks a lot," snarled Gregg. He seemed in a thoroughly edgy mood. "I'm quite capable of doing my own courting, you know."

"You take him up on that, dear," said Ada swiftly. "You're not likely to get a better offer."

"When a chap asks to put his head in the lion's mouth it's

a pretty choosy lion that won't let him," amplified Crook. He turned to Ada. "This is no place for us, sugar," he said, "and they've been open some time."

At the door he turned. "We'll set 'em up for you at The Blue Boar," he offered. "Don't forget you ain't in the metrop now, and they put up the bars at two-thirty."

"Joker!" muttered Dr. Gregg, shoving his hands in his pockets. "All one big laugh to him, I suppose."

The Laughing Cavalier, I thought, but I had the good sense not to say it. There was no mistaking what he had said, but he looked anything but loverlike, standing there with a two-inch-deep scowl on his face. The well-known British phlegm, I imagined, wondering if I'd ever really understand my own compatriots. They seemed to live most of their lives in a sort of code. Involuntarily I grinned.

"You too?" barked Dr. Gregg. "What is it about him that gets you all running? Arthur Crook, the human alligator."

"Oh no," I exclaimed, rather shocked. "He's an old sweetie." The real Julie had said that, I recalled.

"You want your eyes examined," said Dr. Gregg. "You know, I've always sworn, come hell or high water, I wouldn't marry a nurse. I've seen too many good chaps ruined that way. Shop, shop, shop, morning, noon and night. Any story you tell they can cap."

"Not me," I said. "My nursing career hasn't exactly been a shining success. I was thinking of trying for something else."

"I know of an opening," said Gregg—I hadn't yet started thinking of him as Lionel—"I knew it the first day I saw you with Mrs. Duncan. And that's another thing that old phony" (he meant Dr. Mitchison) "has let me in for."

"Aren't you taking rather a lot for granted?" I said, a good deal more coolly than I felt. "It takes two to make a bargain."

"Okay," he said. "Tell me to pack my traps and get out. Go on."

I tried to say it, really I did; because if this was a proposal of marriage it was rather less romantic than buying a bag of buns. But it was no use. I knew—like Crook, with one of those hunches that never let him down—that this man, glaring, unwilling even, was right for me. I wondered why I hadn't known it all along, now it was so obvious. Mind you, I didn't experience the wild ecstasy I'd known with Florian, I didn't want to yell or wave a flag or put my head out of a window and shout the news to all the passers-by—I just felt like someone coming home. I knew that though there was a lot of tanglewood to be cleared away, when I'd hacked my way through he'd be waiting on the other side, if he hadn't actually been with me with another sickle slicing through the undergrowth.

"I wonder if this is how a butterfly feels," I said.

"A butterfly? You won't find many of those in a doctor's household."

"When it emerges at last from its chrysalis and finds the world is full of color and light," I explained. "You are offering me a permanent job?" I added. "I've dotted about from pillar to post long enough."

He reassured me very satisfactorily as to that.

"Everyone will think you're mad, wanting to marry the notorious Julie Taylor," I reminded him.

"I don't," he said, calmly—well, fairly calmly. "I'm proposing to a girl called Solange Peters. I daresay Julie was a peach, and it was too bad what happened to her, but that's past history and not my history."

"You're not going to be able to escape it," I warned him. "It won't be a picnic . . ." I stopped abruptly. But Lionel didn't seem to notice.

"Picnics are for layabouts and kids," he said. "Anyway, that'll be Crook's headache."

It's only fair that Crook should have the last word. When Lionel said, "I suppose we might as well go along and tell them they can start saving for a wedding present," we hurried round to The Blue Boar and found Ada and her escort looking about as cheerful as a pair of professional mutes, with an unopened bottle of champagne on the table between them.

"You've taken your time," Crook said. "Hope I'm never on your operating table. How do you open that thing?"

Lionel showed him in a way that attracted the attention of everyone else in the bar.

Crook screwed up his big nose, opened his mouth and tipped the stuff down. "The things I do for my clients!" he groaned. "Sugar, let's you and me go to the bar and have an honest drink."

I suppose they went, though I didn't see them go. "It's the sun," I explained. "It's in my eyes." It wasn't my fault that everyone else thought it was raining.

››› If you've enjoyed this book and would like to discover more great vintage crime and thriller titles, as well as the most exciting crime and thriller authors writing today, visit: ›››

The Murder Room
Where Criminal Minds Meet

themurderroom.com

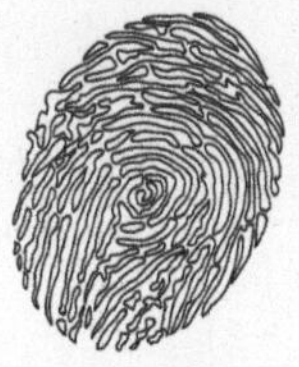

www.ingramcontent.com/pod-product-compliance
Ingram Content Group UK Ltd.
Pitfield, Milton Keynes, MK11 3LW, UK
UKHW022311280225
455674UK00004B/256